D0208770

EGMONT PRESS: ETHICAL PUBLISHING

Egmont Press is about turning writers into successful authors and children into passionate readers – producing books that enrich and entertain. As a responsible children's publisher, we go even further, considering the world in which our consumers are growing up.

Safety First
Naturally, all of our books meet legal safety requirements. But we go further than this; every book with play value is tested to the highest standards – if it fails, it's back to the drawing-board.

Made Fairly
We are working to ensure that the workers involved in our supply chain – the people that make our books – are treated with fairness and respect.

Responsible Forestry
We are committed to ensuring all our papers come from environmentally and socially responsible forest sources.

For more information, please visit our website at www.egmont.co.uk/ethical

Mixed Sources
Product group from well-managed forests and other controlled sources
www.fsc.org Cert no. TT-COC-002332
© 1996 Forest Stewardship Council

FSC

Egmont is passionate about helping to preserve the world's remaining ancient forests. We only use paper from legal and sustainable forest sources, so we know where every single tree comes from that goes into every paper that makes up every book.

This book is made from paper certified by the Forestry Stewardship Council (FSC), an organisation dedicated to promoting responsible management of forest resources. For more information on the FSC, please visit **www.fsc.org**. To learn more about Egmont's sustainable paper policy, please visit **www.egmont.co.uk/ethical**.

Also by Jenny Nimmo

Midnight for Charlie Bone
Charlie Bone and the Time Twister
Charlie Bone and the Blue Boa
Charlie Bone and the Castle of Mirrors

The Rinaldi Ring
The Snow Spider Trilogy
Secret Creatures

For younger readers
Matty Mouse
Delilah
Farm Fun

Charlie Bone and the Hidden King

Jenny Nimmo

EGMONT

Dedicated to the memory of Miriam Hodgson,
a true friend and inspiring editor

EGMONT

We bring stories to life

First published in Great Britain in 2006
This edition published 2007
by Egmont UK Limited
239 Kensington High Street
London W8 6SA

Text copyright © 2006 Jenny Nimmo
Cover illustration copyright © 2006 David Wyatt

The moral rights of the author and illustrator have been asserted

ISBN 978 1 4052 2820 6

7 9 10 8 6

www.charliebone.com
www.egmont.co.uk

A CIP catalogue record for this title is available from the British Library

Typeset by Avon DataSet Ltd, Bidford on Avon, Warwickshire
Printed and bound in Great Britain by the CPI Group

Contents

The children of the Red King, called the endowed

Naren Bloor
Adopted daughter of Bartholomew Bloor, Naren can send shadow words over great distances. She is descended from the Red King's grandson who was abducted by pirates and taken to China.

Asa Pike
A were-beast. He is descended from a tribe who lived in the Northern forests and kept strange beasts. Asa can change shape at dusk.

Billy Raven
Billy can communicate with animals. One of his ancestors conversed with ravens that sat on a gibbet where dead men hung. For this talent he was banished from his village.

Lysander Sage	Descended from an African wise man. He can call up his spirit ancestors.
Tancred Torsson	A storm-bringer. His Scandinavian ancestor was named after the thunder god, Thor. Tancred can bring rain, wind, thunder and lightning.
Gabriel Silk	Gabriel can feel scenes and emotions through the clothes of others. He comes from a line of psychics.
Emma Tolly	Emma can fly. Her surname derives from the Spanish swordsman from Toledo, whose daughter married the Red King. He is therefore an ancestor to all the endowed children.
Charlie Bone	Charlie can travel into photographs and pictures. Through his father he is descended from the Red King, and through his mother, from Mathonwy, a Welsh magician and friend of the Red King.

Dorcas Loom	Dorcas can bewitch items of clothing. Her ancestor, Lola Defarge, knitted a shrivelling shawl whilst enjoying the execution of the Queen of France in 1793.
Idith and Inez Branko	Telekinetic twins, distantly related to Zelda Dobinsky, who has left Bloor's Academy.
Joshua Tilpin	Joshua has magnetism. His origins are, at present, a mystery. Even the Bloors are unsure where he lives. He arrived at their doors alone and introduced himself. His fees are paid through a private bank.
Una Onimous	Mr Onimous's niece. Una is five years old and her endowment is being kept secret until it has fully developed.
Olivia Vertigo	Descended from Guanhamara, who fled the Red King's castle and married an Italian Prince. Olivia is an

illusionist. The Bloors are unaware of her endowment.

The endowed are all descended from the ten children of the Red King: a magician-king who left Africa in the twelfth century, accompanied by three leopards.

prologue

The Red King and his friend walked together through the forest. It was a golden autumn and leaves fell about them like bright coins. The king was tall, his black hair showed not a trace of grey and his dark skin was unlined, but the sorrow in his eyes was centuries old.

Mathonwy, the magician, was a slighter man. His hair and beard were silver-white and his back bent from years spent in the forest. He wore a cloak of midnight blue, patterned with faded stars.

Ten paces behind the men came three leopards; they were old now and not so quick as they had once been, but their gaze never wandered from the figure of the king.

He was their master and their friend and they would have followed him through fire.

Mathonwy was troubled. He knew that this was not one of those companionable walks that he was used to taking with the king. Today their pacing had a deeper purpose. Each step took them further from the world of men, and closer to the forest's heart.

They came at last to a glade where even the dead leaves were silent. The grass was the colour of honey and the hawthorn trees heavy with crimson berries. Mathonwy rested on a fallen tree but the king stood looking up through the bare branches. The sky had turned a burning red but, in a high band of deepest blue, the first star showed.

'Let us make a fire,' said the king.

Mathonwy delighted in bonfires. He sang in Welsh while he gathered the kindling, and the merry song hid the dread in his heart. The dead twigs were tinder dry and soon they had a small blaze going. A thin column of smoke lifted through the trees and the king declared it to be the sweetest scent in all the world.

Now, thought Mathonwy. Now, he is going to ask me.

But it was not yet.

'First the cats,' said the king. 'They cannot survive for much longer in a land of cold winters and callous

hunters. Come here, my good creatures.'

The leopards walked up to the king. They purred as they brushed their heads against his hand.

'It is time for you to wear new coats,' the king told them. 'Find a master who is good, for this one has to leave you now.'

It was said. Mathonwy shuddered. The king was leaving. How empty the forest would be without the companion who had filled his mind with wonders, who had shared his thoughts, answered his doubts, conversed from sunrise to moonset.

The king walked round the fire with long measured strides and the leopards followed him, around and around and around.

'Watch my children,' the king commanded them. 'Seek out the descendants of the children who are lost to me: sons and daughters of brave Amadis and bright Petrello, children of gentle Guanhamara and clever Tolemeo, descendants of my youngest child, Amoret. Help them, my loyal cats, keep them safe.'

When the king stepped away from the fire the big cats continued to circle it. They were running now, leaping and bounding.

The king raised his arm. 'Bright flame, burning sun and

golden star,' he chanted. 'Guard my children with your wild hearts. Live safely in the world of men, but remain forever what you are.'

Mathonwy had seen such spells as these before, but tonight the king's magic had a special beauty. The bounding leopards had become a ring of fire. Sparks flew into the trees and glowing streams festooned the branches, bathing the glade in ever-changing rainbow colours. When the king let his hand fall, the ring had faded; the leopards had gone. Mathonwy rose to his feet. 'Where are they?'

The king pointed to a tree behind the magician. On a low branch sat three cats. One was the colour of copper, one as orange as a flame, the last like a pale gold star.

'Behold! Aries, Leo and Sagittarius. Their coats have changed, but I still know who they are.' The king laughed contentedly, pleased with his spell. 'And now it is my turn.'

Mathonwy sighed. From the folds of his cloak he drew out a slim ash stick – his wand. 'What would you have me do?'

The king looked about him. 'The forest has become my home. The guise of a tree would suit me well.'

'You don't need my help for that,' said the magician. 'Shape-shifting comes as naturally to you as flying to a bird.'

The king regarded his only friend. 'Shape-shifting is not what I need, Mathonwy. I crave an everlasting change. If I am doomed to live forever, then I want to discard my human form, and take on a more peaceful aspect.'

'You want to live forever as a tree?' Mathonwy asked. 'A tree without speech, without movement? What if they come and cut down the forest?'

The king considered this. 'Perhaps I shall learn to move,' he said with his mischievous smile. 'Don't grieve, my friend. Last night I saw a boy in the clouds and I knew that he was one of mine. A future child. And listen to this, Mathonwy: I know that he was from your line too. This knowledge gave me a moment of great happiness. Now I feel the Red King can leave the world.'

'The world and me,' said Mathonwy without bitterness, for he was pleased to know that one day his bloodline would be joined with the king's.

'Don't begrudge me this favour,' begged the king. 'If I do it alone, then I will be tempted to return. Only you can make my transformation permanent. I am so weary, my friend. I cannot carry my sorrows any further.'

Mathonwy gave a gentle sigh. 'I will do as you wish. But forgive me if I do not compose the tree in a way that you imagine.'

The king smiled, but although he fought his sorrow with all his strength it began to overwhelm him and his eyes were clouded with tears.

The magician was filled with compassion for the king and began to work quickly. He touched his friend's shoulders with the tip of his ash-wand, then reached for the crown. But the thin gold band was so embedded in the king's black curls Mathonwy let it rest where it belonged.

The king wore the robes of coarse hemp that he had worn ever since he had come to live in the forest. As he lifted his hands the rough sleeves fell back and beneath his arms slim green shoots sprouted from his body. Mathonwy tapped the shoots with his wand and they began to thicken. The king's head rose, his body stretched, taller and taller, wider and wider. Leaves began to cover the branches; like tiny mirrors they reflected the colours of the autumn forest and the red-gold fire.

The cats watched the transformation of their master with glowing eyes. They watched the magician leap around the king, his wand a streak of sparks, his dark cloak flying, his hair a drift of thistledown. And now the cats began to howl, for their master had all but vanished; only his head remained atop a tree of dazzling splendour. And,

as his dear features gradually faded, the tears that fell from his dark eyes ran a deep berry red.

'Oh, my children!' sighed the king. And then he was gone.

But the tears flowed on, coursing down the furrowed trunk, red as blood.

Mathonwy stared at the tears in dismay. He tried to stem them with his wand, but on they flowed. So, summoning all the wit, the poetry and the magic that was in his soul, Mathonwy cast a spell. 'One day, my friend,' he said, 'your children will come to find you, and oh, what a day that will be!'

A deadly hour

Snow filled the air; thick and fast it heaped itself upon the sleeping city, almost as though it were trying to keep it safe. A blanket of down to smother the wickedness that someone was determined to let loose.

It was the second week in January, a time when snow is not uncommon, and yet this was no ordinary snowfall. On a hill above the city a boy stood with his arms wide, as if for flight. As the wind buffeted his body, clouds of snow billowed into his wide sleeves and under the green cape he wore. Tancred Torsson could summon rain, wind, thunder and lightning, but this was the first time he had attempted snow. And why should he be standing here, in the dead of night,

beckoning snow? Because three cats had climbed up to his windowsill and woken him with their calls. Slipping a cape over his pyjamas, Tancred had rushed out into the dark.

The cats met him at his front door and, while his parents slept on (his father sending thundery snores through the house), he had followed the three bright creatures down a shadowy lane to a windy hillside where he could see the city lights twinkling below him. Once there, the cats stared and stared at Tancred until they had made him understand their wishes.

Tancred did not have the gift of understanding animals but, being a descendant of the Red King, he could, sometimes, follow the gist of their yowling. 'Snow?' he said. 'Is that what you want?'

A loud trill came from the cats, their voices blending musically.

'Never done that before.' Tancred scratched his stiff blond hair. 'But, hey, I'll give it a go.'

The cats purred their satisfaction.

While Tancred set to work, the cats sped down the hillside into the city. The first cat was the colour of a copper sunset, the second like an orange flame, the third a yellow star. They bounded lightly down alleys, through gardens and over stone walls and fences, their paws leaving

scarcely a mark on the first scattering of snow. The tall city buildings were beginning to disappear in a shroud of white silence.

This was an hour like no other. A time when the living were as quiet as the dead. A deadly hour.

The cats ran down Filbert Street. They had nearly reached their destination when a car appeared, moving slowly up the street towards them. It stopped outside number twelve and three figures stumbled out. A man, a woman and a boy. Grumbling and exclaiming at this sudden snowstorm they heaved bags and cases on to the pavement.

'We're just in time,' said the woman. 'Another ten minutes and it would have been too deep for the car.' She climbed the steps up to her front door.

'What a welcome,' muttered the man. 'Let's go back to Hong Kong.' He gave a gruff chuckle and slammed the car door.

The boy carried two cases up the steps, then turned, as if he felt something watching him. He looked across the street and saw the three cats. 'It's the Flames,' he said, 'outside Charlie's house. I wonder what they want?'

'Don't stand out there, Benjamin,' said his mother. 'Come inside.'

Benjamin ignored her. 'Hello, Flames!' he called softly. 'It's me, Benjamin. I'm back.'

A throaty rumble came from the cats. A growl of welcome that also held a note of complaint. 'About time, too,' they seemed to say.

'See you soon,' said Benjamin as his mother hauled him and the cases through the door.

The cats watched the door close. When the lights came on inside number twelve, they turned their attention to the house behind them. A leafless chestnut tree stood in front of the house and they quickly climbed to a wide branch that hung outside one of the dark windows. Sitting in a row, the cats began to sing.

On the other side of the window, Charlie Bone stirred in his sleep. Someone was calling him. Was it a dream? His eyes opened. A sound he recognised came floating through the window. 'Flames?' he murmured. Now he was wide awake. Leaping out of bed, he drew back a curtain and opened the window.

The sight of three shining creatures, veiled in snow, took Charlie's breath away. When he'd convinced himself he wasn't dreaming he asked, 'Aries, Leo, Sagittarius, is it really you?'

They didn't bother to reply. With soft thuds they landed

on the carpet, followed by a cloud of flying snow.

Charlie closed the window. 'You'd better come downstairs,' he whispered. 'It's a night for warm milk and maybe a slice of turkey?' He glanced at a bed on the other side of the room, where a boy lay sleeping, his hair as white as his pillow.

The cats padded after Charlie as he crept downstairs. In the kitchen he warmed a pan of milk and poured it into three saucers. Deep, delighted purring filled the room as the cats lapped the milk. As soon as it was gone, Charlie laid slices of turkey on the empty saucers.

Snowflakes whirled past the uncurtained window, glistening in the beam of the kitchen lamp.

'Something different about that snow,' Charlie observed. 'Should I put two and two together and guess why you've come?' He watched the cats vigorously wash themselves. 'I was twelve last week and where were you then? Parties don't interest you, I suppose?'

Leo, the orange cat, stopped washing and returned Charlie's gaze. Not many cats could look you in the eye like that. Leo's gaze burned with knowledge, with wildness and with memories of a life most mortals could only dream of. Leo was nine hundred years old, as were his brothers.

Aries and Sagittarius now added their intense gaze to

Leo's. Charlie had the impression that they wanted to tell him something. He would have to wake the boy upstairs if he was to understand what the cats were trying to tell him.

Three pairs of golden eyes followed Charlie out of the room. He could still feel them on his back as he climbed the stairs.

'Billy! Billy, wake up!' Charlie gently shook the white-haired boy's shoulder.

'What? What is it?' Billy opened his round, ruby-coloured eyes.

'Ssh! The Flames are here. I want you to come and talk to them.'

Billy yawned. 'Oh. OK.' He tumbled out of bed, still not fully awake.

'You must be quiet,' warned Charlie, 'or Grandma Bone will hear us.'

Billy nodded and reached for his spectacles.

Billy was eight years old and a head shorter than Charlie. He could communicate with animals, but only if they allowed him to. He had always been a little fearful of the Flame cats. They knew when he was lying.

'Come on,' Charlie whispered urgently.

'I've got to find my specs,' said Billy, 'or I'll fall. Ah.

Here they are.' He pushed them on to his nose and crept after Charlie.

The cats watched the two boys enter the kitchen. Three pairs of ears flicked towards Billy when he sat, cross-legged before the stove, neat and alert. Charlie closed the door and sprawled beside the smaller boy.

'Go on, then,' said Charlie.

A sound came from Billy's throat: a soft, lilting mew. *You have news for us?*

Aries replied with a growl that grew in strength the longer he held it. The other cats joined in and Charlie wondered if Billy could take in the chorus of information that came mewing and wailing at him in three different voices.

Billy didn't make a sound. With his arms tucked inside his crossed legs and his chin resting on his clasped hands, he listened attentively. Charlie looked anxiously at the door. He dared not hush the cats but he worried that Grandma Bone would hear their yowling.

Billy frowned as the cats continued in their lilting, anxious voices. When, at last, their speech was over, Billy's eyes were wide with alarm. He turned to Charlie. 'It's a warning.'

'A warning?' asked Charlie. 'What kind of warning?'

'Aries says that something might wake up if they can't stop . . . stop . . . er . . . another thing from being found. And Sagittarius says that if that happens, you must be watchful, Charlie.'

'Watchful? But what am I supposed to watch?'

Billy hesitated. 'A woman – I think. Your –' The next word stuck in his throat.

'My *what*?' Charlie demanded.

'Your – mother.'

'My . . .' Charlie stared at Billy and then at the cats. 'Why?' His voice was husky with dread. 'Is someone going to make her disappear – like my father?'

Billy asked the cats and Leo responded with an apologetic warble.

'Leo says he wishes he could tell you more,' Billy interpreted. 'He will help you to watch.'

Leo gave several loud mews.

'He says that if the shadow has moved, then you'll know it's been released.'

'*What's* been released?' begged Charlie, tugging at his wild hair. 'Can't they be a bit more specific?'

At that moment the door opened and a voice said, 'Will someone kindly turn off that light?'

Charlie leapt to the switch and, as soon as the lamp

over the table had gone out, a tall man in a red dressing gown appeared. He was holding a lighted candle in a brass candlestick.

'I see you have visitors.' Charlie's great-uncle Paton nodded in the cats' direction. 'Morning, Flames.'

The cats trilled a greeting and Charlie said, 'Is it really morning?'

'It's two am,' said Uncle Paton, who didn't seem at all surprised to see Charlie and Billy downstairs at such an early hour. 'I'm feeling peckish.' He crossed the room and opened the fridge. 'I detect an air of mystery. What's been going on?'

'The Flames came to warn me,' Charlie told his uncle, 'about Mum.'

'Your mother?' Uncle Paton turned away from the fridge with a frown. 'Did you say your *mother*?'

'Yes.'

'And a shadow,' added Billy.

Uncle Paton brought a plate of cheese from the fridge and set it on the kitchen table, beside the candlestick. 'I want to know more,' he said.

'Billy, tell the cats to explain,' begged Charlie. 'Ask them what the shadow is.'

But the cats were eager to be gone. They stretched

themselves and ran to the door.

'Wait!' said Charlie. 'You haven't told me about the shadow.'

Aries yowled and Leo scratched the door. Charlie had no choice but to open it. And then the cats were out and bounding through the hall.

'What shadow?' Charlie whispered fiercely as he followed the cats.

Sagittarius growled. Charlie couldn't tell if it was an answer or a demand.

'Let them go, Charlie.' Billy ran and opened the front door. 'They've got to get somewhere else, fast. To see if the thing is found.'

With a sudden chorus of trills the Flames darted through the door and were away up the street; three bright flames swallowed by the whirling snow.

'They didn't explain,' Charlie grumbled. 'Now I'll never know.'

'They did,' said Billy. 'They –'

Before he could say any more a voice from the top of the stairs shouted, 'What's the meaning of this?'

Grandma Bone was an unpleasant sight at the best of times, but after midnight she looked her worst. Her skinny frame was wrapped in a shaggy, grey dressing-gown and her

big feet were encased in green tartan bootees. A long white pigtail hung over her shoulder and her sallow face had blotches of white cream dotted across it.

'Hello, Grandma,' said Charlie, trying to make the best of things.

'Don't be insolent.' Grandma Bone didn't like people being cheerful at night. 'Why aren't you in bed?'

'We were hungry.'

'Rubbish.' She treated everything Charlie said as a lie. 'I heard cats.' She began to descend the stairs.

'They were outside, Grandma,' Charlie said quickly.

She stopped and stared at the glass fanlight above the front door. 'What sort of snow is that? It doesn't look normal.' She had a point. There *was* something different about those spinning flakes, but Charlie couldn't have said what it was.

'It's cold, white and wet,' said Uncle Paton, stepping out of the kitchen. 'What more do you want?'

'You!' snarled Grandma Bone. 'Why didn't you send these boys back to bed?'

'Because they were hungry,' answered her brother in a superior tone. 'Go to bed, Grizelda.'

'Don't you order me about.'

'Suit yourself.' Paton ambled back into the kitchen.

For a moment Grandma Bone remained on the stairs, glaring down at Charlie.

'I'll get a glass of water, Grandma, and then we'll go straight to bed.' Charlie looked at Billy. 'Won't we, Billy?'

'Oh, yes.' To an orphan like Billy, Charlie's strange, quarrelling family was endlessly fascinating. He nodded emphatically at Grandma Bone and added, 'Promise.'

Grandma Bone gave a 'Hmph' of doubt and shuffled upstairs.

Charlie drew Billy into the kitchen again and asked in a whisper, 'What did they say, Billy? The Flames. About the shadow?'

'They just said a word,' Billy replied. 'It sounded like listen. No, something different, an old-fashioned word for listen.'

'Hark?' Uncle Paton suggested.

'Yes, that's it.'

'That's hardly a name, dear boy.' Uncle Paton bit into a hunk of Cheddar. 'It's more of a command. Perhaps you misheard.'

'I didn't,' Billy said gravely.

By now the three cats had crossed the city and were

stepping lightly over the snow that had drifted against the walls of Bloor's Academy. They passed the two towers on either side of the entrance steps and kept going, along the side of the building, until they reached the end, where a high stone wall began. Ivy had taken root in the ancient stones and the cats skimmed up the creeper and dropped down into a snowy field.

On the far side of the field, the dark red walls of a ruined castle could be glimpsed. The cats became cautious. They paced carefully across the white field, their ears tuned to any sound that might come from the ruin. And then they heard the cry.

'I know what you're doing,' shrieked a woman's voice. 'But I can't be stopped, you fools. Did you think that snow would hinder me? Granted, it has slowed me down, but never will it stop me.'

The cats moved closer. Through the great arch into the castle, they could see a dark figure, bent in half, her arms buried in snow up to her elbows. She swayed this way and that, tugging, pulling and moaning with effort. With a sudden, deep groan a large, flat stone was heaved upright, then fell back on to the snow.

The woman stooped and groped in the earth. With a cry of triumph she lifted something out and held it up to the

white air, her hands torn and bleeding from the struggle. 'Mine! It's mine!'

A small shudder passed through the earth; a movement imperceptible to humans but enough to send a tiny thread of fear through every creature in the region. Birds awoke and screamed, small frantic rodents scurried desperately for safety and the mournful howling of dogs carried through the bitter air.

Their eyes bright with alarm, the Flames watched the woman stumble from the ruin. The hem of her black coat was heavy with snow and her lamp swung in the icy breeze. She reached a door in the great grey building that was Bloor's Academy and disappeared. A few minutes later a glimmering light appeared in a high window.

The cats gazed at the window, fearing the worst.

The woman was standing before a gold-framed portrait of the Red King, her lamp illuminating the thick, cracked paint. 'I have it,' she whispered. She was not addressing the king. With her free hand she withdrew an object from the folds of her coat. At first glance it looked like an imperfect circle of rusty metal, no more than six inches across. She held it by a thick oval stem.

The king gazed out of his portrait with dark magnetic eyes. A circle of gold glinted on his black hair and his

red cloak had the appearance of real velvet.

As the woman twisted her metal circle it caught the rays from her lamp and a sudden, bright flash lit the painting. A shadow could be seen behind the king's shoulder. Gradually it defined itself, its outline becoming sharper and brighter.

'Awake, my lord,' the woman urged in a voice heavy with yearning. 'I have found the Mirror of Amoret.'

Slowly the shadow moved. It slipped from behind the king and drifted forward, closer and closer.

The woman gave a gasp of ecstasy. She sighed and swayed; her lamp swung, the circle glittered and the light on the painting danced and flashed. A sudden, thunderous explosion brought the portrait crashing to the floor and the woman screamed.

A shadow rose out of the frame and came towards her.

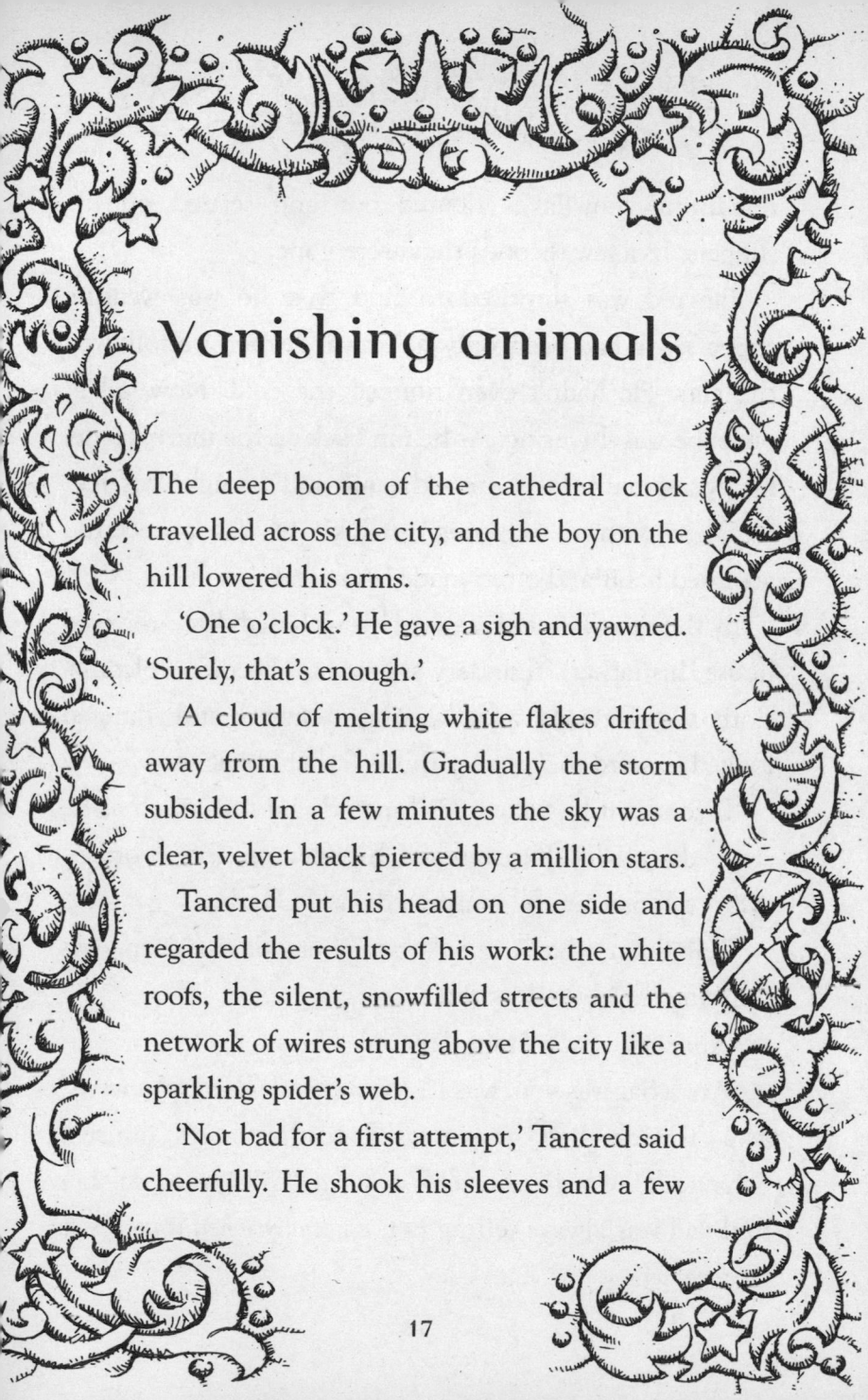

Vanishing animals

The deep boom of the cathedral clock travelled across the city, and the boy on the hill lowered his arms.

'One o'clock.' He gave a sigh and yawned. 'Surely, that's enough.'

A cloud of melting white flakes drifted away from the hill. Gradually the storm subsided. In a few minutes the sky was a clear, velvet black pierced by a million stars.

Tancred put his head on one side and regarded the results of his work: the white roofs, the silent, snowfilled streets and the network of wires strung above the city like a sparkling spider's web.

'Not bad for a first attempt,' Tancred said cheerfully. He shook his sleeves and a few

remaining snowflakes floated out and settled on his slippers. In a few seconds they were gone.

Tancred was surprised to find that he was wearing slippers. He had been only half awake when he followed the cats. He hadn't even noticed the cold. Now, all at once, he was shivering. As he ran back up the narrow lane, he occasionally leapt into the air and brought his feet together with a satisfying 'smack'. It was a recently acquired habit and often made his friends laugh.

By the time Tancred reached his secluded three-towered house, his father's thundery snores had become volcanic. Both the Torssons were weather-mongers and Tancred looked forward to a chat with his father about snow.

'I wonder if he's tried it?' Tancred said to himself as he stepped indoors. He stamped his feet on the doormat. 'Must tell Sander,' he murmured, 'and Charlie.'

'Tell them what?' Mrs Torsson, unable to sleep, was drinking tea in the kitchen.

'About the snow,' said Tancred.

'Ah. That was you, was it? I wondered where you were.' Mrs Torsson had grown used to her son's unusual behaviour. *A boy's got to do what a boy's got to do*, her husband was always telling her, *especially when it comes to the weather*.

'Phew! Dad's making a racket.' Tancred shook his damp cape and hung it on the back of the door.

Mrs Torsson absent-mindedly put a third spoonful of sugar in her tea and then poured a cup for Tancred. He took a chair opposite her and drank thirstily. Snow-making was an exhausting business. He hoped he wouldn't be called upon to do it again too soon.

'The Flame cats were here,' he explained to his mother. 'They wanted snow – don't ask me why. But I get the feeling something's not right down there in the city.'

'Your father said he had a foreboding. He hasn't been sleeping well.' Mrs Torsson shook her head. 'Sometimes I wonder if we should move away from here. You could go to a nice normal school and –'

'I couldn't,' Tancred said emphatically. 'I belong here. Just as much as Charlie and Sander, and Gabriel and . . . and Emma. The Red King lived here and we're his children. We've got to stick together. You *know* that, Mum.'

'Yes, Tancred.' His mother sighed.

Mrs Torsson wasn't the only mother to wish that she and her family were far away from the city. Charlie Bone's mother longed to escape her dreary life in a house that didn't belong to her, in a place that echoed with the

whispers of its terrible past, and where her son had been forced to attend a school run by a malevolent old man.

But Amy Bone had no money and nowhere to run to. Besides, Charlie was perfectly happy. Nothing ever seemed to get him down. He was an extraordinarily optimistic boy. Nothing could shake his conviction that his father was still alive and that, one day, Charlie would find him. It was something that Amy had given up counting on.

It was eight o'clock on Saturday. Apart from Charlie's mother, the occupants of number nine Filbert Street were all asleep. Even Amy's mother, Maisie, could be heard gently snoring as Amy tiptoed past her room.

After a hasty breakfast, Amy left the house and began her ten-minute walk to the greengrocer's where she worked. Not a hint of last night's snowfall remained. The air was chilly and the pavements still damp, but no one would have guessed that, a few hours ago, several inches of snow had covered the city.

'Mrs Bone! Mrs Bone!'

Amy turned quickly. The voice came from a boy on the other side of the road. Could it be . . .? Was it possible?

'Benjamin!' cried Amy, running back towards number nine. 'It's you!'

The boy looked left and right, then dashed across

the road.

'Oh, Benjamin, I'm so, so happy to see you.' Amy gave him a tight hug. She'd never done such a thing before and Benjamin was rather startled.

'Are you all, er, r-right, Mrs Bone?' he asked, embarrassment and lack of breath causing him to stammer. 'I mean are you *all* all right?'

'Charlie's just fine,' said Amy. 'He's still asleep, but I'll let you in and you can surprise him.' She ran up the steps, unlocked the door of number nine and opened it. 'You know where his room is. I'll have to dash now, or I'll be late for work. But go in, go in.' She gave Benjamin a little push into the house and closed the door behind him.

Benjamin looked round the silent hall, pleased to see that nothing had changed. He was a small fair-haired boy with a perpetually lost expression. At the moment he was slightly jet-lagged, but he couldn't wait to see Charlie and Runner Bean, the dog he'd left in Charlie's care.

Benjamin peeped into the kitchen. No dog basket. No bowl. Of course, Runner Bean must be sleeping in Charlie's room.

As he climbed the stairs Benjamin heard footsteps above him, and then Charlie's grandmother, the kind one,

appeared on the landing. She was wearing a bright pink dressing gown.

'Benjamin Brown! What a sight for sore eyes!'

Benjamin was subjected to yet another breathtaking squeeze. Maisie Jones was a round, curly-haired, twinkle-eyed person and the squeeze threatened to send Benjamin tumbling down the stairs.

'You lovely normal boy,' said Maisie. 'No magical endowments for you. No poncy acting, no fiddling flutes, no animal gruntings. You'll do Charlie a power of good. Go on up!'

'Thanks,' said Benjamin, breathless again.

Maisie swayed downstairs, still talking. 'I'll make some toast and a nice cup of tea. Cornflakes? I s'pose it's all noodles now. Do they have noodles for breakfast in Hong Kong?'

'Mrs Jones, where's my dog?' called Benjamin.

But Maisie had disappeared into the kitchen.

Benjamin walked on to Charlie's bedroom. He listened outside the door. Not a sound came from the other side. Benjamin opened the door. He saw Charlie, fast asleep in bed. There was a new bed on the other side of the room and Benjamin could just see a few tufts of white hair poking above the duvet. Billy Raven. There was no sign of Runner Bean.

Benjamin stood just inside the door, wondering what to do. His pale solemn face now wore a look of extreme anxiety. What had happened to Charlie while he had been away? He had a vision of his best friend surrounded by all those peculiar children at Bloor's Academy. The musicians, actors and artists; the weather-monger, the hypnotist and all those other weird things. Perhaps this explained why Maisie and Amy Jones were so pleased to see him. Because he was normal, unlike poor Charlie.

A sudden movement on Charlie's bed caught Benjamin's eye. A white moth fluttered over the duvet. Benjamin had always been told that moths were pests. They made holes. He sprang forward and cupped his hand over the moth.

Three things happened. Charlie sat bolt upright and screamed. Billy Raven rolled out of bed, and the moth bit, yes *bit* Benjamin, who yelled and let go of it.

'Benjamin!' cried Charlie.

'Charlie!' cried Benjamin. 'A moth bit me.'

'It's my wand,' said Charlie.

'Your *wand?*'

'Manfred burnt it and it turned into a moth. You haven't killed it, have you?'

Benjamin shook his head. 'It's on top of your wardrobe. Sorry.'

Benjamin never said things like: how can a wand turn into a moth? Charlie realised how much he'd missed his friend. 'It's really great to see you, Ben.'

'It's great to see you, too. Where's Runner Bean?'

'Ah.' Charlie swung his legs out of bed. 'He's not here.'

'I can see that.'

Billy Raven groaned and sat up. He put his hand up to the bedside table and felt for his spectacles.

'What's Billy doing here?' asked Benjamin.

'Dr Bloor lets me out at weekends now.' Billy found his spectacles and put them on.

'So, where's my dog?' Benjamin persisted, turning to Charlie.

Charlie tugged his tousled hair. He had so much to tell Benjamin he didn't know where to start. He made his friend sit on the bed and, while he got dressed, he explained how Grandma Bone had tried to have Runner Bean put down by the pest controllers. The look of horror on Benjamin's face prompted Charlie to add quickly, 'But Mr Onimous got here first. He took Runner to the Pets' Café, and I go every weekend and take him for a run.'

'Only once a week?' Benjamin said accusingly. 'He needs a walk every day.'

'Well, I can't get out of school, can I?' Charlie lowered

his voice. 'It's not my fault that I have to sleep at Bloor's during the week, is it?'

'No. Sorry. It's great to see you, Charlie.'

'You too,' Charlie said once again.

As soon as Billy and Charlie were dressed the three boys went downstairs where Maisie gave them a huge cooked breakfast. Benjamin gazed dismally at the food. He couldn't eat. His stomach was churning with apprehension. He had to see his dog. Suppose someone had stolen him.

'Mr Onimous would never let that happen,' Maisie patted Benjamin's head. 'Runner Bean's just fine. You'll see.'

Billy and Charlie wolfed down their breakfasts and followed Benjamin, who was already at the front door.

'Where's all the snow gone?' said Benjamin as they raced up Filbert Street. 'Last night it was so deep we could hardly drive through it.'

'The Flame cats had something to do with it,' muttered Charlie.

'You mean like it wasn't real snow?'

'Don't know what I mean,' said Charlie.

When they reached the Pets' Café they found a 'Closed' sign hanging on the door. Charlie pressed his face to the window. Chairs were piled on tables and the counter was bare. But at the back of the café a soft light could be seen

coming through the beaded curtain into the kitchen.

Charlie knocked on the door.

For a moment he thought no one had heard. He was about to knock again when Mr Onimous's small figure appeared behind the counter. The three boys waved and Mr Onimous scurried round the tables to open the door.

'Well, if it isn't Marco Polo himself,' said Mr Onimous, ushering the boys into the café.

'Marco who?' asked Benjamin.

'An ancient traveller, Benjy.' Mr Onimous locked the door. 'A man who went to China before most people knew it was there.'

'I was in Hong Kong,' Benjamin said gravely, 'and I'm not ancient. Please, where's my dog?'

'Ah.' Mr Onimous ran a hand over his stubbly chin. 'You'd better come into the kitchen.'

'Where is he?' Benjamin ran round the counter and past the curtain.

Mr Onimous shrugged uneasily and whispered, 'The dog's gone, Charlie. Goodness knows where.'

'Gone?' Charlie and Billy rushed after Benjamin.

On entering the Onimous's kitchen, the boys beheld Emma Tolly, sitting in the only armchair. Her eyelids were red and wet streaks covered her cheeks.

'Emma, are you OK?' Charlie said and immediately felt foolish because, clearly, Emma wasn't OK.

In a desolate voice Emma said, 'I've lost my duck.' She gave a deep sob.

'What!' Charlie exclaimed.

'Now, now, now. Let's all calm down,' said Mrs Onimous, almost scalding herself as she emptied a kettle of boiling water into a gigantic teapot. 'Sit down, boys, and help yourselves to cake.'

'I don't think I can eat.' Benjamin pulled out a chair and dropped on to it. 'I just want my dog. I've been waiting to see him for seven whole months.'

'Well, you'll just have to wait a tad longer,' said Mrs Onimous somewhat testily. 'As a matter of fact there's been a mass exodus. All the animals have gone and –'

'Even Rembrandt?' squeaked Billy.

'All means *all*, even rats, Billy,' said Mr Onimous. 'But I'm sure there's a simple explanation. In order to think we must remain calm. Pour the tea, Onoria, my darling. Tea is restoring.'

Emma joined the boys at the table, while Mr and Mrs Onimous took a seat at either end. Tea and cakes were passed round, but Charlie was the only one to enjoy the cake. His concern for the animals hadn't managed to spoil

his appetite. Surely, they couldn't all have disappeared. He looked round the cosy kitchen looking for signs of life: a mouse, a spider, the odd fly. But nothing moved on the copper pans above his head, or on the shelves crammed with jars and tins and brightly painted crockery. Finally his glance fell on a lidded basket in the corner and he asked, 'What about the blue boa?'

'Gone, the dear thing,' Mrs Onimous replied sadly. 'They must have left last night, in the snowstorm. I came down early to make a cuppa and the place was deserted. No welcoming barks, no eager scamperings, no happy slitherings.' She blew her very long nose with a loud trumpeting sound.

'Same happened to me.' Emma's blue eyes filled with fresh tears. 'Nancy's always, always, always in her duckhouse in the yard. But it was empty.'

Billy gave a light cough. 'The Flame cats came to warn us, but they didn't say anything about animals disappearing.'

'What exactly did they say, dear?' Mrs Onimous bent her lean frame eagerly towards Billy.

'They said Charlie must watch his mother and a shadow was waking up. A shadow called Hark.'

'Hark?' Mr Onimous raised and lowered his bristly eyebrows. He scratched a whiskery cheek with slightly

furry hands and said, 'I'm in the dark.'

'What was that?' Mrs Onimous suddenly sat bolt upright, craning her long neck towards the far end of the kitchen.

'Scratching,' said Billy.

Now they could all hear it: a very, very distant scratching.

Billy jumped up and rushed to a door that led into the pantry.

'Billy, no . . .' Mr Onimous snatched a torch from a shelf and hopped after Billy, calling, 'Come back, Billy. Do you hear me?'

'It's Rembrandt,' said Billy's faint voice.

Charlie followed Mr Onimous through a long room lined with shelves of dog food and then down a dark passage with an earthen floor and walls of bare rock. The ceiling was only inches above Charlie's head, and it was so dark he could barely see Mr Onimous scuttling ahead of him.

The Pets' Café was built into the ancient city wall, and they were now travelling along an underground passage that led to the very heart of the Red King's castle. By the time Charlie had caught up with Mr Onimous, Billy had reached a small door at the end of the passage. Before Mr

Onimous could stop him, Billy wrenched open the door and leapt into the space beyond. He was now in a cavern whose curved walls were lined with large crates and lumpy-looking sacks.

Mr Onimous stepped into the cavern with Charlie close behind him. In the beam of light from Mr Onimous's torch, Charlie could see that Billy was holding a large black rat.

'Oh, Rembrandt, where've you been?' Billy continued with a series of high squeaks and strange little hums.

The rat responded with a few squeaks of his own, and Billy said, 'He's had a bit of an adventure. He went through – oh . . .' as he said this he turned to see Mr Onimous closing a very small door. Black and scarred with age, the door nevertheless perfectly fitted a gaping hole in the wall.

'Wow! Where does that go?' asked Billy, staring at the door.

'It's just a hole,' Charlie said quickly.

Mr Onimous bent and retrieved a tiny brass key lying on the floor. 'Animals,' he grunted, fitting the key into a tiny lock in the ancient door. 'They're too clever by half. I suppose it was you who unlocked the door, Rembrandt rat.' He pocketed the key.

'Yes, it was him,' said Billy. 'But where *does* that lead to?'

'Billy, I want you to promise me something.' Mr Onimous's genial whiskery features had become almost severe. 'I want you to promise never, ever to tell a single soul about this room or that door.'

'Oh.' For a moment Billy silently gazed at the door, and then understanding seemed to dawn on his eager face. 'It's a secret passage, isn't it?' he whispered. 'To the castle?'

'I'm waiting for your promise, Billy,' Mr Onimous said gravely.

'I promise never, ever to tell a soul about this place or that door,' Billy said in a small voice.

Mr Onimous smiled at last. 'You don't need to know any more. Forget it. Understand?'

'Yes,' came the whispered reply. Though how could Billy possibly forget such an exciting place?

The rat began to squeak again and they all trooped back to the kitchen to find out what he had to say.

'Any news of Runner?' asked Benjamin. 'That's some rat, by the way.'

'Name's Rembrandt,' said Charlie, 'and we think he's got something to tell us.'

Rembrandt was placed in the centre of the table and, when everyone had taken their places, Billy gave the rat a

light prompting hum. Rembrandt looked round at the expectant faces. He was a sociable rat and clearly enjoyed being the centre of attention. With small squeaks, pauses, grunts and twitters he began his story. Gradually the sounds he made formed a pattern that Charlie could almost recognise as speech. Billy sat with his chin on his folded arms, gazing at Rembrandt and listening intently to his voice. When it was clear that the rat had uttered his last squeak, Billy picked him up and put him in his lap. The exhausted creature curled up and fell asleep.

'Go on, Billy,' said impatient Benjamin. 'What did he say?'

'Some of it's hard to explain,' said Billy.

'Try,' urged Charlie.

'Well – he said that last night something – kind of – woke up. And – and the earth shivered.'

'We didn't notice, did we?' Mrs Onimous looked at her husband.

'We're not animals, dear,' he replied. 'Not quite, anyway.'

'*Please*,' moaned Benjamin, 'let him go on!'

With a shake of her smooth, feathery hair, Mrs Onimous pointed her very long nose in Benjamin's direction. 'I'm sorry to interrupt, I'm sure,' she said tartly.

Benjamin ducked contritely and then quietly begged,

'I just want to know about my dog.'

Billy took a breath and continued, 'Anyway, Rembrandt says that they were very frightened, him and the boa and Runner Bean, and instinct made them want to go – somewhere else. So Rembrandt got a key.' Billy paused. 'I think he said it was in your bedroom, Mr Onimous.'

'Little devil,' muttered Mr Onimous.

'And he unlocked a door,' Billy went on quickly, 'and they all went into a tunnel and – they went through the castle ruin, and all the mice and squirrels and birds and rabbits, and everything else that lived there, they all went too, and . . . and this is the hard bit, I think they went down a cliff – where the river roars – and over a bridge.' Billy took off his spectacles, which had steamed up. He rubbed them against his sleeve and put them on again. 'Imagine all those animals pattering over a bridge.'

'Maybe some swam,' Charlie suggested.

'And some would fly,' added Emma.

'Yes, birds would.' Billy glanced at the frowning Benjamin and hurriedly continued, 'And after a bit, they found somewhere safe. And that's where they are now: Runner Bean and the blue boa, and your duck, too, I expect, Emma.'

'Where?' Benjamin spread his hands.

'I don't know, do I?' Billy replied. 'I mean, Rembrandt didn't tell me any names. He came back here because he wanted me to know what had happened. But he thinks the others might stay there.'

Benjamin was speechless with dismay. In fact everyone was silent, until Emma asked, 'Why? Why do they want to stay?'

Billy stroked his rat's glossy coat. 'I think Rembrandt was trying to say that it's a kind of – sanctuary.'

'Sanctuary? I never heard of such a place in this city,' said Mrs Onimous.

'But it isn't in the city. It's out there, on the other side of the river.' Billy gazed over their heads to an imaginary paradise, floating somewhere in space.

'Billy, old fellow, there's nothing on the other side of the river,' said Mr Onimous. 'It's a wilderness.'

With a cry of despair, Benjamin buried his face in his hands.

The girl in the sunshine coat

Wilderness. The word was in everyone's mind but no one would say it out loud, just yet. By now, the city was crowded with Saturday shoppers and when the four children emerged from the Pets' Café, they headed for the quiet street that led to Ingledew's Bookshop.

Every weekend Emma helped in the shop where she lived with her Aunt Julia. Emma's aunt was wise and kind. She had read almost all the rare and ancient books on her shelves, and her knowledge of the city and its past was prodigious. She was bound to know about the wilderness across the river. There was also a strong possibility that Charlie's Uncle Paton would be in the shop.

And so, without even discussing it, the children gravitated towards the two people who might be able to tell them what had happened to their animals.

Exhausted by his long journey, Rembrandt had fallen into a deep sleep. He lay curled in Billy's pocket, incapable of uttering another squeak.

As they drew near to the shop, the noise of the city receded and they became aware that something was wrong. None of them could say what it was, but in one way or another they all felt very uneasy.

'It's kind of spooky up here.' Benjamin wrinkled his nose. 'It never used to be.'

'There are no birds,' said Emma. 'They've all gone.'

They had reached the wide cobbled square in front of the cathedral where, usually, at least a dozen jackdaws could be seen, strutting across the cobbles, or shouting from the rooftops. Today there was not even a pigeon.

'No cats either,' Charlie observed. 'There's always a cat mousing round the cathedral.'

'And dogs.' Benjamin spun on his heel, staring round the square. 'On Saturdays people walk their dogs here. So, where are they?'

Billy spoke the words on everyone's mind. 'In the wilderness.'

Charlie felt a prickling sensation at the back of his neck. Someone was watching them. He whirled round, just in time to see a figure in yellow disappear into an alley. 'We're being followed,' he said quietly. 'I saw a yellow floaty thing, down there.'

No one looked where Charlie was pointing. They ran for the bookshop as though a monster were on their trail. Charlie followed them, stumbling down the steps into the shop and bumping into Benjamin, who let out a yell of warning.

Distracted by the sudden commotion, Paton Yewbeam, balanced precariously at the top of a stepladder, began to sway dangerously and the armful of books he'd been placing on a high shelf almost slipped out of his grasp.

'Paton, look out!' Julia Ingledew sprinted across the room and steadied the ladder.

'What's the trouble, you lot?' Uncle Paton deposited the books and came down the ladder.

All four children spoke at once, causing Uncle Paton to cover his ears and exclaim, 'For pity's sake, one at a time.'

'Let's take a break,' Miss Ingledew suggested.

They all piled into the small sitting-room at the back of the shop and, while the boys made themselves comfortable among the books on chairs and sofa, Emma

described her morning, from the discovery of Nancy's empty duck-house to the absence of birds and animals in the city.

'I knew something was amiss,' Uncle Paton said thoughtfully. 'But I couldn't put my finger on it. I lose a few details when I'm wearing my dark glasses.'

'But do you know anything about the wilderness across the river?' Charlie asked his uncle.

'I've never ventured that far,' Uncle Paton said regretfully. 'And why the animals should choose to go there, I have no idea.'

'They were frightened,' said Charlie.

'But we don't know why,' said Emma.

'Yes, we do,' put in Billy. 'Rembrandt told us. Something woke up and the ground shivered.'

'I'll never see Runner Bean again,' moaned Benjamin. 'Oh, why couldn't he have waited for me?'

Miss Ingledew, who had been tidying small areas of the room, all at once stopped and looked hard at Billy. 'Shivered? Did you say shivered?' she asked Billy.

'Actually, Rembrandt said it,' Billy told her.

'Ah. You have a theory about the ground, don't you, Julia?' Uncle Paton sat back with a smile.

They waited for Miss Ingledew to explain.

'You can make fun of me, but I have my reasons.' She bent over her desk and began to shuffle papers into a drawer.

After a short and anxious interval, Charlie begged, 'Please tell us about your theory, Miss Ingledew. We won't make fun of it.'

Miss Ingledew pushed a lock of luxuriant chestnut hair away from her face and straightened up. 'Very well, but I'm sure you've heard it all before, Charlie.' She sat on the arm of Paton's chair. 'As you know, the Red King, from whom you are all descended – except for you, of course, Benjamin – well, when the queen died and the king left to mourn alone in the forests, his ten children fought amongst each other until five of them left the castle forever. But the fighting didn't stop. It continued for centuries, yes, centuries.'

There was a buzz of surprise as the children uttered cries of 'Wow! Centuries?' 'D'you mean like hundreds and hundreds of years?'

Charlie said, 'It's kind of happening now, isn't it? I mean with the Bloors trying to control everyone, and Uncle Paton fighting them when they go too far . . .'

'And your ghastly Grandma always against you,' said Benjamin.

'Shush!' Uncle Paton lifted his hand. 'If you want to hear what Miss Ingledew has to say, kindly let her continue.'

The children immediately fell silent.

Miss Ingledew smiled round at everyone. 'As I said, the killing went on for centuries. The land around the castle was a constant battleground until, in the eighteenth century, a fire destroyed almost every building in the city. Only this small area around the cathedral was saved. Everything else had to be rebuilt. It was at this time that the Bloor family erected a grand mansion in the grounds of the ruined castle.'

'Bloor's Academy!' Charlie proclaimed.

'Exactly,' Miss Ingledew confirmed. 'Although at that time it was called Bloor House, I believe.'

Benjamin, who was now scowling with impatience, said, 'I don't see what has all this got to do with the ground shivering.'

'No, of course not. I'm sorry. I'll explain,' said Miss Ingledew. 'It has to do with the history: all the troubled lives, the hatred, the fear, all buried under the ashes, under the ground and under the city, all . . .' she pressed the fingers of her two hands together, 'all contained and yet . . .' She glanced at Billy's ashen face. 'Oh dear, I'm frightening you.'

'You're not. You're not,' cried Billy. 'Please go on.'

Miss Ingledew continued hesitantly, 'Well, it occurred to me that certain of the more evil spirits – could be – er, restless . . .'

'Like someone turning in their grave,' Charlie suggested eagerly.

'That's one way of putting it.' She gave a light chuckle. 'But really, Charlie, I meant that something, or someone, might have woken them up.'

'And that's why the ground shivered,' Billy broke in. 'The Flame cats said they had to stop something being found.'

'A key, no doubt,' said Uncle Paton with a small yawn.

Charlie knew that his uncle's slightly bored tone belied his curiosity and he asked, 'You don't mean an actual key, do you?'

'No, Charlie. More of an artefact, an item that would connect an ancient spirit with our world.'

Billy suddenly leapt up. 'Animals can sense things, you know. That's why they've all gone. If something from the past has woken up, it's brought memories with it: battles and fires, the pain and the terrible sounds. No wonder they ran away.'

'I don't see how all this helps me,' cried Benjamin. 'I mean, maybe I'll never, ever find my dog again.'

The dreadful prospect of a city without animals of any kind suddenly dawned on everyone at the same time.

'It's like being under a curse,' Emma remarked.

Uncle Paton didn't hold with such pessimism. 'You're all being too gloomy,' he said. 'I'm sure the situation's temporary. Pretty soon that rat will wake up and tell you where they've all gone.'

But Rembrandt didn't wake up. He lay in Billy's pocket all day, his only sign of life a very weak heartbeat.

On Sunday, a north wind blew clouds of freezing sleet into the city, and only the foolhardy ventured out.

Charlie and Billy played video games while Rembrandt, tucked in Billy's bed, emitted a faint ratty snore. A particularly violent gust of wind sent a slate crashing into the road and Charlie went to the window. There, sheltering beneath the bare chestnut tree, he saw the figure in yellow again. He was quite sure it was the person he had glimpsed ducking into an alley the day before. But this time, in spite of the sleet, he got a better look at her. If he wasn't mistaken she was Chinese. Her coat was sunshine yellow. It had a loose hood, and her black shoulder-length hair was held away from her face by a shiny butterfly clip.

When the girl saw Charlie she smiled and raised her hand. Charlie waved back. As soon as he did this the

girl's smile widened, and then she ran off.

'Wait!' cried Charlie.

'Who are you talking to?' asked Billy.

'That girl.' Charlie rushed out of the room. He leapt downstairs and ran across the hall. Flinging open the front door, he called up the street, 'Wait! Who are you?'

But the girl in the sunshine coat kept running until she was out of sight.

'What girl?' asked Billy when Charlie returned.

'Just a girl. She seems to know me, but she ran off.'

Rembrandt gave a sudden squeak and sat up.

'Look, he's awake.' Billy picked up the rat and began talking in his strange, piping rat-speak.

Rembrandt appeared to be listening. When Billy fell silent the rat replied with a few weary squeaks.

Billy frowned. 'He says he can't remember anything.'

'What! He can't remember how he got to the sanctuary, or whatever it was?'

Billy spoke to Rembrandt again. He was answered in the same weak tones of an exhausted rat.

'He's got a picture of the place in his head, but he's completely forgotten how he got there.'

'Then how are we going to find the other animals?' Charlie demanded.

'Don't know. But Rembrandt couldn't walk all that way again, even if he wanted to.' Billy lifted one of the rat's feet. 'Look, his pads are really sore, and he's lost a claw.'

Charlie observed the rat's small feet. They certainly looked the worse for wear. He dropped gloomily on to his bed and thought of Benjamin, waiting seven long months to see Runner Bean, only to find that the dog he idolised had vanished. Charlie felt responsible. Perhaps if he had taken better care of Runner, he wouldn't have run away.

'It's not your fault, Charlie,' said Billy gently. 'Grandma Bone would've killed Runner or sent him to a dogs' home. And anyway, he was happy at the Pets' Café.'

'I wonder if the animals will come back,' mused Charlie, 'or if they've all gone for good.'

Later that evening Maisie came to fetch Rembrandt. She told the boys she would keep the rat in her room, safe from Grandma Bone, and return him to Mr Onimous on Monday.

In the meantime, Charlie and Billy had to pack ready for the new school term. They worked in silence, folding their blue capes and white shirts, and tucking books, shoes and socks into the bottom of their bags, each of them thinking of the new term ahead. Charlie wondered what the situation would be like in the King's Room, where the

descendants of the Red King held their silent battles during homework hours. At the end of the previous term, Charlie and his friends had seemed to gain the upper hand, but he knew the peace was temporary. The other five had been revealed as powerful enemies. There was bound to be conflict among the children of the Red King.

The next morning, when Charlie stepped inside the tall doors of Bloor's Academy, he noticed that many of the children looked depressed. The rule of silence was not the only reason for the gloomy atmosphere. Shoulders were hunched, eyes downcast, and huge sighs were emitted as children found their way through the crowd and into the right cloakrooms.

'Deary me, what a gloomy shower!' Manfred Bloor pushed his way through the throng. 'What's the matter with you all? Give us a smile, Emma! Gabriel Silk, you look like a wet week. Move out of my way, you moron.'

Manfred had suddenly come face to face with Lysander Sage. Charlie noticed that his friend was now almost as tall as the headmaster's son. Lysander, wearing a look of grim determination, silently stood his ground.

'Move!' bellowed Manfred.

'Say please!'

The children round the two young men instantly drew

back, leaving Manfred and Lysander isolated in the centre of the hall. Manfred's pale face had turned bright red. He scowled at Lysander, his black eyes narrowing and his eyebrows drawn into a furious line above his long nose.

Charlie held his breath. If Lysander didn't move quickly he'd be hypnotised. Everyone in the hall was aware of the danger. Many of them had already been the victim of Manfred's paralysing gaze, including Charlie.

Move, Sander, move, Charlie silently implored his friend.

But Lysander wouldn't give way.

Manfred opened his mouth. A horrible gurgle came out. He was trying to threaten detention but, with a snort of contempt, Lysander slipped away and went into the green cloakroom.

Charlie stood still, amazed by what he had seen. Manfred Bloor had failed to hypnotise or intimidate Lysander, and now he appeared to be in shock. He glared into the distance, horror and disbelief written across his bony face.

Billy tugged Charlie's cape. 'We'd better get out of here,' he whispered.

His warning came too late.

'What are you gawping at, Bone?' shouted Manfred, now even more furious than before.

'Nothing . . . I just . . . I thought I'd lost something.'

'Your wits most likely.' Manfred turned abruptly and marched over to the Prefects' Room.

Charlie felt like shouting something rude at his back, but Billy pulled him into the blue cloakroom. They were met by a buzz of conversation. At least ten children had lost their pets. Gabriel Silk looked even more forlorn than usual. Twenty of his gerbils were missing, also three ducks and his mother's pet goat.

'That's not as bad as losing our dog,' whined Gwyneth Howells, a moaner if ever there was one.

'Losing a cat's worse than losing a dog,' argued a small girl in a cape that was two sizes too large for her.

Fidelio Gunn was tuning his violin, oblivious to the conversation going on around him.

'Fido, what about your cat? Pudding, isn't it?' Charlie sat on the bench beside his friend.

'Pudding? What about her?' Fidelio bent over his violin and tightened a string. 'She's fine. Deaf as a post, of course.'

'You must've heard what's been going on. Everyone's pet has . . .' Charlie paused, struck by a sudden thought. 'Of course, your cat's deaf.' He pictured Fidelio's house, crammed with musical children, strumming and drumming, singing and thumping. Gunn House positively

rocked with sound – but surely, not at midnight.

'Did anything special happen in your house on Saturday night?' Charlie asked.

'Yeah.' Fidelio hummed a note. 'Felix had his band over. They were in the cellar but they still made a helluva noise. Dad sent them packing round about one a.m.'

'That accounts for it,' said Charlie. 'Pudding wouldn't have felt a thing.' He stood up, aware that the cloakroom was now empty. 'Come on, we'll be late for assembly.'

At first break an atmosphere of gloom lay over the playing field. Charlie was surprised by the number of children who kept a pet of some sort. He passed little knots of dejected owners discussing their lost animals: dogs, cats, rabbits, even iguanas, snakes and bushbabies. Where had they gone, and why? Would they come back, and when?

Charlie had no doubt that the finger of suspicion would eventually fall on the Children of the Red King. They were usually blamed for unusual happenings.

Miss Chrystal, the violin teacher, gave Charlie a cheery wave from the door. 'Are you all right, Charlie?' she called. 'You look lost.'

'I was just looking for Fidelio, Miss,' said Charlie.

'Ah. He's waiting for a music lesson. I'm late.' Miss Chrystal popped back inside.

Charlie envied Fidelio. He had the youngest and prettiest music teacher in the school. Charlie had old Mr Paltry with his bad temper and smoker's cough.

'Hi, Charlie!'

Charlie turned to see Tancred and Lysander walking round the field together. Tancred beckoned to him. When Charlie ran up to them, Lysander's usual welcoming smile was absent. He stared moodily into the distance, as if Charlie wasn't even there.

'Hey, it was great, you standing up to Manfred like that,' Charlie said encouragingly.

Still no smile. 'Yeah.' Lysander stared grimly ahead.

'His parrot's gone,' Tancred explained. 'You know – Homer.'

'All the animals have gone,' said Charlie. 'They went during the snowstorm on Saturday. But we'll get them back, I know we will.'

Tancred said quickly, 'About the snow, Charlie. It was me. I brought it, but I swear I had nothing to do with the animals.'

'*You!*' said Charlie. 'No wonder. I thought there was something weird about that stuff.'

Tancred looked slightly offended. 'I thought I did a pretty good job, actually.'

'But why snow?' asked Charlie.

'The Flame cats made me do it.' Tancred ran a hand through his spiky yellow hair. 'I'm not sure why.'

'They came to see me, too,' said Charlie, almost to himself. 'Maybe they were trying to stop something from being found, and the snow helped, for a while, but in the end someone got to an object that connects our world to a kind of – ancient spirit.' Charlie drew breath.

The two older boys were staring at him with a mixture of fascination and disbelief.

'Go on,' said Lysander.

'Well, when that happened, the earth shuddered. At least that's what Rembrandt told Billy. The animals felt the shudder and they were all so frightened they fled.'

'Where to?' Lysander demanded. 'My parrot's gone and I want him back. I need him.'

Charlie gave a defeated shrug. 'Rembrandt said they all went across the river. He came back, but now he can't remember how he got to – wherever they all went.'

'Useless rat,' Lysander grunted.

Charlie was disappointed to find a tough character like Lysander so dependent on a parrot. He was about to defend Rembrandt when the horn sounded for the end of break and the boys headed back towards the school.

As a crowd of children filed through the garden door, Charlie was astonished to see a familiar figure walking among them. It was Benjamin's mother, Mrs Brown.

'That's your friend's mum, Charlie,' Tancred observed. 'Is Benjamin coming to Bloor's?'

Charlie shook his head. 'No. He would have said. What's she doing here?'

'She's a private investigator, so she's probably investigating,' said Lysander. 'Hey, maybe she's come to find out about the disappearing animals. They probably think it's one of us.' He gave a bitter laugh.

Mrs Brown suddenly looked over her shoulder and met Charlie's gaze. She quickly turned away and stepped through the door.

'She doesn't want to know me,' said Charlie incredulously.

'You're under suspicion, Charlie Bone,' said Tancred with a mocking grin. 'See you later, animal evaporator.' He flew after Lysander, who was already several strides ahead.

'What . . .' Charlie stood with his mouth open.

Tancred was joking, of course, but it was no joke to have your oldest friend's mother deliberately avoiding you.

'Trust you to be last.' Asa Pike, the head prefect, smirked at Charlie from inside the hall. 'I'm going to lock this door in ten sec–'

'NO!' Charlie leapt over the step and skidded to a halt beside Asa.

'Did you have a nice Christmas holiday?' There was a sneer behind Asa's every remark.

Charlie chose to ignore the sneer and replied, 'Great, thanks. And you?'

Asa's weaselly face twitched. He tucked a greasy strand of orange hair behind his ear and said, 'Course. Get moving or you'll be late for class.'

Charlie hastened across the hall, leaving Asa to lock the door. There was something unusual about the prefect's behaviour. He had seemed nervous and ill at ease. Asa was the oldest pupil in the school and should have been head boy but, having failed all last year's exams, he had been passed over for Riley Burns, a bossy know-all and champion athlete.

Could Asa's humiliation have accounted for his nervousness? Charlie wasn't sure. And then a thought struck him. When dusk fell, Asa had been known to change his shape; he could become a long-snouted, crook-backed, wolfish creature. Perhaps, like other animals, he too had felt the earth shudder. Charlie decided to observe the prefect during homework, when they would sit at the same table in the King's Room.

That evening, Charlie was the first person through the black doors of the King's Room. He looked around the high-ceilinged, circular room, its curved walls lined with shelves of leather-bound books. There was space for only one picture: a huge gilt-framed painting of the Red King.

Charlie liked to sit where he could see the painting and, as he arranged his books on the large round table, the other endowed children began to arrive.

First came Joshua Tilpin, a small boy with a mousey face, big ears and crooked teeth. As usual, he wore a dusting of chalk, paper, leaves and twigs. Joshua was magnetic in more ways than one. Next came the telekinetic twins, Idith and Inez, and then Billy Raven made a furtive entrance. Sidling towards Charlie, he whispered, 'I've got something to tell you.'

But Charlie barely heard him. He was staring at the king's portrait. He knew it so well. He had gazed so often at the dark face, its features blurred by cracks in the ancient paint. The king wore a slim gold crown and a red cloak, its deep folds darkened and stained with age. Charlie had longed to enter the painting and walk in the distant world of the Red King, but something always prevented him. A dark shadow stood behind the king, a mysterious figure that blocked Charlie's every attempt

to reach his ancestor. But now . . .

Charlie's eyes widened. Dizzy with shock, he gripped the back of his chair. The shadow had moved. Only slightly, but Charlie knew the painting so well it was obvious to him. Once the shadow had been a hazy shape, standing behind the king. Now it appeared to be larger and more defined, as though it had taken a step forward.

'The shadow,' he breathed.

Leaning close to him, Billy said softly, 'I was going to tell you.'

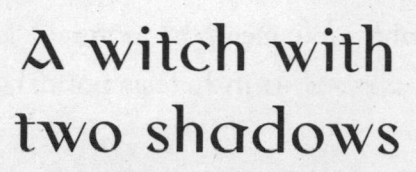

A witch with two shadows

'Billy Raven, are you talking?' Manfred Bloor strode into the room. He was carrying a large black briefcase, brand new by the look of it.

'Er – not really. I was just sort of asking Charlie to move a book.' Billy's red eyes blinked nervously.

'Silence is golden, remember that, Billy.' Manfred settled himself on the opposite side of the table.

'Yes, Man– sir.' Just in time, Billy remembered that Manfred must now be called 'sir'.

Gradually, the King's Room filled up. Lysander was the last one in. He closed the door with a backward kick, causing Manfred

to storm, 'For pete's sake, can't you behave normally, Lysander Sage?'

'Depends what you mean by normal,' Lysander said airly. 'I mean none of us in here is normal, are we? Not even you.'

Thrown offguard, Manfred stared at Lysander with an expression of horror. But quickly regaining his composure, he snarled, 'I've had enough of your cheek, Sage. That remark will cost you. Now sit down and shut up.'

Shrugging his shoulders, Lysander sat beside Tancred and, watched by the rest of the room, arranged his books on the table.

The oppressive atmosphere in the King's Room grew steadily worse. To Charlie, the children sitting on either side of Manfred seemed especially smug tonight. They kept darting secretive looks at each other, and then glaring across the table at Charlie and his friends.

Dorcas Loom had once been a round and rosy, perpetually smiling girl. Now she was a heavy-set, glowering twelve year old, with matted blonde hair and an unhealthy indoor pallor. She sat between the identical Branko twins, Idith and Inez, the black-haired, doll-faced children who only smiled when someone was in trouble.

One of the twins (who knows which) was watching

Charlie now, as his gaze slid up to the Red King's portrait. He couldn't concentrate on his work at all. The changed position of the sinister shadow in the painting filled his thoughts. How had it happened? And why? Manfred had told him that the shadow was Borlath, the king's oldest son and a brutal tyrant. But Charlie's instincts told him that this was not true. Who, then, was the shadow?

'Bone! Do your work!' Manfred's voice brought Charlie back to earth.

'I w-was,' he stuttered.

'No you weren't. You were staring at that painting again. You're always doing it. Well, give it up, Charlie Bone, because that's one picture you're never, ever going to enter. Understand?'

'If you say so.' Charlie bent over his work. He had resisted the urge to mention the shadow, although he longed to know how the others would react. Apart from Billy, had any of them even noticed that the shadow had moved?

As soon as homework was over, Charlie gathered up his books and quickly followed Billy out of the room.

'Did you see the shadow?' he asked Billy, as the smaller boy hurried along the passage. 'Is that what you wanted to tell me?'

'I'm not very observant,' Billy said warily. He stopped and looked over his shoulder. 'What are they waiting for?'

Looking back, Charlie saw Gabriel, Emma, Tancred and Lysander standing outside the King's Room.

'Did you see that?' Emma called to Charlie.

'What?' said Charlie, irritated by the distraction and desperate to find out more from Billy.

'Asa came and locked the door as soon as we left the room,' Emma told him.

'And the others are still in there,' added Gabriel. 'What are they up to?'

'Who cares.' Lysander strolled away from the group.

'I care.' Tancred's cape billowed out and a strong breeze whistled through everyone's hair. 'What are they doing? I want to know.' He put his ear to the door, which suddenly opened, causing him to fall forward, straight into Asa Pike.

'Shove off, spy!' hissed Asa, pushing Tancred backwards.

With a yell of rage, Tancred stumbled back, lost his balance and sat down hard on his bottom.

'And that goes for all of you.' Asa glared down the passage. 'Unless you want detention.' He slammed the door and locked it loudly from the inside.

Tancred got to his feet and was about to approach the

King's Room again, when Emma put a hand on his arm. 'Don't, Tanc,' she said. 'It's not worth it.'

Charlie could see that Tancred was just itching to bang on those tall black doors, but something in Emma's quiet voice stopped him. 'OK. You're right, Em. I'm just playing into their hands.'

Emma helped Tancred to gather the books and pens he'd dropped and, with a pile of homework tucked under his arms, the storm boy joined the group making its way to the dormitories. When they had crossed the landing above the hall, the two older boys left the others and mounted a staircase to the upper floors. A little further on, Emma began to climb a second staircase to the girls' dormitories.

'Night, Em. See you –' Charlie broke off.

'What is it?' Emma looked over her shoulder.

The passage was very dim, and the doors leading off it hardly discernable, but Charlie knew what he had seen. 'Mr Brown,' he whispered. 'Benjamin's dad. He went into one of those store rooms. He was following us. I'm sure he was.'

'Weird,' said Emma. 'But we can't do anything about it now.' She yawned. 'I'm off. Night, boys.' She disappeared up into the shadows of the next floor.

Charlie and Billy continued down the long gloomy passage to the dormitory they had shared the previous

term. Lists had been pinned to the doors and they soon found that they would be together again.

Gabriel was already in the dormitory. He was sitting on one of the beds, sniffing the air. 'There's a funny smell in here,' he said.

'Smell or not, we're the first ones here, so we get first choice of a bed.' Charlie consulted his watch. 'Hey, Manfred let us out early.'

'So that he could have his secret talks with Asa and co, no doubt,' Gabriel suggested. He went into the bathroom and gave a shout of surprise. 'Uurgh! What a stink. It's that dog again.'

'Oh, poor Blessed, I forgot him.' As Billy ran to the bathroom he almost tripped over the short, fat dog that came waddling out as fast as its stubby legs could carry it.

'What's he doing here?' Gabriel exclaimed. 'How come he didn't disappear with the rest of the animals?'

'I was going to tell you.' Billy patted the old dog's head. 'He came in when I was unpacking my bag, and I kind of, accidentally, shut him in the bathroom when I went to homework.'

'That doesn't explain how he avoided the great animal exodus,' said Gabriel as he returned to the bathroom.

'He's old,' Charlie pointed out. 'A lot of the old ones

couldn't make it, or didn't feel the shudder, or whatever it was.'

Billy heaved Blessed on to the bed he had chosen for himself. 'Actually, he did feel the shudder,' he told Charlie. 'But he was with Cook and she made him stay where he was. When it was all over, he crept out and saw something that made him very, very scared. Didn't it, Blessed?'

The old dog gave several low grunts and made himself comfortable on Billy's pillow. Charlie sat on the end of the bed next to Billy's. He didn't understand how Billy could tolerate the terrible smell that Blessed must leave on his pillow, let alone the dirt, hairs and probably fleas.

'Well, what did he see?' Charlie asked Billy.

The small albino lowered his voice. 'He saw a witch with two shadows.'

'What!' cried Charlie.

Gabriel sprang out of the bathroom. 'What happened?'

Charlie repeated what Billy had told him.

'What d'you mean, a witch?' Alarm spread across Gabriel's long face, making him look like a startled rabbit. 'How did Blessed know it was a witch?'

'That's my word for it,' Billy admitted. 'Blessed's word was more like devil-woman.'

'Devil-woman.' The hairs on the back of Charlie's neck

prickled like a bramble bush. 'That's worse.'

'And what's all this stuff about two shadows?' asked Gabriel, hoping to calm himself with a rational explanation. 'D'you think he was seeing double? I mean he's a pretty ancient dog, isn't he?'

'His eyesight's just as good as mine.' Billy adjusted his round-framed spectacles and spoke to Blessed in a whining sort of mumble.

Blessed gave a worried howl, then rolled on to his back and emitted a series of staccato-like barks.

'Definitely two shadows,' said Billy, when the old dog's voice had subsided. 'Because one of them turned into something else while the devil-woman's shadow stayed with her.'

'What did it turn into?' asked Gabriel and Charlie in unison.

'For a dog he described it very well,' Billy said appreciatively. 'He was in the hall, behind that old chest. The woman came down the main staircase with these two shadows spread across the flagstones in front of her. And when they reached the main doors this . . . other one kind of stood up. First it was grey, like a cloud of dust, and then it was green with golden patterns on it.'

Billy glanced at Blessed and lowered his voice. 'He said

it was a dressing gown, but I think he means that it was a long kind of medieval robe.' He gave Blessed a friendly grin. 'It's not his fault. I mean, he's never seen a medieval robe. I mean *I've* only ever seen pictures of –'

'Could you please go on about the shadow?' begged Charlie.

'Sorry. But dogs' feelings are important.' Billy gave a light cough. 'Anyway, he said that it had a man's face and brown hair, almost to its shoulders, and its shoes were long and pointed, and –'

The door suddenly burst open and a crowd of boys streamed into the room.

'Uuurgh! Not that smelly old dog again,' said the first boy, a large, chunky character who had earned the name 'Bragger' Braine.

Blessed gave a whine of dismay, tumbled off the bed and padded through the door as fast as he could.

'It's disgusting,' grumbled Bragger, making for the bed furthest from Billy's. 'That dog has the most evil smell in the world.'

'I can think of worse,' said Fidelio, putting his bag on the bed Charlie had saved for him.

'Mummy's given me some air-freshener,' Rupe Small, a diminutive first-former piped up. 'It'll soon smell better in

here, Bragger.' He produced an enormous pink can and proceeded to spray the room with an even worse scent than Old Dog.

'It's called Sweet Petal,' Rupe called happily, while eleven boys dived on to their beds and covered their faces with pillows, pyjamas and anything they could lay their hands on.

Choking cries of 'Stop that!' 'It's worse!' 'Give it up!' 'Someone strangle him!' came from the victims, while Rupe blithely filled the dormitory with the suffocating scent of Sweet Petal.

Nothing, it seemed, could stop the determined sprayer, until a series of ear-splitting screams issued from the floor above. Caught in mid-puff, Rupe stood with his mouth agape while boys flung themselves off their beds and piled past him.

Charlie was the first to reach the girls' floor. He stood at the top of the stairs, rocking on his feet and perilously close to a backward tumble, while Gabriel, propping him up with both hands, peered round him into the passage beyond.

'OH, GRIEF! OH, MUM!' screeched Gabriel, collapsing on to the line of boys standing behind him.

Oblivious to the yells of pain and anger below, Charlie stared incredulously at the creature in front of him. A

greenish-grey alligator of gigantic proportions blocked the entire passage. It blinked its yellow eyes and opened a cavernous mouth, crammed with more evil-looking razor-sharp teeth than Charlie had even seen, even in horror movies.

The floor behind the monster was littered with prostrate figures in various items of nightwear, while the terrified faces of girls who hadn't yet fainted kept peering out of their rooms, screaming and withdrawing. The passage echoed with the drumbeats of hastily slammed doors.

All at once, the giant creature gave a throaty bellow and came charging at Charlie. Clinging to the stair-rail, but unable to move, Charlie screamed so loudly the creature actually stopped in its tracks.

'WHAT'S GOING ON?'

Charlie recognised the voice of his great-aunt Lucretia, the matron. Knowing how much she disliked him, he doubted if she would come to his rescue, but to his amazement, the monster began to de-materialise. Beginning with its tail, invisibility slid up its warty back and over its gnarled head until it was completely swallowed in nothingness.

By the time Lucretia Yewbeam had climbed over the injured boys and reached Charlie, the passage was empty,

except, of course, for the unconscious girls.

Taking in the dreadful scene before her, the matron cried, 'CHARLIE BONE, WHAT, IN THE NAME OF ALL THAT'S GOOD, HAVE YOU DONE?'

'Me?' croaked Charlie. 'Nothing.'

'Do you call that nothing?' The matron pointed at the fallen girls, some of whom were now regaining consciousness.

'I didn't do *that*,' said Charlie.

'He did,' said a sly voice. Dorcas Loom had emerged from one of the dormitories. 'He made an alligator. Well, that is to say, he created the illusion of one.'

'I never,' cried Charlie. 'You know I didn't. I got here minutes after you all started screaming.'

'That doesn't mean that you didn't do it,' said Dorcas.

'Go to the headmaster this instant.' The matron glowered down at Charlie.

'Why?' asked Charlie, genuinely surprised.

'To explain what you've done.'

'But . . .' Charlie looked up at the cold face looming over him. They were all the same, his grandmother and his three great-aunts. They would always be against him. To argue would be useless.

He was about to go down the stairs when a voice

sang out, 'He didn't do it, Matron. Honestly. I know he didn't.'

Charlie turned to see Olivia Vertigo bouncing along the passage. She was wearing the most incredible pair of pyjamas. They were black velvet embroidered with huge golden flowers and exactly matched her black-and-gold striped hair.

'Mind your own business, Olivia,' barked the matron.

'But it is my business,' Olivia protested. 'Dorcas was lying. Charlie's innocent.'

'Innocent, my foot.' The matron gave Olivia a violent shove. 'Get to bed.'

'Thanks for trying, Liv,' said Charlie. 'By the way, you look fantastic.'

'I told you to see Dr Bloor,' shrieked the matron. 'Now, GO!' She grabbed Charlie's shoulder and sent him stumbling down the stairs.

Fidelio was waiting outside the dormitory. 'Good luck,' he called.

Charlie grinned. 'Dr Bloor doesn't scare me.'

They could hear the matron marching along the passage above them, barking out orders and hauling whimpering girls to their feet.

'Poor things!' Charlie muttered as he left the noises

behind him. When he came to the main staircase he heard a light footstep below him and looked down. The hall appeared to be deserted. Charlie began to descend. He was halfway down when he saw a figure dart into the blue cloakroom. Mr Brown, if Charlie was not mistaken.

Did Benjamin know that his parents were working at Bloor's? Charlie wondered. He had reached the small door that led to the Bloors' apartment in the west wing. A single, dim light showed the way to the base of the west tower. From here a spiral staircase climbed to the turret, but at the first floor, Charlie turned through an arch into a thickly carpeted corridor.

It was only now that he began to hear his own heartbeat thumping in his chest. He hated this part of the academy. For all its comparative warmth and comfort it made him feel like a trespasser. He began to wonder how he could prove his innocence without revealing the identity of the true culprit. For that must remain a secret at all costs.

Olivia had discovered her endowment the previous term. Only Charlie, Fidelio and Emma knew about it, and they decided to keep it a secret. The fewer the people who knew about it, the better. Olivia had promised to use her gift only in the most desperate circumstances, so what had

possessed her to conjure up an alligator, right outside the girls' dormitories?

Charlie had reached the lofty oak-panelled door of Dr Bloor's study. He knocked tentatively.

'Enter!' Dr Bloor's frosty voice came from within the room.

Charlie entered and stood just inside the door. His heart sank when he saw old Ezekiel sitting by the fire in his wheelchair. He looked even older than his one hundred and one years, with his skull-like face and sparse white hair.

'What brings you here so late in the day, Charlie Bone?' Dr Bloor demanded.

'Matron sent me.' The words stuck in Charlie's throat and came bubbling out as if he were gargling.

'What?' Ezekiel put a hand to his ear. 'Speak up, boy.'

'Matron sent me,' shouted Charlie.

'No need to shout,' said Dr Bloor, 'we're not deaf.'

'No, sir.'

'So? Come on, why did Matron send you? What have you done now?'

'Can you never keep out of trouble?' Ezekiel gave Charlie a black-toothed grin.

'I try,' said Charlie. 'But sometimes I am falsely accused.'

'I hope you're not blaming members of staff.' The

headmaster gave Charlie one of his dead-eyed glares.

Charlie shifted from foot to foot. 'Not exactly.'

'Not exactly. What have you been accused of, Bone?'

'Of making girls faint, sir.'

Dr Bloor raised an eyebrow. 'And how, pray, did you achieve that?'

'That's just it, sir. I didn't,' Charlie blurted out. 'There was this alligator in the passage, an illusion and –'

'What?' Ezekiel whirled his wheelchair away from the fireplace and drew up in front of Charlie. 'So it's you. You, who have been creating illusions, frightening people to death.'

'NO!' cried Charlie. 'It's not. I can't. If I could, I'd have done it ages ago.'

Ezekiel Bloor's small black eyes darted over Charlie's face, as though seeking the truth from his slightest change of expression.

'He didn't do it, Grandfather,' said Dr Bloor. 'I believe it's someone who has only recently discovered their endowment. And Charlie knows who it is.'

'Yesss!' Ezekiel spat the word. 'Yess! He knows. Who is it, Charlie?'

'I *don't* know.'

'Liar!' The old man's cane was hidden in the folds of his

tartan rug and Charlie didn't see it until, in a blur of white, it slashed across his knees.

'Owww!' yelled Charlie.

'You know who it is,' said Ezekiel. 'And now we must know. We have to, you see. Every child who is endowed must be known to us.'

'Well,' said Charlie, thinking fast as he rubbed his knees, 'I haven't a clue. Nor have any of us. It took us completely by surprise. I mean we knew there were twelve of us – if you include Manfred – so imagine how we felt when, out of the blue, someone started creating illusions.' Charlie paused, worried that he had gone too far. 'Perhaps it's one of the teachers.'

'Don't be silly!' Ezekiel lifted his cane but Charlie stepped out of the way just in time.

'Let it go, Grandfather.' Dr Bloor spoke slowly, his tone full of menace. 'We'll find out in time. And then, oh dear, they'll be in for it. Nasty, crafty, sneaking child. And you'll be in for it too, Charlie Bone, for lying.'

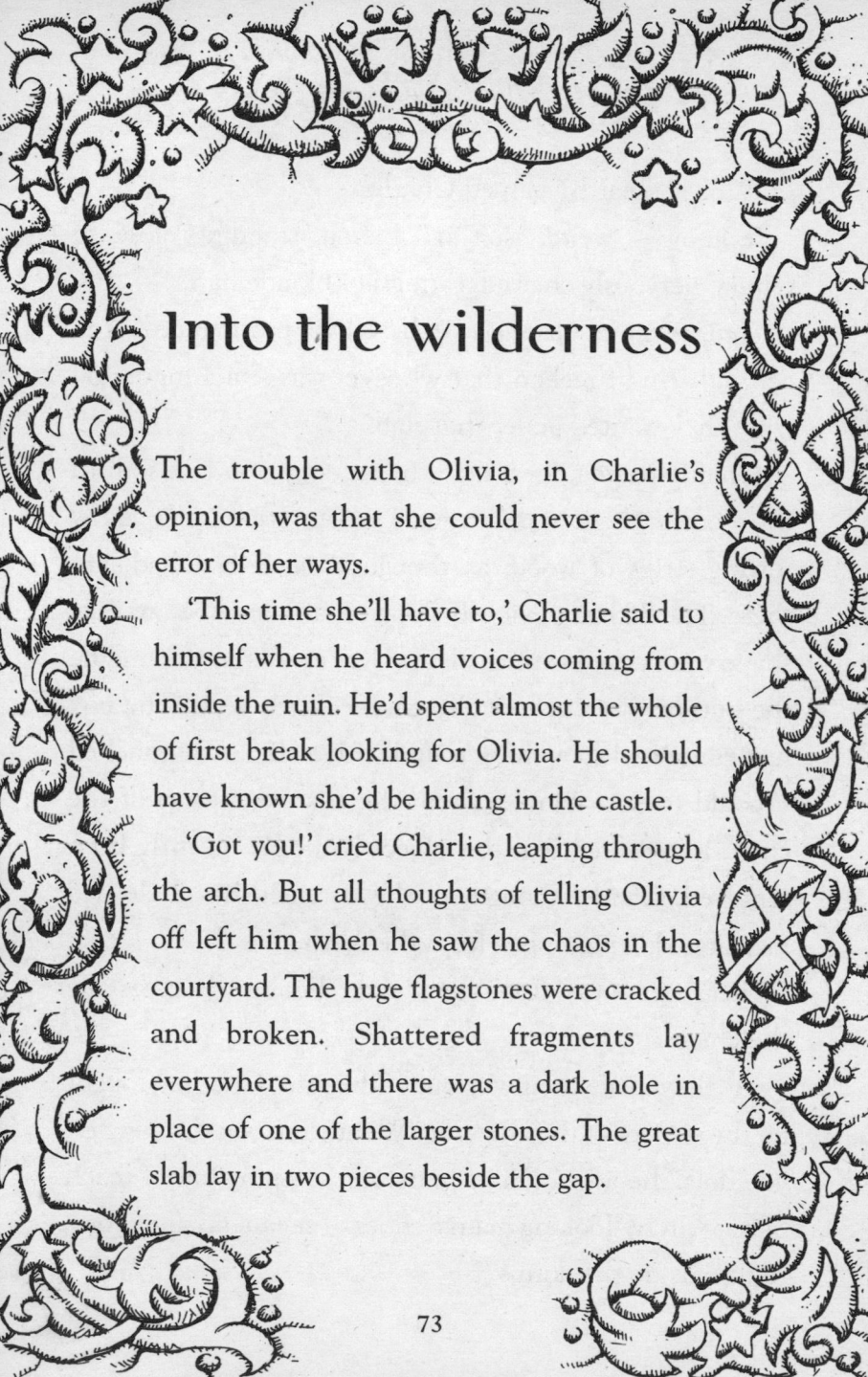

Into the wilderness

The trouble with Olivia, in Charlie's opinion, was that she could never see the error of her ways.

'This time she'll have to,' Charlie said to himself when he heard voices coming from inside the ruin. He'd spent almost the whole of first break looking for Olivia. He should have known she'd be hiding in the castle.

'Got you!' cried Charlie, leaping through the arch. But all thoughts of telling Olivia off left him when he saw the chaos in the courtyard. The huge flagstones were cracked and broken. Shattered fragments lay everywhere and there was a dark hole in place of one of the larger stones. The great slab lay in two pieces beside the gap.

'What on earth?' gasped Charlie.

'I know – weird, isn't it?' Emma, standing close to Olivia, nervously chewed a strand of blonde hair.

'This is the result of a search,' Olivia pronounced. 'You can tell. And I reckon that whoever was searching found what they wanted under that slab.'

Charlie peered down into the rectangle of dark soil. In the centre there was a square indentation defined by rotting strips of wood, as though a small box had lain there. The lid had obviously decayed and now the box-like shape was packed with earth and leaves. But in the middle the outline of a circle could still be clearly seen. The box had contained something round with a slim oval attached – could it be a handle? From the sharp contours of the circle it appeared that the object had only recently been removed. Charlie thought of the 'artefact' his uncle had mentioned being ripped from the earth.

'Let's get away from here,' said Emma. 'It gives me the creeps.'

As they made their way out of the ruin, Charlie brought up the subject of the alligator. 'What were you thinking of, you dolt?' he asked Olivia, carefully stepping out of reach of her witchy-looking mauve shoes. 'I mean, an alligator – right outside the dorms.'

'I was sick of all the moaning.' Olivia adjusted the mauve bandanna on her head. 'They were all going on about their lost kittens and disappearing dogs and stuff and . . .' a wicked sparkle came into her eye. 'Did you know that the Looms' revolting Rottweilers were missing? Dorcas has never liked them but she was grizzling like a drain. 'Oh, my poor brothers, they've lost their dogs.' So I thought an alligator would cheer her up.'

Olivia was a brilliant actress and Charlie couldn't help smiling at her impression of Dorcas Loom. 'You'll scare someone to death, Liv, and then what'll we do? You'll be found out and then you'll be finished. The Bloors are desperate to know who's creating the illusions.'

Olivia grinned. 'I won't be found out.'

'You might,' said Emma. 'And then you won't be able to help us. Remember, you're our secret weapon.'

Olivia gave a huge sigh. 'OK. I promise to cool it for a while, but I tell you, it's so much fun scaring people out of their wits. People who deserve it, of course.'

Charlie looked away from her. 'Being endowed isn't supposed to be fun.' He could hardly believe what he had just said. The words just popped out of his mouth without his knowing they were there.

'That's a very un-Charlie-ish thing to say,' Olivia remarked.

'Charlie shrugged. 'Perhaps it's the new Charlie speaking. I'm twelve now.' He began to race away from them.

'Don't let your age be a burden, Charlie!' Olivia called after him.

Charlie turned and gave her a wave. 'Are you nuts?' And yet, when he thought about it, his own endowment had certainly not proved very helpful just lately.

Olivia kept her promise. For the rest of the week no alligators appeared outside the dormitories, no dinosaurs roamed the gardens and no medieval warriors galloped through the school, brandishing axes (one of Olivia's specialities).

If Blessed had seen the shadow again, he was keeping it to himself, and Charlie's chief concern became the baffling presence of Benjamin's parents.

On Friday, when Charlie asked Billy if he'd like to stay the weekend, he was surprised by the answer.

'Mrs Brown has asked me to keep Benjamin company,' Billy said brightly. 'You see, he's lonely without his dog.'

Charlie felt surprised and guilty all at the same time, and yet it wasn't his fault that Runner Bean had run away.

He, Charlie, was Benjamin's friend. Why couldn't he keep Benjamin company?

But all he said was, 'Oh. All right then.'

Back at home, Charlie sat at the kitchen table while Maisie stirred eggs in a saucepan on the stove.

'It's been a funny old week,' said Maisie. 'No birdsong, no cats on fences, no dogs on leads. I never realised the difference they made. It's lonely without them, you know. People are saying that the city is dying.'

'Mm,' Charlie mumbled. He was wondering if he would see the girl in the sunshine coat again.

'They've had the police on to it; and animal welfare and council workers and private detectives, and Lord knows what else.' Maisie brought a dish of scrambled eggs to the table and peered into Charlie's face. 'What's up, then, Charlie? Had a bad week?'

Charlie shook his head. 'Not really.'

'Benjamin coming over?'

Charlie shrugged. 'Billy Raven's staying with Ben this weekend.'

'Well, there's a turn-up.' Maisie raised her eyebrows. 'Didn't know they were friends.'

'And Fido's playing in the band,' Charlie went on sadly.

'You do sound sorry for yourself.' Maisie sat beside

Charlie. 'Come on, eat those lovely eggs. Much better for you than patti- di- fwa-gra, or whatever it is Grandma Bone has such a passion for.'

Charlie managed to raise a smile. He was about to start his meal when Uncle Paton marched in and, flinging open the fridge door, declared, 'I'm starving. My hamper's not coming today, they tell me. Hope you're not too disappointed, Charlie?'

Every Friday Uncle Paton had a large hamper of delicious food delivered from a store in the city. Charlie had been so immersed in his own problems he had quite forgotten to look forward to it. 'What happened?' he asked.

'Owner dropped dead,' said Uncle Paton.

Charlie put down his fork. 'Just like that? Dropped dead? Was he in the store? Were people scared?'

'Yes, is the answer to all those questions,' Uncle Paton replied.

'It was in the papers,' said Maisie, 'along with the missing animals. What a week.'

'What did he die of?' Charlie found he couldn't eat.

'Ah. There's the mystery.' Uncle Paton brought a plate of cheese and biscuits to the table. 'Can I eat your eggs, Charlie?'

Maisie slapped Paton's hand, which had begun to inch

its way towards Charlie's plate. 'The boy needs his food,' she said sharply. 'Charlie, eat up.'

'Didn't the doctors know?' Charlie put a forkful of egg into his mouth. He was worried about this store owner who had inexplicably dropped dead.

'His heart stopped beating for no reason,' said Uncle Paton. 'Very fit man apparently. Regular jogger. Very sad. Luckily, no family, though. The new owner has already taken the reins – a relative, I'm told. They'll be back to normal next week and we'll get our weekend treats.' This time it was Uncle Paton who peered into Charlie's face. 'Feeling your age, Charlie? Twelve isn't the end of the world, you know.'

'Twelve,' Charlie repeated. 'I was two when my dad disappeared. Ten years ago. Ten. Is that a lucky number, do you think?'

Paton's jovial expression softened. 'Ten?' he said thoughtfully. 'Well, the Red King had ten children, but it's a matter of opinion whether this was lucky.'

'Hardly,' muttered Maisie.

Someone could be heard climbing the steps up to the front door and, as Charlie turned to the window, he saw Benjamin and Billy get into the Browns' car. Where were they off to? he wondered. A movie? The bowling alley?

Amy Bone came in looking weary after a week of weighing vegetables. As usual, she made the best of things. 'Pineapples,' she said cheerfully, plonking a bag of prickly shapes on the table. 'It'll make up for the hamper not coming.' She pecked Charlie's cheek. 'You look glum, Charlie.'

'Good to see you too, Mum.' Charlie took his plate to the sink.

'Are we going to see Benjamin this weekend?' asked Charlie's mother. 'You two must have a lot to catch up on.'

'No.' Charlie turned and, with his back to the sink, he gave his three relatives a challenging stare. They looked up expectantly.

'I won't be seeing Benjamin because he blames me for Runner Bean's vanishing. Fidelio is playing in a band and Billy Raven is staying with the Browns. Oh, and by the way, Benjamin's parents are working at Bloor's now.'

'Extraordinary,' Paton declared.

'But I won't be lonely,' Charlie went on, 'because I'll go to Ingledew's Bookshop. OK?'

'Of course, it's OK, Charlie,' his mother said quietly.

Pronouncing Ingledews to be the best place in the world, Uncle Paton got up, patted Charlie's shoulder and began to forage in the fridge again.

And that was that.

Except that Charlie never got to the bookshop because, early next morning, a light tap on his window led him into an adventure that would ultimately change his life. And a good many other lives besides.

The tap came at dawn. Charlie woke up. In the gap between the curtains he could see the white moth fluttering against the window pane. At first Charlie thought that the delicate beat of wings on glass had woken him. But then there came another tap, this time sharper and louder.

Charlie went to the window and looked out. The chestnut tree was covered in a crisp white frost. In the grey dawn light, Charlie could make out a figure standing beneath the tree's icy branches. It was the girl in sunshine yellow. Her hood was thrown back and she had a thick multicoloured scarf wound round her neck and covering her mouth. She waved at Charlie.

He opened the window. 'Hi! What d'you want?'

The girl pulled her scarf away from her mouth. 'Charlie Bone, I want to take you somewhere.'

Charlie was suspicious. 'Why?'

'Don't you trust me?'

'I don't know you.'

The girl frowned. 'You will have to trust me, if you want to find the animals.'

'The animals!' cried Charlie. 'You know where they are?'

'Sssh!' The girl put a finger to her lips. 'Are you coming?'

'You bet.'

Charlie hurriedly threw on his warmest clothes: thick socks, thick sweater, boots and padded jacket. As he passed the kitchen he thought of leaving a note, but what could he say? Better to let his mother believe he had gone to Ingledews, he decided.

The girl was waiting for him at the foot of the steps. Her glossy black hair was tucked into her scarf and her dark eyes held a mischievous twinkle. She held out her hand. 'Good to meet you, Charlie Bone.'

Charlie took her hand. 'And who are you?'

'Naren, the Chinese word for sunflower. They grew beside our door. Come. Let's go before the city wakes.'

The girl began to run up Filbert Street with Charlie panting behind her, amazed by the speed of her small springy feet in their black boots. When she reached the High Street, Naren waited for Charlie to catch up. And at last he managed to blurt out, 'Why me? Why did you choose me to find the animals?'

'Because you are Charlie Bone,' said Naren, 'so you are the right person.'

'I don't understand.'

'My father knows you. He worries for you.'

'Your father?' Charlie's heart leapt. 'He's not *my* father too, is he?'

'No. Not yours.' Naren lowered her gaze. 'Sorry, Charlie.' She looked up again. 'But he is a friend of your father.'

'Really? Can he tell me where he is?' Charlie was tense with hope.

'No. Sorry, sorry. He *was* a friend of your father. But now your father is lost.'

'Yes,' sighed Charlie.

'My father, too, was lost. But now ... come, the animals.' Naren darted off again, but this time she kept pace with Charlie and, as they travelled through the city together, she told him how she had been watching Charlie and his friends, Children of the Red King like herself. She told him how she had longed to speak to them. 'But my father said I must not approach you,' she said sadly.

'Why,' asked Charlie, 'if he knows me? And if you are one of us.'

'He will explain.' Naren put on a little burst of speed. As she ran, she said, almost in a whisper, 'He will be angry with me, for he forbade me to enter the city.'

Charlie glanced at her small anxious face, but asked no

more questions. Naren was leading him though an unfamiliar part of the city. Rows of bare trees reached into the cold sky, and the houses were partially obscured by tall hedges laced with frost. Naren slowed her pace and carefully picked her way round the icy patches on the pavement. She took a sudden turn to the left and Charlie, following, found himself on a narrow track that wound down and down and down. He could hear a loud rushing sound that grew more intense with every step he took.

Naren reached a set of railings and, looking over her shoulder, she declared, 'We're halfway there. But now we must be most careful.'

'Only halfway?' Charlie slithered up to her and grasped the railing. Looking down, he saw, perhaps sixty feet below him, a wild torrent of water. White foam gushed and bubbled over the dark rocks that thrust their way through the rapid rush of the river and Charlie was mesmerised by the dreadful pounding of the water. 'The river,' he gasped. 'I didn't know it was so close.'

Naren gave him a mysterious smile. 'Now we must cross it.'

'Must we?' Charlie said doubtfully.

'My home is on the other side.'

He looked across the chasm. At the top of the opposite

cliff a dense forest stretched as far as he could see. 'You live over there?' he asked in disbelief.

'People can live in forests.' Naren's smile widened.

'Yes, but that one?' Charlie stared at the distant mass of trees. 'I heard it was a wilderness.'

'Maybe it is.' She tugged his arm and pointed downwards. 'There's the bridge. Come on.'

Charlie leant over the railings and saw a thin strip of wrought iron suspended above the river. It looked old and dangerous. 'That?' he squeaked.

'There's a big bridge further on,' said Naren, 'but it's full of noisy traffic. I like this one, and so do the animals.'

'Oh, the animals.' Charlie remembered why he was standing above this turbulent river with a girl he'd only just met. He followed Naren's perilous route down the cliff face until they reached the iron bridge. Close up, it looked even more treacherous. The rail dripped with icicles and the flooring was grey with frost.

There was a sign hanging on a wire across the entrance to the bridge. It said, DANGER. UNSAFE BRIDGE.

But Charlie wasn't going to be outdone by a small Chinese girl. The rusty iron rang with the sound of Naren's boots as she tripped across and Charlie, swallowing hard, clanged after her.

They were halfway across when he thought of the promise he'd made on his twelfth birthday. He'd told his mother that he wouldn't make any more hasty decisions; that he'd stop to consider the consequences before he rushed into things. And yet, here he was, walking across an unsafe bridge above a river that could quite definitely drown him were he to fall into it.

Naren looked back. 'Why have you stopped?' she called.

'I was just admiring the view,' Charlie said airily.

'Come on.'

At that instant one of the supports that held the metal rail fell out and clanged on to the rocks below. The whole bridge shuddered and a shower of icicles spun down into the void.

Charlie froze.

'It's OK.' The girl smiled encouragingly. 'We're not heavy, you and me. The bridge will hold us.'

Gritting his teeth, Charlie strode after her.

When he got to the end of the bridge he hid his relief by swinging nonchalantly between the two final posts, and jumping on to a welcome strip of firm rock.

Naren laughed. 'Now, another climb,' she said.

The sky had become lighter and the climb to the top of

the cliff didn't seem nearly so hazardous as the descent on the other side.

At the top of the cliff they were surrounded by huge naked trees. A faint path led through the forest and Charlie, stepping behind Naren, became aware that the place was full of sound. From the bare branches, clusters of chattering birds watched the children passing beneath; even the dead grass rustled with life. Rabbits hopped beside the path, a stag peeped from behind a tree, and then, gradually, the wild sounds were drowned by an incessant and exciting barking.

A few seconds later, Runner Bean burst through the undergrowth and leapt up at Charlie, yelping with joy.

'Runner!' cried Charlie, hugging the big yellow dog.

'He's yours?' asked Naren.

'No. He belongs to my friend. But I feel kind of responsible for him, because Benjamin, my friend, has been away.'

'That dog was the first,' said Naren. 'Over the bridge he came, and the others followed: dogs, cats, ponies, goats, rabbits, everything. We heard them coming and ran to the cliff to look. It was quite a sight, all those animals under the moon, running across the bridge.'

'But why did they come here?'

'Because it's safer. Can't you feel it? Over there, in the city, something evil has woken up. My father will explain.'

Before Charlie could ask any more questions, Naren turned quickly and began to bound along the path. Runner Bean leapt beside her, but Charlie followed at a slower pace. He gazed up at the canopy of branches above his head. Yes, it did feel safer here. There was a calmness, a wonderful sense of protection. He wondered what sort of man he was about to meet. If Naren was descended from the Red King, then, in all probability, so was her father. Was he a sorcerer? A hypnotist? A were-beast?

A fence came into view, and an open gate. Charlie's heart began to pound. Naren was standing just inside, but Runner Bean waited for Charlie and together they walked through the gate into a wide enclosure.

At the far end stood a small cottage, with red-brick barns on either side. Smoke drifted from the cottage chimney and the slate roof was covered with birds. Animals of every description filled the enclosure. There were ponies cropping the sparse winter grass, dogs feeding from stone troughs and cats sitting on the fence.

A grey bird sailed out of a window calling, 'Dog ahoy!'

Surely it had to be Lysander's parrot, Homer.

Charlie barely registered the existence of the other creatures. His attention was held by a figure standing in front of the cottage door. The man was of medium height with a brown weathered face and a shock of white hair. In spite of the cold he wore only a tartan shirt over his muddy jeans. His tanned skin emphasised the colour of his vivid blue eyes, eyes that stared at Charlie with shock and recognition.

And Charlie noted the large axe, held across the man's chest. He looked all too ready to use it.

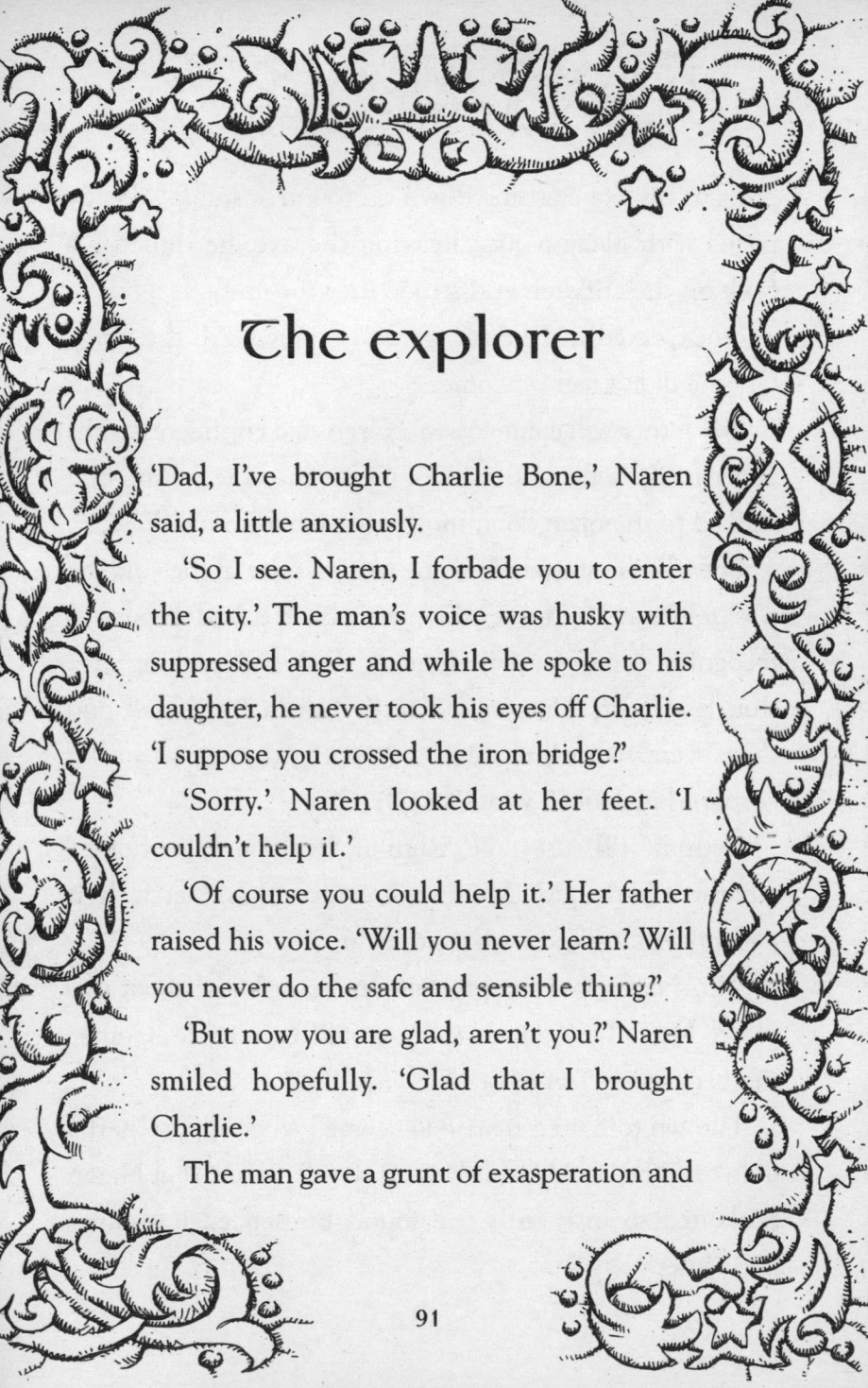

The explorer

'Dad, I've brought Charlie Bone,' Naren said, a little anxiously.

'So I see. Naren, I forbade you to enter the city.' The man's voice was husky with suppressed anger and while he spoke to his daughter, he never took his eyes off Charlie. 'I suppose you crossed the iron bridge?'

'Sorry.' Naren looked at her feet. 'I couldn't help it.'

'Of course you could help it.' Her father raised his voice. 'Will you never learn? Will you never do the safe and sensible thing?'

'But now you are glad, aren't you?' Naren smiled hopefully. 'Glad that I brought Charlie.'

The man gave a grunt of exasperation and

brought his axe crashing down on to a tree stump, already pitted with blade marks. Leaving the axe, he turned his back on the children and strode into the cottage.

Unexpectedly, the door wasn't slammed. All the same, Charlie didn't feel welcome.

'My father will calm down,' Naren said confidently. 'His anger is like a flame that dies. Come into the warm.' She walked to the open door, motioning Charlie to follow.

But Charlie stayed where he was. In spite of the cold, he was reluctant to leave the animals. He had begun to recognise some of them. Emma's duck was pecking at a trough of corn. Homer had settled on a fence-post and there were two white rabbits cropping the grass in a far corner; they looked very like Olivia's.

'I think I'll just take Runner Bean and go home,' Charlie told the girl. 'My friends can come and fetch their pets now that I know where they are.'

'No,' Naren said sharply. 'No one must know about this place. My father's anger, then, would be terrible. Come,' she beckoned. 'You must talk with him.'

The white-haired man had seemed so grumpy, Charlie didn't feel he could possibly want to talk to him, but Naren beckoned so insistently, he found himself edging closer and closer.

Runner Bean came as far as the door, but wouldn't follow Charlie when he went into the house. Naren took off her boots in a small stone-flagged hall, and Charlie did the same. And then Naren opened a second door, and when Charlie stepped through it, he found himself in a warm, bright kitchen.

A kettle boiled on an iron range, and burning logs blazed in the grate beneath it. An oil-lamp sitting on a round table gave the room a smooth, mellow glow.

Naren's father sat in a chair by the stove, while a grey-haired woman bent over him, talking urgently. She looked up when she heard the children enter, and gave Charlie a smile that banished all his uncertainty. Like Naren, the woman appeared to be Chinese.

Charlie would have spoken to the woman but something happened that he was quite unprepared for. He became aware that pictures covered every spare surface of the walls. It was as if a hundred windows were showing him a different view of a mountain. There were mountains bathed in sunlight, mountains ice-white in moonlight, snow-fields streaked with purple shadows and splashed with fluttering rainbow-coloured pennants. So many breathtaking peaks, so many splendid ranges.

In one of the pictures a mountaineer waved at the camera.

His dark glasses were pushed up over his blue woollen hat and he was laughing. Charlie could hear his voice. There were movements in the room around him, and then the kitchen swung violently from side to side and vanished. Charlie was alone, sailing towards the distant mountains.

Cold, cold air stung his cheeks and rattled in his lungs. He was flying over dazzling white snow while the man's laughter grew louder.

Someone tugged Charlie's arms. It really hurt. He wished they would let go. He tried to shrug them off but he was too weak. So he let himself be tugged and pulled and shaken and shouted at, until he had to open his eyes. And there he was, standing just inside a kitchen door, with a pair of blue eyes peering anxiously into his, and a face that wasn't grumpy any more.

Naren's father took Charlie's arm and set him in a chair by the stove.

'I thought I was on a mountain.' Charlie looked up at the pictures on the wall. 'You were there, Mr . . .?'

'I know,' said Naren's father. 'You chose a fine time to travel, Charlie Bone. Gave us all a nasty fright.'

'Oh. Do you know about it, then?' asked Charlie in surprise. 'My travelling, I mean.'

'Yes. I've heard.'

The Chinese woman said, 'You are welcome here, Charlie.' She glanced at the man with a frown. 'My husband worries for Naren, but he should not have been angry with you.' Shaking her head in a worried way, she pulled out a chair and sat at the table. 'That was not right.'

Naren put her arm round the woman's shoulders, saying, 'Sorry. My fault. Sorry, sorry, Mother.'

'Erm . . . who exactly are you?' Charlie asked the man.

'My name is Bartholomew. I'm Ezekiel Bloor's son.' When he saw the look of alarm on Charlie's face, the man added quickly, 'Don't worry, I'm the black sheep of the family, or perhaps the white. I haven't seen my father for years, or my son. They are as far removed from me as the moon from the earth.'

'But why . . .' Charlie looked round the room. 'How come you're here?'

'Ah.' Bartholomew moved to the window and gazed at his animal visitors.

'He will tell you,' Naren said. 'Won't you, Father? You must tell Charlie.'

Bartholomew strode back to them. 'Yes.' His tone was solemn and a little regretful. 'I must.' He drew a chair close to Charlie's and began to talk.

While Charlie listened, Naren's mother gave him a

bowl of delicious, steaming tea, and then a cake of sweet, fulfilling munchiness. He had never tasted anything so wonderful, but he could only nod his thanks, for he was incapable of dragging his mind away from Bartholomew's incredible story.

It began with a wedding. Bartholomew Bloor married Mary Chance on a rainy autumn morning. No one was happy about it except for the bride and groom, who were so in love they hardly noticed the weather. Ezekiel Bloor and his Yewbeam cousins despised the bride, who was a pretty, but impoverished dancer. And Mary's parents feared for a daughter who was marrying into such a strange, unsociable family.

'For a while they left us alone,' Bartholomew said with a sigh. 'And then I heard about the expedition. My mother used to take me with her when she collected rare plants in the mountains of Bavaria. Ever since then I have loved mountains. After my mother died, I spent all my holidays climbing with friends. We went to Snowdonia, the Alps and the Pyrenees, but my dream, always, was to climb in the Himalayas.

'One day a letter came from one of my mountaineering friends. Harold, my son, was eight at the time. He was serious and stolid. He didn't share my love of travel. He

hated camping, hiking, even picnies.' Bartholomew gave a rueful laugh. 'Imagine a child not liking picnics.'

Naren clicked her tongue. 'Imagine!'

'The letter told me about an expedition,' Bartholomew went on. 'There was a place for me. They were leaving for the Himalayas in a month.'

Charlie munched the sweet cake as quietly as he could – and waited.

Bartholomew's voice faltered before he said, 'Mary told me it was the chance of a lifetime, and I'd always regret it if I didn't go. So I did.' He stood up and began to pace the room. 'Things went well until the night of the storm. It was ferocious and terrifying. An avalanche killed two of our party, and I was swept into a ravine. For two days I lay there, unable to move. I was rescued by a man from an unknown tribe of extraordinary people.'

Bartholomew came and sat down again. He told Charlie how the mysterious tribe had cared for him. Both his legs were broken and a gash on his head gave him constant pain, but at the end of a year he was well enough to travel. A young tribesman took him to a mountain path that led out of the valley and, after several weeks, he reached a town with a telephone.

'I was full of excitement, longing to speak to Mary

again, to tell her I was alive and coming home.' Bartholomew shook his head. He ran a hand through his white hair and covered his eyes with the other.

At first Charlie was afraid to ask a question. He looked at Naren and her mother, but they seemed unable to speak, Bartholomew was so distressed. Eventually, curiosity got the better of Charlie and he ventured, 'So what happened?'

Bartholomew looked up. 'Your grandmother, Grizelda Bone, answered the phone. She was in my house, on the point of selling it. She told me that everyone believed I had died in the avalanche. When Mary heard she went into an empty theatre and danced and danced herself to death.' Bartholomew took a deep breath. 'My son was living in Bloor's Academy, cared for by Ezekiel and Grizelda. And very happy he was too, apparently.'

Charlie was too shocked to speak.

'So I didn't come home,' Bartholomew continued. 'I became an explorer. I went on travelling until I came to China, where I lived for many years until I met my second wife, Meng.' He looked over to the grey-haired woman, who smiled at him. 'One day, after a terrible flood, a flower from the sun walked into our home. Her parents had been swept away by the water. She was four years old and called herself Naren – a sunflower.'

'Yes, me!' cried Naren. 'And they adopted me, and here I am.'

Charlie looked round at her and grinned. 'But why did you all come back here?' he asked.

'Ah.' Bartholomew went to the window. 'That's something I can't explain. I had to be close to the place where the Red King's children were born. From this side of the gorge we can see the castle, or what's left of it. But we're safe from the city and those two terrible families. And we're safe from,' he paused, 'from something I heard about, when I was in Italy. A thing they called "the shadow". I dream about it sometimes.'

A sudden chill entered the cosy room, as though an invisible door had fallen across the window. Charlie shivered. 'A shadow stands behind the king in his portrait,' he said. Bartholomew nodded. 'You've seen it then.'

'We think,' Charlie hesitated, 'it seems as if he's back. The shadow has moved, you see, and we think – well, that is, a rat told my friend Billy (Bartholomew didn't bat an eyelid) that the earth shuddered. And then a dog...' Charlie repeated Blessed's story about the shadow that had turned into a man.

Naren's mother put a hand to her mouth and Bartholomew closed his eyes against an unimaginable horror.

'They say it's Borlath,' Charlie went on, 'your ancestor – and mine too, I suppose, as we're kind of cousins.'

'It's not Borlath,' the explorer said grimly. 'The king's shadow was a man who tore the Red King's family apart. I forget his name.'

'I never heard of him before,' said Charlie. 'He's not in my uncle's history books.'

'Histories are written from a certain point of view,' Bartholomew said dismissively. 'They are edited, embellished, shorn of the facts. Only the traveller can find the truth, Charlie, for the truth is in men's heads and in their hearts. Do not always put your trust in words that you see on paper.'

'I s'pose I'm a traveller, in a way,' said Charlie.

'You certainly are. And who knows, you may discover more about the Red King than I have, in all my years of travelling.'

'Only if I can get past the shadow,' Charlie murmured.

'Ha! We're back to the shadow.' Bartholomew suddenly rose to his feet with a closed look on his face.

All Charlie's questions were swallowed in a gulp. Instead, he spoke about his life since his father disappeared, about Bloor's Academy and the endowed children who had become his friends.

'You will find your father, Charlie,' Bartholomew said with conviction, 'because of the way you are, and because of the loyalty you have inspired. Lyell is an extraordinary man. It's a miracle he remained so decent surrounded by all those vipers. I am old enough to be his father, but in a few short weeks we became the best of friends. You were a year old, Charlie, when I paid my family a brief visit. They wanted nothing to do with me. My son barely acknowledged me. I suppose, in a way, Lyell became the son I'd lost. I took him climbing with me . . .' Bartholomew's voice trailed off, then, with a big shrug, he said, 'Time for you to go home, Charlie. And not the way you came.'

'Can I –?' began Naren.

'No,' her father said sternly. 'You will stay here with your mother. And you will never cross that iron bridge again.'

Naren grinned sheepishly at Charlie. 'But the animals, Father. Charlie must take them back with him.'

'Not *all* the animals,' laughed her mother.

'Just the ones that belong to my friends,' said Charlie. 'You haven't seen any gerbils, have you?'

'Lots!' Naren ran into the passage and, pulling on her coat and boots, called, 'The barns are full of them. Come and see.'

Hurriedly putting on his outdoor clothes, Charlie followed Naren across to a large barn standing at right-angles to the house. As he stepped into the barn, an army of small rodents scampered across the dusty floor, leaping for hay bales or burrowing under logs.

'How on earth am I going to sort them out?' groaned Charlie. 'My friend's lost more than twenty.'

'Who's going to know which is which?' said Naren.

'Gabriel knows his gerbils intimately,' said Charlie with a sigh.

At this Naren gave such a peal of merry laughter, Charlie began to giggle.

It took them almost an hour to catch twenty-five vaguely recognisable gerbils, two white rabbits, a duck, a grey parrot and a blue boa. Boxes were found, and a cage for the boa. 'Don't fancy that thing creeping round my neck while I'm driving,' said Bartholomew, as he helped Charlie to coax the snake into a cage. But the boa was an amiable creature and would never have harmed a friend. None of the family was surprised to learn that it was probably a thousand years old. On his travels, Bartholomew had met creatures of an even greater age.

A battered-looking van stood in the yard behind the house, and the boxed animals were carefully packed into

the back. Charlie took a seat beside Bartholomew, Homer perched on the boa's cage and Runner Bean sat on Charlie's lap.

The van spluttered into life and rolled across the yard. All at once, Naren was running beside them. 'Don't close . . . tonight,' she called.

'What?' Charlie wound down the window.

'Give me something of yours,' Naren called.

Almost without thinking, Charlie tore off his glove and tossed it through the window. The van lurched out of the yard and on to a rough track. Charlie turned in his seat and looked through the back window. He saw Naren pick up the glove and wave it happily. Meng stood behind her, a hand hesitantly raised. The van turned a sharp bend and the two figures disappeared from view.

'Why did she want something of mine?' Charlie asked Bartholomew.

'She wants to keep in touch.' Bartholomew gave Charlie an enigmatic smile.

'But a glove? And what mustn't I close tonight?'

'Your curtains, Charlie. Let the moon shine in.'

'But –'

'Look to your right,' Bartholomew commanded.

Obediently, Charlie looked past Bartholomew. At first

there was nothing to be seen but trees and then, on the other side of the gorge, a square reddish-coloured tower came into view.

'The Red Castle,' Charlie exclaimed.

'The very same,' Bartholomew agreed.

'And there's a part of the wall,' cried Charlie.

The van slowed down so that he could see the tumbling remains of a massive wall, built on the very edge of the gorge. Sections of the wall could be glimpsed for at least a mile and then, gradually, the huge stones were lost in a sea of trees.

'I never realised it was so big,' breathed Charlie.

'Vast,' said Bartholomew. His voice softened. 'And I believe the king is still there, or certainly his spirit. He is hidden for now but, perhaps soon, he'll show himself, especially if the shadow is back.'

'The queen's there, too,' said Charlie.

Bartholomew turned to him with an enquiring frown, and Charlie told the explorer about the white horse that had carried Billy and himself to the Castle of Mirrors.

'The Queen.' Bartholomew's blue eyes glittered. 'That is truly wonderful.'

They drove on in silence for a while and then Bartholomew said gravely, 'Charlie, it's very important that

no one finds out about me and my family. Promise not to tell a soul where we live, or where you found the animals.'

Charlie thought of his friends, and Uncle Paton. 'I promise,' he said reluctantly.

After another mile they left the track through the wilderness and joined a road that eventually took them to the wide stone bridge. Charlie thought it best to take all the animals to the Pets' Café where their owners could come and collect them. He directed Bartholomew to the end of Frog Street, but the explorer wouldn't leave his van.

Before Charlie got out, Bartholomew popped something into his top pocket. 'I don't have any photographs of your father,' he explained, 'but he took that one. I have always kept it and it just occurred to me that it might help you, Charlie.'

'Thank you.'

'Please get out now. I don't want anyone to see me.'

With the boa's cage hanging on one arm, and a box of rabbits and gerbils on the other, Charlie shouted goodbye as the van sped away. Then he trudged down Frog Street with Runner Bean bounding ahead and Nancy the duck waddling obediently behind him. The wilful parrot, however, kept disappearing and shrieking rude words from lamp posts and windowsills.

Charlie had almost reached the Pets' Café when he became aware of footsteps on the cobbled street behind him.

'Stop right there, Charlie Bone,' said a voice.

Charlie stopped and looked round. Dorcas Loom and her two large brothers came striding towards him. Between the two Looms marched Joshua Tilpin.

'Where are our dogs, Charlie Bone?' asked Albert, the tallest and ugliest Loom.

'Yeah. How come you've got your dog and all your friends' pets?' demanded Alfred, the shorter, wider youth.

'What have you done with the animals, Charlie?' said Joshua with a mean sort of grimace. 'Come on, tell us!'

'Nothing,' said Charlie. 'I just happened to find these.' He glanced at Nancy, who came swaying to his side.

'Oh, just *happened* to find them, did you?' said Dorcas.

A growl rumbled in Runner Bean's throat, and Homer shrieked, 'Battle stations!'

'Stop that thing jabbering,' snarled Albert. 'If you don't tell us where our dogs have gone, we'll take yours. We'll take 'em all, unless you speak up.'

'Tell us,' Alfred demanded, 'or else . . .'

The four of them began to close in.

Trapped in the snow

Charlie stood his ground. It isn't easy to run away when you're carrying a cage and a large cardboard box, and expecting a duck to keep up with you. There was only one solution.

'Runner, get them!' Charlie commanded.

The big dog didn't need any encouragement. He rushed at the Looms, barking furiously. But Albert and Alfred hadn't trained four Rottweilers for nothing. Albert grabbed Runner's collar and tugged him to the side of the alley, where Alfred chained him tightly to a lamp post.

Frantic with rage, Runner Bean's howls were enough to raise the town, but no friendly policeman appeared and no one

came to the door of the Pets' Café. Homer, however, was a bird of action. He hurtled out of the sky and dug his talons into Dorcas's curly head.

'Get off! Get off!' screamed Dorcas.

Joshua grabbed Homer by the neck and squeezed. The parrot's grey eyes bulged. He choked and spluttered, his talons clawing the empty air as Joshua pulled him off Dorcas and shook him from side to side.

The boa gave an angry hiss when his cage was dropped, and Charlie was tempted to release him, but he couldn't risk another creature being injured. Putting the box of rabbits and gerbils beside the boa, Charlie ran at Joshua.

'Let him go!' he cried, trying to tear Joshua's fingers away from the parrot's neck.

Charlie didn't stand a chance. Alfred pulled his arms behind his back, and Albert punched him in the stomach.

'Oooooow!' Charlie sank to his knees, doubled up in pain.

Albert grabbed the cage and led the way out of Frog Street. Alfred followed with the box. They marched up the narrow street, herding poor Nancy in front of them, while Dorcas helped Joshua to stuff Homer into his rucksack.

'You can keep the dog,' Alfred called back to Charlie,

'for now.' His footsteps stopped abruptly. 'What the . . .?' His voice shook a little.

Charlie looked up.

At the end of Frog Street, three glowing forms had appeared.

'Flames,' breathed Charlie.

A deep sound rumbled down the narrow alley: the low, angry growl of a wild creature. A second growl joined the first, and then a third increased the sound. The dreadful chorus grew louder. Joshua and the Looms stepped back. Faster and faster they moved. Before they could turn away, a streak of colour, bright as a flame, divided into three and flew towards the boys, landing on their shoulders.

Screaming with terror, Joshua and the Looms flailed wildly as the dazzling creatures bit into their necks.

'Help us, Dorc,' yelled Albert.

Sobbing regretfully, Dorcas bolted without a backward glance.

By now, Albert had dropped the cage and Alfred had cast aside the box. A yellow cat still clung to Joshua's rucksack and, blubbering with fright, the boy yanked it off his back and tore after the Looms, who were sprinting up the alley faster than they had ever believed they could move.

'What was that all about?' said a voice behind Charlie.

Mr Onimous stood in the doorway of the Pets' Café. He was wearing a fake (Charlie hoped) fur dressing gown and bore a striking resemblance to a mole. 'It's hardly breakfast,' he said, 'and Saturday at that. We were having a lie-in.'

'The Looms got me.' Charlie stood up, rubbing his stomach. 'Them and that freak Joshua Tilpin.'

'I see you have a duck – and a dog – oh, and our blue boa. Onoria will be overjoyed.'

Runner barked with delight as Charlie untied him.

'I think I've got them all,' said Charlie, looking into the box. 'Olivia's rabbits and Gabriel's gerbils.'

'That rucksack is talking to itself,' Mr Onimous anxiously observed.

Charlie picked it up and undid the strap. Homer shot out and flew into the air, swearing horribly. Mr Onimous put his hands over his ears. 'That parrot's language!' he protested. 'Where did he learn such disgusting stuff?'

'In the army,' said Charlie. 'That's what Lysander told me.'

'Tch! Tch!' Mr Onimous carried the box and the cage into the café while Charlie coaxed Nancy through the door. Runner Bean needed no coaxing. He rushed into the café, round the counter and into the kitchen, where he

knew he would get a chocolate drop at the very least.

Mrs Onimous, in a pink kimono, was frying bacon when Charlie and her husband walked in. 'The animals are back!' she cried. 'Oh, the pets, the loves. Chocs for Runner, toast for Nancy and something special for Boa. Where did you find them, Charlie?'

Charlie pretended he hadn't heard. 'Could you spare a couple of carrots for the rabbits, and maybe an apple for the gerbils?'

'Of course, Charlie. But where were they?' Mrs Onimous persisted.

'Um. That's difficult to say.'

The Onimouses asked no more questions for the moment. They set about feeding the animals and Charlie. Mrs Onimous was just pouring a second cup of tea when an oily voice from somewhere inside the café said, 'Hello!'

'We're closed,' called Mrs Onimous, frowning. Lowering her voice, she said, 'I hate people catching me in my kimono.'

'I'm sure I locked the door, dear.' Mr Onimous tiptoed out of the kitchen, returning a few moments later with a surprised look on his face, and a parrot on his head. 'Must have flown in before I closed the door,' said Mr Onimous. 'Another beak to feed, my darling.'

But Homer didn't wait to be served. He swooped on to

the table and carried a piece of toast up to a high shelf, where he tore it apart, muttering all the while.

'How rude,' said Mrs Onimous, probably referring to his behaviour, although it could have been his language.

When all the animals had settled down, Mr Onimous once again asked Charlie where he had found them. Charlie struggled with an answer. He knew he could trust the Onimouses, but he had promised Bartholomew not to tell a soul about the house in the wilderness.

'On the bridge,' Charlie said at last. 'I heard Runner's bark and – just went there.'

'Just went there,' said Mrs Onimous suspiciously. 'And just happened to find all the animals belonging to your friends, but no others? No kittens, or mice or puppies belonging to anyone else?'

'Er, no,' said Charlie.

'Leave him be, Onoria,' said Mr Onimous. 'I think he's made a promise to someone. Am I right, Charlie?'

Charlie shuffled his feet. 'Well, yes. And I would tell you, really I would, but I can't, you see.'

'Can't trust us?' sniffed Onoria.

'No, no. That is, I mean yes, of course I can, but . . .'

'Charlie, lad, don't get in a frazzle,' Mr Onimous said soothingly. 'You take that dog back to Benjamin, and we'll

hang on to the others until your friends come to collect them. We'll take good care of them, won't we, darling?' He turned to his wife.

'I'm not sure about the parrot,' Mrs Onimous glanced upwards. 'But I'll do my best.'

'Thanks! You're both the greatest!' Charlie grabbed Runner Bean's collar and led him out of the café.

When they reached Filbert Street, Charlie was reluctant to go straight to number twelve. Benjamin's parents were behaving so strangely, he wondered if he would be welcome there. 'But you are Ben's dog,' Charlie said to Runner Bean, 'so perhaps you'd better go home.'

The big dog's excited bark clinched the matter.

Mrs Brown opened the door to Charlie. 'Charlie, how wonderful. You've found Benjamin's dog.' She was all smiles.

Charlie couldn't understand it. One minute Mrs Brown was ignoring him, the next she was welcoming him into her house as if he were the best thing to arrive since mobile phones were invented. 'Benjamin, it's Runner Bean!' she called up the stairs.

'What!' came an excited shriek.

The next moment, Benjamin was half falling, half leaping down the stairs, while Runner Bean bounced up to meet him, howling with joy.

'Charlie, did you find him? Where was he? Oh, thanks, Charlie. Thanks, thanks, thanks! You're the best!'

Dog and boy rolled down to the hall where Charlie stood, not quite knowing what to say.

'Where did you find him?' Benjamin begged.

'Oh, just in the street,' Charlie said awkwardly. 'He was probably on his way here.'

'In the street?' Mrs Brown's grey eyes narrowed. 'Are you sure?'

'Of course.' Charlie didn't like the way Benjamin's mother was eyeing him.

'And what about the others? I've heard no birds. I've seen no dogs in the street.'

Mrs Brown looked so suspicious Charlie felt like backing right out of the front door. But the next minute he found himself saying, 'I don't know anything about the others. I found Runner Bean, and I brought him back. If that's not good enough for you, well, too bad!' He turned to the door.

'Charlie,' cried Benjamin, grabbing his arm. 'Of course it's good enough. Come upstairs with Billy and me.'

'Yes, come on,' called Billy from the top of the stairs.

Mrs Brown's mouth formed a tight little line and, without another word, she marched into the kitchen.

Charlie kicked off his boots and ran upstairs. As soon as

he was safely inside Benjamin's overheated room he flung off his heavy jacket and burst out, 'Ben, what is it with your mum? Did you know that she was working at Bloor's, and your dad?'

Benjamin looked uncomfortable. 'Billy told me. But I swear I didn't know before. When I asked Mum about it she just said it was a job, like any other.'

'But they're detectives, Ben,' said Charlie. 'They must be investigating something.'

'Yes, they must,' said Billy.

'Well, I did overhear them say something,' Benjamin admitted.

'What? What?' Charlie bounced down on the bed between Benjamin and Billy.

Rembrandt, who had been snoozing in Benjamin's slipper, woke with a start and scuttled under the bed, while Runner Bean, delighted that the rat had decided to play, squeezed in after him, barking with joy.

'Leave it!' Billy shouted desperately. 'If you hurt my rat I'll kill you, you mangy dog.'

'Billy!' said Benjamin in a shocked voice.

Before an argument could develop, and seeing that everything had gone quiet under the bed, Charlie said quickly, 'So what did you hear, Ben?'

'Well, I was outside their bedroom, so I didn't hear too well, but Mum said something about illusions. Billy told me they'd been appearing at Bloor's, so I went a bit closer and I heard Dad say he had an idea. He was on to them, he said. He knew who was doing it, but he just needed one more illusion to –'

'The illusions!' Charlie leapt off the bed. 'They're trying to find out who's doing it, the sneaky –' He stopped, realising what he'd said.

'It's not Mum and Dad's fault,' said Benjamin. 'They're only doing it for the money.'

'Is it you, Charlie?' asked Billy. 'It is, isn't it?'

'No, it's not.' Charlie shook his head. 'I can't create illusions.'

'But you know who it is, don't you?' pressed Benjamin.

'No,' said Charlie.

'You wouldn't tell us even if you did know who it was,' said Billy.

Charlie glanced at Billy. 'No, I wouldn't.'

'I don't blame you,' Billy said a little sadly.

Runner Bean was snoring under the bed and Rembrandt, seizing his chance, was on the move again. He appeared close to Charlie's foot, chewing something.

'What's he got?' asked Benjamin.

'Looks like a photo,' said Billy.

'PHOTO?' Charlie grabbed the rat. 'No, no. It is. It's my photo. My only chance.'

Rembrandt, surprised by the look in Charlie's eye, opened his mouth, and the little square of paper fluttered to the floor. Charlie plonked the rat on Billy's lap and scooped up the photograph. Luckily, only one corner had been chewed. Bartholomew was right. It wasn't a good shot. A cloud of snow almost obscured the lonely figure in the foreground.

'I forgot about it.' Charlie hugged the photo to his chest. 'How could I? He put it in my pocket, and when I took my coat off it must have slipped out.'

'Who put it in your pocket?' asked Benjamin.

'What?' Caught offguard, Charlie mumbled, 'Oh, no one, really. I mean, I put it there.'

Benjamin stared at him. 'You're being a bit secretive, these days,' he said. 'We are your friends, aren't we?'

Before Charlie could answer, Rembrandt and Runner Bean were at it again. The rat had leapt on to a shelf, and Runner Bean, barking wildly, was on his hind legs, sweeping his paw along the shelf. Books and toys came crashing down, and the next minute, the door was flung open, and an angry Mrs Brown stood on the threshold.

'Benjamin!' shouted his mother. 'Can't you control that dog? Your father and I are trying to write up our reports and our vocabularies are all over the place.'

Benjamin blinked. 'D'you mean dictionaries, Mum?' he asked.

Mrs Brown stamped her foot. 'Take him out!' She stood back and pointed to the stairs. 'Now!'

Without another word, the three boys put on their coats and went downstairs to pull on their boots. Billy tucked Rembrandt into his pocket, and Benjamin put Runner Bean on his leash. Then they all went out into the frosty air.

A smart-looking van pulled away from the opposite kerb as the boys emerged, but Charlie thought nothing of it at the time. He told the others he couldn't come to the park because he had something urgent to attend to, and with resigned shrugs his friends accepted that Charlie's problems were more important than a game in the park.

A low buzz of excitement came from the kitchen of number nine. In spite of his impatience to study Bartholomew's photo, Charlie was drawn towards it. He found his family gathered round a large food hamper on the kitchen table. Grandma Bone was sitting by the stove, with her back to them.

'Look, Charlie, Paton's hamper!' said Maisie in a tone that was almost reverent. 'It arrived five minutes ago.'

The lid had been opened and displayed within was a large bottle of champagne, surrounded by a great many packages of exotically labelled food.

'There's a note,' said Amy, reaching between a glittering bag of nuts and a jar of glacé fruits. She pulled out a gold-edged card and handed it to Uncle Paton.

'Rather florid handwriting,' Paton remarked, examining the card.

Set within a border of glittering golden feathers were the words,

Dear Mr Yewbeam,
An unluckie deathe delayed your Friday Festival. I
hope this caused you no distresse. Here is fare to
gladden hearts and set alle to rite.

'Terrible spelling,' Charlie observed. 'I could do better than that in my second year.'

'Aren't we the cleversticks,' said Grandma Bone, without bothering even to look over her shoulder.

'Oh, look, King Prawns!' said Maisie. 'They're still frozen. Shall I put them in the freezer, Paton?'

'Mm.' Uncle Paton licked his lips. 'Leave them to defrost. I'll have them for lunch.'

The hamper had arrived at just the right moment for Charlie. While Maisie and his mother were still exclaiming over every carefully wrapped morsel he crept up to his room, relieved that no one had asked where he had been all morning.

As soon as he had closed his door, he took out the photograph and sat on his bed. He saw a man standing, half-turned towards the camera. In spite of the snow that speckled the foreground, Charlie could tell that it was Bartholomew. He was wearing a woollen hat, a padded jacket and long, laced boots.

Charlie brought the photo closer to his face. The white moth flew across the room and settled on his arm.

'My father took this photo,' Charlie told the moth. 'He was right there, looking through the viewfinder at Bartholomew Bloor, and – "click" – catching him forever, just like that. So if I go in and turn around to look at the camera, I'll see him, won't I? What do you think?'

The moth moved protectively on to his wrist and Charlie smiled at the soft touch of its feet. He was so tense with excitement his hand began to tremble and the moth moved again, until its shining wings fluttered

at the tip of Charlie's forefinger.

'It'll be all right, won't it?' Charlie could already hear the crunch of snow and someone breathing, steadily, into his ear. He always relished the moment when, just after the sounds reached him, he found himself floating into a picture.

'Here goes,' he said. His body became weightless and he was engulfed in the thick fog of time. Now began the slow whirling tumble towards Bartholomew's solitary figure – and the man behind the camera.

Laughter. Laughter that was both merry and gentle. Did he recognise the voice? Charlie could hear Bartholomew's gusty chuckles, but the laughter came from another voice.

'Give it up, Lyell. The snow's too thick.'

No answer.

'You'll drop the camera. Put on your gloves. Your hands will freeze.'

No answer. Only the soft laughter.

Charlie wondered if Bartholomew could see his face in the thick mist of snow. When he 'travelled' only his face could be seen by the people he 'visited', and this could be a little unnerving.

A bitter wind blew the snow into Charlie's eyes. He

tried to rub them but his hands were numb with cold. 'Bartholomew!' he called.

Bartholomew couldn't hear him. The explorer swung away, calling, 'Come on, Lyell. You've got your picture.'

Now was the time for Charlie to turn. Now, surely, he would see the man behind the camera.

He turned.

He saw a man in a fur-lined hood. His chin was tucked into the padded collar of his jacket, and the rest of his face was obscured by the camera.

'Lyell!' called Bartholomew. 'The light's going. We must get back.'

Again the soft laughter and then, 'I'm coming.'

Whose voice was that? Did Charlie recognise it? The camera was lowered and tucked into a pocket. The hood fell over the man's eyes. He pulled on a pair of gloves, keeping his head lowered.

'Dad!' called Charlie. 'Dad!'

The man walked forwards. He walked right past Charlie, his head bent against the driving snow.

'Dad!' Charlie reached out a hand and caught a handful of ice.

The man raised his face to the sky, as though he'd heard a voice in the turbulent air. His hood fell back, but Charlie

saw only a blur, like a face behind frosted glass. And then it was swallowed in snow.

'Wait!' cried Charlie. When he opened his mouth, tiny particles of ice slipped out. They fell on to the snow with a sinister tinkle. Charlie's chest felt as though it were stuffed with knives. 'Where am I going to go?' he croaked.

Back to where you came from, said the voice of reason, but Charlie's brain was so befuddled with cold he couldn't think how to get there.

I'm going to die of cold, he thought. But they say it's a nice way to go. He closed his eyes. It was peaceful in the dark. Soon he would be asleep.

Something bit Charlie's hand. He tried to drag it away, but the something clung on. Now it was stinging his fingers, crawling over his face, tugging his hair, nipping his chin.

'Let me sleep,' moaned Charlie. The cold enveloped him in such a comforting blanket.

'Come back!' The whisper seemed to be made of fine silk, soft and utterly compelling. Charlie felt himself lifted. He rolled through the air, getting warmer and warmer. Warmer, warmer, until . . . he opened his eyes.

He was lying on his bed. The moth hovered above him, its wings a brighter silver than ever before.

'You did that,' Charlie said incredulously. 'You brought me back.'

The moth settled on his hand. It had no voice and yet a link in their understanding enabled Charlie to hear an answer.

'*I did.*'

Charlie sat up. 'So if you're with me when I travel, I'll always be able to get back?'

To this there was no answer because a scream rose through the house; a scream of such anguish and terror Charie felt that it had stopped his heart.

It was his mother's voice.

Frozen Maisie

Charlie leapt down the stairs; stumbling, tumbling, tripping and bouncing. The Flames' warning rang in his ears: *Watch your mother*. He hadn't watched. He had thought her safe inside the house. And how could he watch her everywhere?

It was Amy's scream, but it was Maisie who was in trouble. When Charlie burst into the kitchen, the first thing he saw was Maisie, standing very still in the centre of the room. She was facing the door and seemed to be staring straight at Charlie. Her mouth hung open and there was a look of astonishment on her face. Amy and Uncle Paton stood on either side of her. Amy's hands were clasped but Uncle Paton held his

out before him, as though he didn't quite know where to put them.

'What is it?' cried Charlie. 'What happened?'

'We are not – quite sure,' said Uncle Paton.

'She's frozen,' Amy whimpered. 'Maisie's frozen.'

Even Grandma Bone had risen from her chair. 'What's she done, silly woman? She's done something she shouldn't have.'

'For pity's sake, Grizelda,' roared Uncle Paton. 'Maisie's in trouble.'

'Huh!' Grandma Bone turned her back. 'You'd better do something about it. She's beginning to drip.'

Charlie touched Maisie's arm. She was wearing her pink angora sweater and the soft furry pile had turned to bristling, icy spikes. He had a terrible thought. A moment ago he had been travelling into a world full of snow. Had he, somehow, taken Maisie with him? He touched her face. It was as cold and hard as a block of ice.

'Charlie, don't,' sobbed his mother. 'Don't touch her, it's too – dreadful.'

Grandma Bone was right. Maisie was, indeed, beginning to drip. A little pool of water had formed around her feet.

'Perhaps she's thawing out,' said Uncle Paton. 'Let's speed it up. We'll get her closer to the stove.'

With some difficulty Amy and Uncle Paton manoeuvered Maisie over to the stove. Uncle Paton turned up the dial and heat poured into the room. In a few minutes it was so hot, everyone was flinging off their cardigans and sweaters, but although Maisie continued to drip, very slightly, round her shoes, she remained as hard as an iceberg.

'It's a spell.' Charlie's mother covered her face with her hands. 'It has to be. But why Maisie? She never hurt a soul.'

'Charlie, have you been visiting that sorcerer again?' Uncle Paton's tone was severe.

'N-no,' said Charlie, a little uncertainly.

'But you have been "travelling"?'

Charlie nodded. He could feel Grandma Bone's eyes upon him. 'I didn't visit any sorcerer,' he said quietly, 'but I did go somewhere very cold.'

'Where?' demanded Grandma Bone.

'Oh – just into a Christmas card,' said Charlie. 'Just for fun. There's nothing wrong with that, is there?'

'You shouldn't use your endowment for fun,' she snapped.

'OK, OK,' Charlie mumbled. He noticed that the table was laid for lunch. The contents of the hamper had been shared out, and each person's favourite food set neatly beside their plates. Paté for Grandma Bone, venison pies

for Maisie and Charlie, tuna for Amy and prawns for Uncle Paton. The lid of the prawn jar had been removed and two large prawns lay on the cloth, as though they had been accidentally dropped.

'Uncle Paton, have you eaten any prawns?' asked Charlie.

'No, I . . .' Paton saw the prawns. 'Good Lord, who . . .' He bent down and peered into Maisie's open mouth. 'A prawn!' he cried. 'She's been at my prawns.'

'Paton,' Amy chided. 'Please! You wouldn't begrudge my poor mother a few prawns.'

'My dear, you misunderstand,' said Paton. 'Maisie was eating prawns when she – when she succumbed to this terrible affliction.'

Amy looked up. 'Poisoned?' she gasped.

'A bit more than poisoned,' said Paton. He turned to his sister. 'Grizelda, do you know anything about this?'

'Don't be ridiculous.' Seizing her plate of toast and pâté, Grandma Bone marched out of the kitchen, growling, 'I'm not staying here to be insulted.'

No one else dared to touch their food. They put every last morsel back into the hamper, and Paton rang the store. Fifteen minutes later, a young man arrived in the van Charlie had seen driving off an hour before. Paton handed him the hamper at the front door. 'A member of my family

has been taken very ill,' he told the young man. 'We believe your prawns were responsible. I want them analysed as soon as possible.'

'It's Sunday,' said the youth, who looked nervous and confused.

'Someone may be dying!' roared Paton. 'Get it done!'

'Yes, sir,' mumbled the youth. 'The hospital, perhaps.' He walked shakily down the steps and placed the hamper on the passenger seat, before driving off.

Charlie had an idea. 'The Flame cats,' he suggested. 'They'll help.' He flung on his jacket, rushed out and headed for the Pets' Café. The cats were not always to be found there, but he didn't know where else to look.

Before Charlie had reached the end of Filbert Street, he sensed that the Flames were already near. His gaze was drawn to the roof of a house he was passing, and there they were, at the very apex, their bright forms etched against the grey sky. As soon as they saw Charlie they leapt one by one into a nearby tree, and climbed neatly down through the tracery of branches until they stood at Charlie's feet.

'Flames, I need your help!' Charlie turned and raced back to number nine, and the cats ran with him; Aries slightly in front, as usual, Leo and Sagittarius at either side.

When all four bounced into the hall, Grandma Bone

shouted, 'Not those vile creatures. Get them out!'

The Flames marched up to the open sitting-room door and gazed in with their fabulous glittering eyes. Grandma Bone stepped back, bleating, 'Take them away.'

The Flames growled at her, and she pushed the door shut with the toe of her shiny black shoe.

Charlie grinned. He led the cats into the kitchen where they immediately saw what had to be done. They ran to Maisie and surrounded her, mewing softly.

'Oh, Charlie, can they really help?' Amy clasped Charlie's hand.

'Those cats can work miracles,' said Uncle Paton confidently.

The cats seemed perplexed. What could only be described as a frown passed over their furry faces. Their golden eyes travelled up the length of Maisie's motionless form until they came to her astonished frozen eyes. They mewed again.

For a full minute the cats studied Maisie's stiff fingers, her plump legs, her icy pink sweater and her neat grey curls. They stepped closer and sniffed, their black noses wrinkling in distaste.

Charlie held his breath. Could the Flames melt Maisie? He watched Aries stand on tiptoe and arch his back. The

copper cat began to pace round Maisie's feet in their new red trainers. She had been so proud of them, Charlie thought. Hopefully, she still was.

Leo and Sagittarius followed Aries. The cats' gentle pacing became faster. Soon their bodies resembled leaping flames. Maisie appeared to stand inside a circle of fire. Tiny, glowing sparks flew up to the ceiling and Charlie could hear the hiss and crackle of flames.

'She blinked!' Amy's voice was hoarse with excitement. 'Did you see that?'

Charlie looked at Maisie's face. She blinked twice.

'I saw it,' cried Charlie. 'She blinked.'

'She did indeed,' Uncle Paton agreed.

'She's melting.' Amy sighed happily.

'Clever Flames. Hooray!' said Charlie.

Maisie closed her mouth and something like a smile crinkled each corner.

They waited for more. Nothing happened. The blinking stopped; the mouth remained closed and the rest of Maisie's features stayed stubbornly frozen.

The whirling flames began to lose their brilliance. The frenzied leaping slowed, and the three cats, taking on their true forms, walked once, twice, three times round Maisie's sturdy legs, and then sat down. They looked exhausted.

Aries lifted a paw and licked it gingerly. Leo and Sagittarius sprawled side by side and looked up at Charlie, as if to say, *We tried. We can do no more.*

'You did your best,' said Charlie. 'I know you did.'

'She nearly came back,' said his mother. 'If only they could try just once more.'

'They can't,' said Charlie. 'They gave it everything. They can't do any more.' He went to the fridge and got out some ham, which he chopped into cubes and placed on a saucer. He put the saucer close to the cats and they gobbled it hungrily.

Uncle Paton sat down and grimly folded his arms. 'It was meant for me,' he said bitterly. 'I'm sure of it. I'm the one who eats prawns. Someone tampered with them, and it must have been one of them – or should I say one of us, the endowed. Why else . . .?' He raised his hands and let them fall into his lap.

'We must get a doctor,' said Amy. 'Now. Before it's too late.'

Uncle Paton nodded. 'We must. But it will have to be someone we can trust to be discreet.'

A ray of hope lit Amy's face. 'I know someone. He looks as if he's used to keeping secrets. He buys a lot of vegetables and one day he gave me his card. He's

Doctor . . . something unusual.'

'Could be a doctor of maths or music.' Charlie didn't want to raise his mother's hopes.

'But it's worth a try.' Amy ran to the phone in the hall.

While Amy was on the phone, Grandma Bone shouted, 'Have they gone, those beasts?'

The Flames growled at the sound of her voice. Leo gave the saucer one more lick before leaping after his brothers into the hall. They held their tails high and their heads erect. They might have failed this once, but they still had their pride. Charlie quietly thanked them, and let them out.

'He's coming.' Amy replaced the receiver. 'His name's Doctor Tanaka.'

Doctor Tanaka was a young man with a broad smiling face and a neat grey suit. At first glance he didn't seem to be at all the sort of person who could deal with anything out of the ordinary. But Amy hadn't been wrong. When he saw poor frozen Maisie, Dr Tanaka merely lifted an eyebrow. 'Ah!' he said. 'Cryogenics. Reducing a person's temperature to below freezing, but in this case, supernaturally.'

'Will she – die?' asked Amy, hardly able to say the last word.

'Not necessarily,' replied the doctor in his light, efficient voice. 'When the power is broken, she will return.'

'The power,' Charlie murmured.

Doctor Tanaka turned to him and smiled. 'The power,' he repeated. 'Someone in this city is extraordinarily, supernaturally powerful. I know, of course, that there are quite a few unusual people about. Children of the Red King, I believe they are called. In fact I am probably standing in a house where one – or two – are living?'

Paton inclined his head.

'In my experience there is no power on earth that cannot be broken,' the doctor went on cheerfully. 'And two endowments are better than one.'

'In the meantime,' said Amy, glancing at Maisie, 'what should we do with my mother?'

'Make her comfortable,' said the doctor.

It was decided that the bath would be the best place for Maisie, owing to the droplets that continued to pool around her feet. Before he left, Dr Tanaka helped Uncle Paton to carry the icy body upstairs. They had to wear gloves and it was no easy task to manoeuvre her into the bath. Charlie gently pushed a cushion under Maisie's head, and Amy covered her with a blanket.

'I hope I will have the pleasure of buying many more

vegetables at your excellent shop,' the doctor told Amy before he left.

'I hope so, too,' said Amy, returning the doctor's elegant bow.

No sooner had the doctor gone, than a phone call from the store informed Paton that the prawns held no toxic substances whatsoever. They had been fed to laboratory rats with no ill effects. In fact, the rats had thoroughly enjoyed them and, if anything, had become slightly bushier and brighter after eating them.

'They were probably starving,' muttered Charlie.

'It only took one prawn,' Uncle Paton declared. 'And Maisie had to eat it. My money's on Venetia.'

'But Great-Aunt Venetia only poisons clothes,' Charlie reminded him. 'Why should she change to prawns?'

'No idea,' growled Paton.

Charlie felt uncomfortable using the bathroom with Maisie in it, so he went up to the top floor, where his mother and Maisie slept, and used their toilet. So did Paton.

That night, Grandma Bone grumbled that it was too cold on the top floor and she needed a bath. 'Kindly remove the frozen person,' she demanded.

Paton refused and Grandma Bone had to use the toilet next to the cellar. She went without a bath.

Charlie felt his eyes closing as soon as he got into bed. He sleepily ran through the day's events and suddenly remembered Naren. Was it only that morning he had crossed the bridge into the wilderness?

What had she said? 'Don't close your curtains tonight.' So what could her endowment be? Could she fly, or send messages on moonbeams? Wearily he staggered out of bed and went to the window. The white moth drifted on to one of the curtains as he drew them back. Outside a dusting of frost already glittered on the branches of the chestnut tree. It was going to be another cold night.

Charlie climbed back into bed and fell asleep.

He awoke to find the room bright with moonlight. As he gazed about him he saw thin black shadows snaking towards his bed. Charlie shrank against the pillows as they climbed the bedpost and crawled across the covers. Like tiny, oddly-formed creatures, they swarmed over Charlie's hands and ran up his sleeves, but he could feel nothing.

'Shadows,' he thought. 'Only shadows.'

He watched the tiny shapes move on to the wall behind him. They began to jostle each other, almost as though they were seeking the right place in the swirling crowd. As Charlie gazed in amazement at the moving shadows he became aware that the shapes were letters. Gradually, their

feverish activity began to slow and Charlie could make out the words of a message:

'It's me, Naren. This is what I can do. Were you scared when you saw my little shadows? If you whisper at the wall I shall hear you.'

'Hello, Naren,' Charlie whispered uncertainly.

The letters rearranged themselves and Charlie read:

'Hello, Charlie. I hope you got back safely. If anything troubles you, let me know and I can tell my father. Although he hates to come into the city, he will help you.'

Where to begin? wondered Charlie. He decided to tell Naren about frozen Maisie. When he had whispered every detail of his grandmother's terrible misfortune, the shadows on the wall remained perfectly still for a full minute, as though Naren were trying to make sense of the message.

At last the letters began to move. This time the words were formed very slowly.

'What you say about your . . . grandmother is . . . so bad . . . I will talk . . . to Bartholomew . . . Tomorrow . . . perhaps . . . he can send advice.'

'But I'll be in school tomorrow night. How can you –' Charlie heard footsteps in the passage outside his room. Suddenly the door opened and he whispered, rather

louder than he intended, 'Goodbye!'

Grandma Bone walked in. 'Who were you talking to?' she demanded.

'No one, Grandma,' said Charlie. 'Maybe I was talking in my sleep.'

'But you're not asleep. You're sitting up in bed. What's that on your wall?' Grandma Bone peered at the wall above Charlie's head.

Charlie glanced over his shoulder, hoping desperately that Naren's letters had disappeared. Luckily, she must have understood his hurried goodbye, because the tiny shapes were beginning to fade.

'They're shadows, Grandma,' Charlie said quickly, 'from the branches of the chestnut tree.'

'Stupid boy! You've left your curtains open. How can you sleep with the moon pouring in like that?' Grandma Bone strode across the room and pulled the curtains tightly together. 'Now, go to sleep.'

Charlie lay down and closed his eyes. When Grandma Bone had gone he opened them, briefly. The room was so dark he couldn't even see the wall. In another second, he was asleep.

Next morning Charlie was so tired he completely forgot about frozen Maisie, and then he walked into the

bathroom and saw her lying there. Her face looked bluer than the day before, or was it his imagination? He found he couldn't even brush his teeth with Maisie's icy stare at his back, so he nipped up to the top floor.

Amy was still in the kitchen when Charlie went down to breakfast. 'I'm not going to work,' she told Charlie. 'I can't with Maisie like she is. Oh, Charlie, what are we going to do?'

A pot of parsley sitting on the windowsill gave Charlie an idea. 'Vervain,' he murmured. 'Do you remember, Mum, when Uncle Paton was bewitched last year?'

'As if I could forget,' she said.

'And I stole some vervain from Great-Aunt Eustacia's garden, and we made some tea and —'

'Uncle Paton was cured!' cried Amy.

'Well, Fidelio's mum put some in a pot for future use,' Charlie went on excitedly. 'If you went to Gunn House, I bet Mrs Gunn would still have some. Fidelio says she puts it in his sandwiches sometimes, as a kind of pick-me-up.'

'Charlie, you're a genius!' His mother gave him such a squeeze he swallowed half a slice of toast in one go.

'I'll go straight round to Mrs Gunn after breakfast,' said Amy happily. 'In fact I'll go right now.' She looked out of the window. 'Billy Raven's outside. You will keep

Maisie's little problem a secret, won't you?'

'Course,' mumbled Charlie. As if he'd want anyone else to know his grandma was permanently occupying the bathroom!

Amy dashed into the hall and flung on her coat. As she let herself out, Charlie could hear Billy's small voice asking if it was all right for him to come in.

'Of course, Billy, of course!' said Amy.

The front door slammed and the next minute Billy was standing in the kitchen, looking sheepish.

'Benjamin doesn't have to go to his school for another half an hour,' Billy said dejectedly, 'so Mrs Brown said I'd better come over to you, so we could catch the Bloor's Academy bus together.'

'Couldn't she take you?' Charlie spread honey on his second piece of toast.

Billy shrugged. 'Don't think she's going in today.'

'Well, we've got another three minutes,' Charlie said cheerily. 'D'you want some cereal? It's got strawberries in it.'

'No thanks.' Nevertheless, Billy came and sat at the kitchen table. He was wearing a blue duffel coat that looked several sizes too small for him.

'Did you have a good weekend, then?' Charlie asked.

Billy gazed sadly at Charlie's toast. 'Well, yes, in a way. But Rembrandt wasn't very happy. Can I stay with you next weekend, Charlie?'

'OK.' Charlie swallowed his last bit of toast and licked his fingers. 'We'd better get going.'

Billy got up and made for the door. 'Can I use your toilet?'

'NO!' cried Charlie. 'That is, yes. Use the one next to the cellar.'

Billy stood motionless beside the door. 'What's wrong with your upstairs toilet?'

'Blocked,' said Charlie.

While they ran up Filbert Street together, Charlie tried to get more information out of Billy. Why hadn't he enjoyed his stay with the Browns? And what had happened to Rembrandt?

'I enjoyed most of it,' panted Billy. 'But Benjamin's mum and dad asked me so many questions, and Runner Bean and Rembrandt kept arguing, and it's really tiring listening to animals argue.'

'It must be,' said Charlie sympathetically.

'Runner Bean's so boisterous,' went on Billy. 'Rembrandt's quite exhausted.'

'Did you leave him with the Browns?'

'No, he's in my pocket.'

Charlie stopped running. 'Billy, you can't keep a rat in the dorm.'

Billy drew up beside him. 'I know, I know. I'll give him to Cook when we're in the canteen.'

Charlie thought this could be risky, but said no more.

'Runner Bean's not a very nice dog, you know,' Billy muttered as they began to run again.

'He's a great dog,' said Charlie. 'You're just looking at it from a rat's point of view.'

'Don't see how else I can look at it,' argued Billy.

The blue Academy bus arrived at the top of Filbert Street and the two boys raced towards it.

When they got to school, they found that Dorcas Loom had done her worst. The story of Charlie and the animals had spread through the academy. Every cloakroom was full of it. Charlie Bone had been seen with all his friends' pets, so where were the others?

At first break, when Charlie stepped outside, a large gang approached him. He saw Dorcas and Joshua with a Branko twin on either side of them. And Charlie's old enemy Damian Smerk was there, with Bragger Braine and Rupe Small behind him. There were at least ten others, some of them fourth and fifth formers whom Charlie only

knew by sight. Joshua's magnetism had obviously drawn them together. They weren't the sort who would normally bother with a mere second-former like Charlie.

Asa Pike pushed his way to the front of the group. 'So, Charlie Bone, what have you got to say for yourself?' he snarled.

Before Charlie could speak, a gust of wind rushed round his ankles and Asa staggered backwards as a blast of cold air practically knocked him off his feet.

Behind Charlie, a familiar voice said, 'He's got nothing to say. So shove off!'

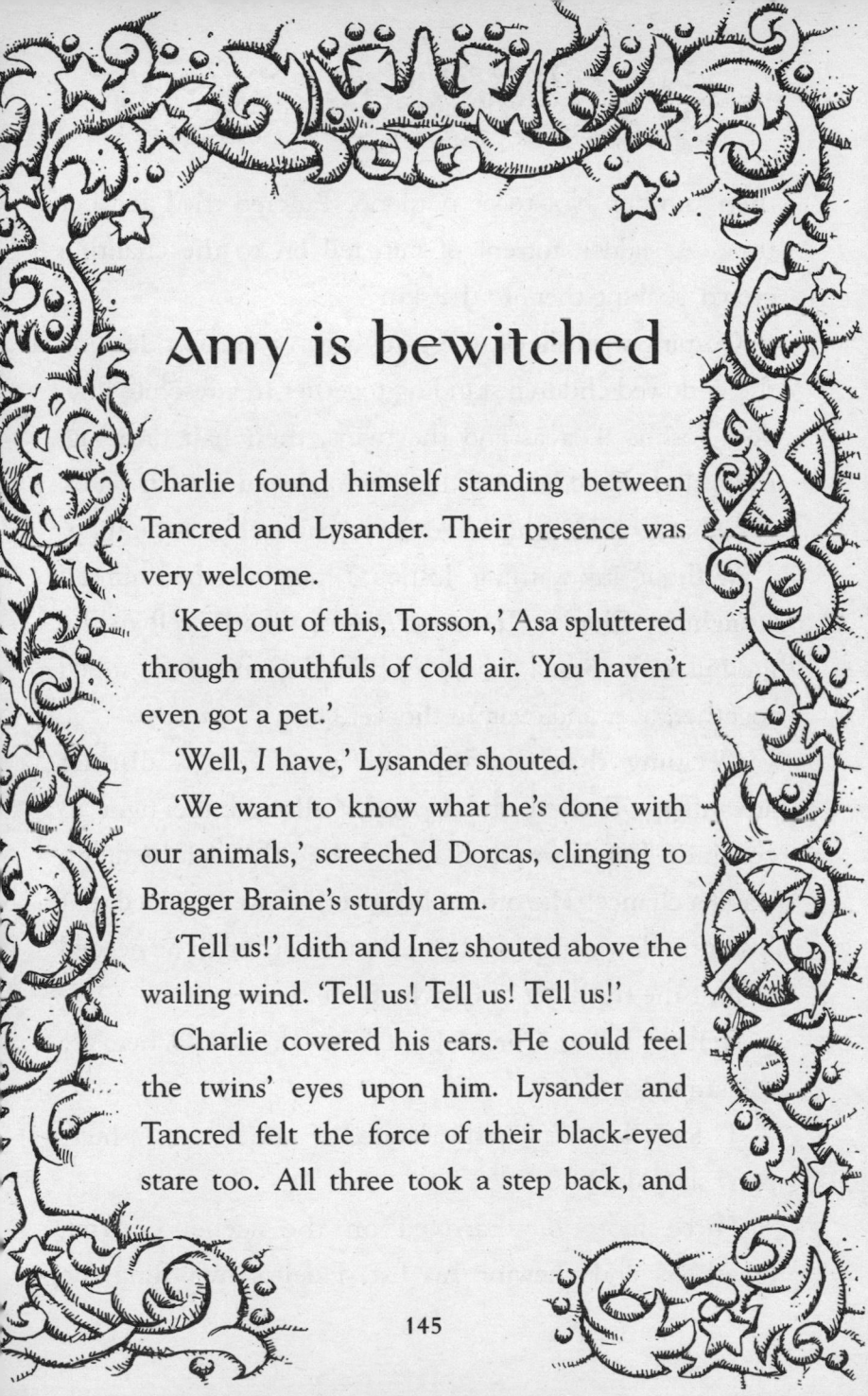

Amy is bewitched

Charlie found himself standing between Tancred and Lysander. Their presence was very welcome.

'Keep out of this, Torsson,' Asa spluttered through mouthfuls of cold air. 'You haven't even got a pet.'

'Well, *I* have,' Lysander shouted.

'We want to know what he's done with our animals,' screeched Dorcas, clinging to Bragger Braine's sturdy arm.

'Tell us!' Idith and Inez shouted above the wailing wind. 'Tell us! Tell us! Tell us!'

Charlie covered his ears. He could feel the twins' eyes upon him. Lysander and Tancred felt the force of their black-eyed stare too. All three took a step back, and

then another. Not to be outdone, Tancred tried another trick. A sudden torrent of rain fell on to the chanting crowd, soaking them to the skin.

Gasping with shock, the gang began to scatter, leaving the endowed children standing together in a resolute line. Asa, Joshua, Dorcas and the twins, their hair dripping, their clothes sodden and their faces gleaming with water, glared at Charlie, who couldn't stop himself from smiling.

Without any warning, Joshua Tilpin launched himself straight at Charlie. Taken off guard, Charlie fell to the ground with Joshua on top of him. The two boys rolled together, over and over, in the wet grass.

Deciding that Charlie's size gave him a distinct advantage, Tancred and Lysander allowed the fight to continue. Joshua was such a weedy boy, they felt he didn't stand a chance. The others, however, were convinced that Joshu's endowment would give him the strength he needed to beat the truth out of Charlie Bone.

'Tell us! Tell us, Charlie Bone,' they droned. 'Where are the animals?'

'I don't know.' Charlie landed a punch on Joshua's puny shoulder.

Three more boys arrived on the scene: Gabriel, breathless and chewing his fist, Fidelio, mouthing the

words, 'what's going on?' and Billy, creeping between the two of them, and anxiously swaying from foot to foot.

Fighting Joshua was like heaving a ton of bricks about. How could such a small boy weigh so much? Charlie wondered. He pummelled his adversary's back, he pulled at his skinny arms, kicked his twig-like legs. But Joshua seemed to suck all the energy out of him. When he lay on Charlie's chest, Charlie felt as though a massive wall was crushing the life out of him. He struggled to get his breath, his hands clawing the air and then, with one mighty effort, he bunched up his fist and punched it into Joshua's face.

'Aieeee!' Joshua's screams were unearthly. He rolled off Charlie, clutching his nose.

Charlie staggered to his feet. He felt five hands patting him heavily on the back and almost fell on his face again.

Lysander gave a whoop of victory. 'Well done, Charlie!'

'Serves the little scab right,' added Tancred.

Joshua was still on the ground, snivelling miserably. Dorcas helped him up and he stood glaring at Charlie as he wiped his bloody nose. 'One day I'll get you, Charlie Bone,' he grunted. His tone was full of menace, but he looked so pathetic, Fidelio burst into laughter.

'HOW DARE YOU!' No one had noticed Miss Chrystal striding up.

'You, Fidelio, of all people! How dare you laugh at an injured boy?' She turned to the others. 'What's been going on?'

Everyone shouted at once, one side accusing Charlie, the other denying he had done anything wrong.

Miss Chrystal held up her hand. 'Asa, you're a prefect. Why didn't you stop the fight?'

Asa was momentarily at a loss. At length he said, 'I tried, but this lot,' he indicated Dorcas and the twins, 'wanted to know why that lot,' he pointed at Charlie and his friends, 'had got their animals back. It's generally believed, Miss, that Charlie Bone has got something to do with all those pets disappearing.'

Miss Chrystal swung round and stared coldly at Charlie. 'Have you?'

Charlie was shocked by the expression on Miss Chrystal's normally pretty face. She looked cold and spiteful. Her pale blue eyes were half closed and her shapely mouth had become a thin, hard line.

'I haven't got anything to do with animals coming or going,' Charlie claimed.

Miss Chrystal stared at him for a bit longer and then

marched off, without another word. Curiously, Joshua ran after her. Grabbing her arm, he cried, 'I'm hurt. You've got to do something.'

Miss Chrystal stopped and spoke to him in a low voice. Charlie couldn't hear every word, but he thought she said, 'Pull yourself together, Josh. Remember who we are.'

Joshua's arm dropped to his side and he looked down, biting his lip.

The horn sounded for the end of break and, as everyone made for the door, Charlie saw Miss Chrystal fondle Joshua's hair. She looked up and caught Charlie watching her. This time her expression was one of outright hatred.

'Round one to you, Charlie,' said Fidelio as they stepped into the hall. 'Well done!'

Something told Charlie that there were many more rounds to come and it was by no means certain that he would win the next one.

Charlie's mother was, at that moment, helping Mrs Gunn to tidy her chaotic kitchen. For all its mess and muddle, Amy found it a very comforting place. Mrs Gunn had become her closest, perhaps her only, friend, and Amy often popped over to see her after work.

Amy picked up a guitar that was balanced precariously

on top of ten assorted mugs on the kitchen table. She placed the guitar beside a double bass standing in the larder. Then, skidding over a jammy knife, she bent and retrieved it, along with three other knives, two dirty spoons and an apple core.

'I don't know how you do it, Chloe.' Amy dropped the cutlery into a sink already piled high with dishes. 'Eight children to clean up after. As soon as you've finished they'll be back for tea, and you've got to start all over again.'

'Not Fidelio.' Mrs Gunn brushed cornflakes off three of the chairs. 'He's at Bloors, remember. And Felix is away a lot now, with his band, so that only leaves six.' She removed a flute and three music books from the worktop and tucked them into the washing machine.

'Will they be safe in there?' Amy asked anxiously.

'Safe as houses,' said Chloe. 'Pudding's inside and she'd let me know if I started a wash.'

A large grey cat jumped out of the washing machine.

'Oh, well,' Chloe said cheerfully. 'Let's have our coffee.'

Amy wiped a blob of butter off one of the chairs and sat down. Chloe sang as she filled the kettle. She sang most of the time, as did her husband, a music teacher at the local school. Every one of their children was musical, but Fidelio was the star. A musical genius.

Chloe knew that her fourth child would go far.

Outside the kitchen window a row of green herbs could be seen, sprouting from their terracotta pots. Alas, the herb that Amy had come for had vanished.

'Who would have taken that vervain?' asked Amy, sipping her coffee.

'No idea,' said Chloe. 'It was there two nights ago. I used some in a salad. I'm so sorry, Amy. What are you going to do next? You can't leave your mother in the bath indefinitely.'

Amy gave a sigh of despair. 'Oh, Chloe, I don't know *what* to do.'

'I think you should go and see the manager at Kingdom's. If someone tampered with those prawns, the store is responsible.'

'They say they're not.'

'Then tell the police,' Chloe advised.

'I can't. Don't you see – it's . . . it's a spell. Dr Tanaka said as much. The police can't deal with spells.' Amy drained her cup. 'I'd better go, Chloe. I don't like leaving Maisie for too long. She just might melt, and she'll be so frightened if she's all alone.'

'Especially if that mother-in-law of yours is on the prowl,' said Chloe grimly.

Amy intended to go straight home and yet, when she found herself walking down the High Street, something made her turn and look at a splendid building on the other side of the road. Green marble pillars stood on either side of the entrance, and every one of the ninety-nine windows sparkled with a soft light, the sort of light that tells the world the room beyond holds treasures that most people can only dream of.

Amy crossed the road. She stepped into the recess behind the pillars. Green and gold marble swirled above her head and beneath her feet. Two doormen wearing green frock coats and shining top hats stood on either side of a gleaming oak door. Their white-gloved fingers rested lightly on the large bronze door handles.

'Are you going in, Madam?' asked one of the doormen in a bored voice.

'Yes, I am,' said Amy decisively.

He was obliged to open the door.

Amy walked in. She had only twice been into Kingdom's. Once, long ago, with her husband, Lyell. It was here that he had spent a whole month's salary on the diamond ring that Amy still wore on the third finger of her left hand. Surprising tears came to her eyes and she quickly brushed them away.

All around her, velvet-covered counters displayed exquisite jewellery, silk scarves and extravagantly packed oils, creams and perfumes. Hand-written cards with names that Amy had never heard of, and prices she dared not think of, peeped slyly from behind leather boxes, coloured bottles, glittering tins and velvet bags.

Lanterns hung low over every counter, casting a brilliant light on the displays beneath, while the assistants stood in shadow. Only a pair of pale hands could occasionally be glimpsed, hovering over the counters. Amy wondered if the hands had been specially chosen.

She decided to approach the hands that dealt with jewellery. She was, after all, wearing a ring that had once nestled on that very counter. Leaning under the lantern, she peered up at the shadowy face of someone blonde, who looked remarkably severe.

'My name is Mrs Bone,' said Amy, 'and I'd like to see the manager.'

'Why?' asked the blonde person.

'We've had a case of food poisoning.'

'Food's in the basement.' The blonde's expression didn't change.

'I know, but I want the manager,' Amy insisted.

The blonde sighed, picked up a receiver discreetly

covered in velvet and pressed a knob. 'I've got a lady here who wants to see the manager,' she said in a superior voice.

Amy couldn't see the twelve cameras situated in the dark faraway ceiling. She didn't hear them swivel smartly to focus on her. But, all at once, she found herself caught in a fierce beam of light that came from somewhere high above.

'Oh!' cried Amy. 'What did I do?'

The assistant didn't reply. She was still talking into her velvet-covered instrument.

Amy didn't know that she was being watched on twelve different monitors by someone on the top floor. She was unaware that even in her shabby winter coat, without make-up or properly combed hair, she was still beautiful.

'The owner wants to see you.' The blonde assistant smacked her phone back on to the counter.

'The *owner* . . .' Amy faltered. 'The owner, I didn't know he lived here. I just wanted to talk to the manager.'

'Top floor,' snapped the assistant. 'The lift's over there.' She pointed to a distant light.

'Thank you.' Amy began to wish she hadn't come into Kingdom's. What could anyone do, after all? They couldn't break spells. Unless, of course, there was a sorcerer hidden somewhere on the top floor?

She reached the lift and pressed a button. The door slid

open and she stepped into a small room with mirrored walls, a marble floor and a ceiling decorated with golden birds. Birds that looked remarkably real — apart from the gold paint.

Amy got out on the top floor. She was now standing almost ankle-deep in black fur — what sort of fur she couldn't guess. A door opened to her right and a man walked out — the most handsome man Amy had ever seen. She patted her hair, twitched her coat and glanced at her scruffy shoes.

The man gave a small nod. 'Mrs Bone?' He had brown hair that, somehow, looked gold. His face was tanned and his eyes were a deep olive green.

'Yes, that's right. Mrs Bone,' Amy said timidly.

The man bowed and, sweeping out an arm, indicated that she should enter his room.

Amy ploughed through the black fur and walked into a room carpeted, this time, in white fur.

'Oh,' she said, looking down, 'how . . .'

'Har . . . Hart Noble.' The man took her hand and bent over it like a hungry animal. 'The carpet is Arctic Bear.'

Amy gasped. 'But I thought . . .'

'Please sit down.' He gently removed her coat.

Amy sat on the edge of a sofa that appeared to be covered in — could it be pony skin?

'Tell me your troubles.' Hart sat beside her. He was wearing a white silk shirt and a waistcoat that must have been sealskin.

While Amy told him about frozen Maisie and the suspect prawn, Hart took her hand and gazed into her eyes. She felt she was drowning in a deep green pool. At the end of her story he got up and fetched two glasses of champagne from an ivory table at the back of the room.

Amy sipped her drink and looked about her. The room was entirely walled in mirrors, and every piece of furniture appeared to have been made from an animal. Tusks, bones, skins, feathers and furs. If she had listened very carefully, she might have heard their cries. But Amy was falling under a spell.

A second glass of champagne was poured. When Amy looked at her reflection she saw someone she barely recognised: a beautiful woman with shining hair and sparkling eyes; even her old pink cardigan looked new.

Hart brought her a plate of tiny morsels covered in a spicy glaze. Amy devoured them, moaning with delight. When he told her that they were made of eagle meat she didn't turn a hair.

He persuaded her to talk about her life, and Amy found herself remembering things she had forgotten for years.

She didn't notice the light fading from the windows, and only realised how long she had been talking when she found herself sitting in candlelight.

'My goodness, it must be late.' Amy got to her feet rather unsteadily.

Hart helped her on with her coat and escorted her to the lift. 'Adieu,' he said, elegantly blowing her a kiss.

Amy walked through the store in a daze. Outside the pavement sparkled with frost. 'Beautiful,' she said aloud. 'I'm walking on stars.'

'Stars?' said an old lady, passing by. 'It's perishing cold, that's what it is. You've been bewitched.'

When Amy got home she went straight up to her room and took off her diamond ring.

A stab of pain made Charlie wince.

'What's up? Eaten too fast?' joked Fidelio.

They were sitting in the canteen after tea. Everyone else had left, except for Billy who was, at that very moment, furtively handing Rembrandt to Cook.

'I think my mum would call it indigestion,' said Charlie, rubbing his chest. But he wasn't sure what it was. And he didn't know why, when the pain had gone, he felt as if something precious had been lost.

Cook came round the counter and sat at their table.

'What's going on, Charlie?' she asked. 'Rumours are flying thick and fast. They say that some of the animals have come back, very particular animals in fact. Runner Bean has been mentioned, along with Lysander's parrot, Nancy duck, Gabriel's gerbils, et cetera. How come all the others are still lost?'

'Blessed's here,' Charlie said evasively.

'Course he is. I made sure of that. He's scared stiff of something, though.'

'I don't think Charlie can tell us anything,' said Fidelio. 'Even I don't know.'

Cook shook her head. 'You haven't gone and sworn a silly oath, have you, Charlie?'

'Not exactly,' said Charlie.

'Well, take care, my dear. There's trouble brewing. You'd better find an answer for the Bloors or they'll force it out of you in a very unfriendly fashion.' Cook returned to her kitchen with one hand over the large pocket in her apron. 'All right, you'll get some supper in a minute,' she said to the pocket as she disappeared through the swing door.

The trouble that was brewing came to the boil after supper. Instead of dismissing the children when they had finished eating, Dr Bloor clapped his hands for

silence and began to pace round the platform that held the staff table.

From the three long tables in the dining hall, three hundred children watched the headmaster in his black cape, his head down and hands clasped behind his back. He was a large man with a neat grey moustache and iron-grey hair, cut very short. Today his face was a pinky-red. When he came to rest, at last, he stared at the children on the Drama table, directly in front of him.

'There cannot be one of you who is not aware of the catastrophe that has struck this city. Eh?' He put a hand behind his ear. 'What did you say?'

'NO, sir,' shouted the children in purple capes.

Dr Bloor walked to his right until he reached the centre of the platform. 'And what do you say?' he demanded of the children in Art.

'NO, sir,' shouted the children in green.

Dr Bloor took several more paces to his right. He was now standing in front of Charlie, who had been the last in and was forced to sit in one of the unlucky seats just below the staff table. Fidelio was sitting opposite him.

'And what about you?' Dr Bloor's pinkish complexion darkened. 'Have you heard about the city's problems?' He stared hard at Charlie.

Charlie thought the question was personal and asked, 'D'you mean the animals, sir?'

'Of course I mean the animals.' Dr Bloor gave a little jump of fury. 'Stupid boy.'

'In that case, yes, sir,' said Charlie.

The other children on the Music table repeated, 'Yes, sir.'

The headmaster then said something very surprising. 'It is, of course, a catastrophe when beloved pets disappear. It is especially distressing for the elderly whose pets have become their only companions. However,' Dr Bloor walked across the platform, 'it happens sometimes and it can't be helped.'

Charlie was baffled. Did the headmaster know what had caused the animals to run away? He certainly didn't seem suprised by their disappearance.

Dr Bloor suddenly swung round and walked back to stand in front of Charlie. 'But it is unforgivable when someone finds a pet or two, belonging to their friends, and will tell no one where he found them.' The headmaster stuck his chin out and stared at Charlie. 'Where did you find the pets, Charlie Bone? The city councillors want to know. Where did you find the dog, the duck, the parrot, the rabbits and gerbils, and the snake that belongs to my grandfather?'

'I just found them, sir . . . wandering around,' said Charlie. 'STAND UP, BOY!'

Charlie stood up.

'I'll repeat my question,' said Dr Bloor. 'Where did you find the animals?'

Charlie gritted his teeth. 'I could bring back the snake, sir, if you like.'

'We don't want the snake. It's a feeble thing now, by all accounts.' Dr Bloor stamped his foot. 'AND DON'T CHANGE THE SUBJECT!'

'No, sir.' Charlie looked away from the headmaster's angry red face. 'Perhaps the animals will just wander back, sir, like the ones I found.'

'Well, if they don't, Charlie Bone,' Dr Bloor leant closer to him, 'if they don't, there's a room in the attics where a boy can be kept until he tells the truth.'

'Yes, sir,' said Charlie in a choked voice.

'DISMISS!' roared the headmaster.

Three hundred children leapt to their feet and began to stack the dirty plates.

'What are you going to do?' Fidelio asked Charlie as they made their way out of the dining-hall.

'Don't know,' said Charlie. 'I'll have to think about it while I'm doing homework. That is, if I can think. It's going to be nasty in there tonight.'

But it wasn't as bad as Charlie had feared. Perhaps

Joshua and Dorcas had enjoyed the headmaster's scolding so much, they felt that Charlie had got all he deserved for the time being.

Charlie appeared to be working hard on his history project, but his thoughts were far away. How could he get all the animals back? And how could Maisie be unfrozen? When he thought of Maisie, lying so still in the bath, it made him shiver. And then the horrible feeling that he'd lost something precious gradually overwhelmed him.

After homework, Charlie trudged back to the dormitory in a daze. Someone jogged his elbow and he realised that Gabriel was walking beside him.

'Thanks for getting my gerbils, Charlie,' Gabriel said quietly. 'I won't ask where you found them.'

'That's OK.' Charlie felt better when he saw Gabriel's cheerful face. 'I left them in the Pets' Café. You can collect them at the weekend.'

'Great. D'you think you'll be able to get the others back?'

Charlie gave a huge sigh. 'How can I, Gabe? Think about it. Almost every bird in the city, every rat, mouse, frog, toad, dog, cat – you name it – has run away. How can I get them *all* back without . . . without . . .'

'Telling where they are,' said Gabriel. 'I see your problem.'

It didn't bother Charlie that half the boys in his

dormitory wouldn't speak to him. He had too much on his mind. Long after lights out, he lay awake, and when he was quite sure that all the others were asleep he tiptoed across to the window and opened the curtains, just wide enough to let a slice of moonlight creep into the room. The light fell in a thin band right behind his bed.

Charlie climbed under the covers and waited. Would Naren find him? Would she send a message? Because he badly wanted to talk to her. He had almost given up hope when tiny black shadows began to tumble over the sill and into the room. Charlie watched them crawl across his bed and up on to the wall. At last they came to rest and he could read the words:

'How are you, Charlie?'

'I'm in trouble,' Charlie whispered. 'I've got to get the animals back, Naren, and soon, or they'll lock me up.'

The little shadows quickly rearranged themselves, and Charlie was astonished to read,

'They're on their way. Tomorrow every lost creature will be back in the city.'

'How?' asked Charlie.

'Three bright cats arrived. Magical cats. You should have seen them, Charlie. They sat in our yard and called in such loud, beautiful voices, all the animals gathered around and

followed them out of our gate. What a sight! Birds in the air, creatures running, scuffling, leaping –'

A sudden shriek ripped through the dormitory. Charlie whispered 'Goodbye', and the words began to fade.

'What was *that*?' cried Rupe Small. 'It was horrible.'

By now the whole room was awake.

'The wall was covered in – in stuff – animals or something,' said Rupe. 'Charlie Bone was talking to it.'

'Urgh!' 'What?' 'Yuk!' 'Trust Charlie Bone!' came from one side of the dormitory.

'Shut up and go to sleep,' said Fidelio. 'You were having a nightmare, Rupe Small.'

'I WAS NOT!'

The door opened and Lucretia Yewbeam's tall shadow fell across the room. She turned on the light. 'What's going on?' she demanded.

Rupe pointed at Charlie. 'There was stuff all over the wall, and *he* was talking to it.'

The matron's eyes narrowed. 'What was it, this *stuff*?'

'Nothing, Matron,' said Charlie.

'I saw it,' said Bragger Braine. 'It disappeared when Charlie whispered to it.'

'It was just flies,' said Charlie. 'I don't know where they came from.'

'Don't lie,' said his great-aunt. 'There are no flies. It's winter. They're all dead.'

To this, Charlie could find no answer.

The matron walked over to Charlie's bed and stared down at him. 'It's always you, isn't it? Keeping other people awake, disturbing their sleep. I don't know what you were doing and I don't really care. It's detention for you, Charlie Bone. You'll spend half your weekend in school.'

'But I can't,' Charlie protested. 'My grandmother's ill.'

'Your grandmother is perfectly well,' said the matron, walking away.

'No, not your sister. Not Grandma Bone. I mean Maisie, my other grandmother.'

'Oh, her,' the matron said carelessly. 'What's the matter with her?'

'She fr-c-caught a cold,' stuttered Charlie.

'A cold? Hardly a matter of life and death. Go to sleep.' The matron turned out the light and closed the door.

As Charlie slid under the covers he heard something that made his heart leap. An owl hooted, and then another.

'They *are* coming back,' he thought, and at last he drifted off to sleep.

The hundred heads

If Charlie had looked out of his window, he would have seen an astonishing sight. The sky was crowded with birds. Their voices were silent but the air hummed with the sound of beating wings. Gradually, small groups began to swing away from the vast flock. They flew down and settled on walls, trees, fences and buildings. Once there, they tucked their heads under their wings and fell asleep. Soon, only the owls were left awake.

Down in the city, light sleepers found themselves drawn to their windows. They were rewarded by a sight they would never forget. Lines of solemn, silent creatures moved through the city. They were led by

three cats whose coats were so bright that the air around them shone with fiery colours. As they made their way along the streets, the animals began to find their homes. They bounded through windows, they walked into gardens, kennels and stables, and the marvelling watchers heaved a sigh of relief. The city wasn't dying after all.

The news travelled fast. By first break even the children in Bloor's Academy had heard about the great return. Laughter was heard in the canteens and classrooms; smiles were seen on the faces of children who had said they would never smile again. Charlie was relieved, even though some of his classmates still looked at him with suspicion.

Just when one problem had been solved, Charlie was presented with another. Detention. He was desperate to find out if Maisie had melted, and he also felt he should be at home to watch over his mother.

At lunchtime, Charlie found Billy in the canteen eating one of Cook's new specialities. Potato hedgehogs.

'They're not really hedgehogs,' Billy said gravely. 'It's just that they've got these nice crispy tips.'

While Cook was serving Charlie, she said quietly, 'I hear the animals are back.'

Charlie nodded. 'The Flames brought them. But I've got detention this weekend, so . . .'

'What?' Cook lowered her ladle. 'You can't have.' She looked very surprised.

Charlie was about to ask why, when behind him Gabriel said, 'I'm dying of hunger. Move on, Charlie.'

Charlie took his plate of hedgehogs to Billy's table. In a few minutes, Fidelio and Gabriel had joined them.

'D'you know what's happening this weekend?' Billy asked the others.

'I've got detention,' said Charlie.

'No, I didn't mean that.' Billy squared his shoulders and said importantly, 'It's the Hundred Heads' Dinner on Friday, and the Grand Ball on Saturday. I heard Dr Bloor reminding Matron about it. He was cross because she'd given you detention, Charlie, and he didn't want any children in the building. But Matron said it was against her principles to take back detentions. And Dr Bloor walked off in a huff. He said she'd got to keep you out of the way. I expect he meant me, too, because I'll be here if you are, won't I, Charlie?'

Charlie felt quite out of breath when Billy finally came to a halt.

Gabriel said, 'Billy, I've never heard you say so much all in one go.'

Fidelio asked, 'So what are the Hundred Heads' Dinner and the Grand Ball?'

'Well,' began Billy, 'I found out a bit more from Manfred.'

'From *Manfred*!' said the others in shocked voices.

'He likes to feel important, so I thought he'd be very happy to tell me,' said Billy, 'and he was. He said every ten years there's a reunion. Head teachers from a hundred other academies come here to talk about their pupils and things.'

'What other academies?' said Charlie.

'Where all the other endowed children go,' said Billy.

'There are *others*?' said Charlie in surprise.

'Of course, there would be,' Gabriel said thoughtfully. 'When you think about it, there must be hundreds of children like us, all over the world. I mean the Red King had ten children and if they all had children, nine hundred years ago . . .'

'Wow!' Charlie's mouth dropped open. 'Am I stupid, or what?' They couldn't all come to Bloors, could they? Not if they lived in China or Africa.'

'Or even Scotland, or Ireland,' said Fidelio.

'Phew! I just never thought.' Charlie shook his head in wonderment.

They tucked into their hedgehogs, each one of them thinking about those other academies, other children and other headmasters.

'I'm going to get into that Hundred Heads' Dinner somehow,' said Charlie. 'There's a lot I want to find out.'

'Me too,' said Billy.

Charlie gulped down his last lump of hedgehog and smiled. The weekend wasn't going to be so bad, after all. Perhaps his mother had found the vervain, and when he got home Maisie would be her old self again.

The pupils at Bloor's Academy were left in no doubt that a momentous event was about to take place in their school. By the time Friday arrived, the ceiling of the great hall glittered with a thousand lanterns. Swords, crossbows, scimitars, spears and many other impressive-looking weapons had been retrieved from chests and cupboards. Burnished to an awesome brightness, they hung on the oak-panelled walls, where they drew gasps of terror and admiration. An army of cleaners had polished the flagstones to a slippery shine, and the children were commanded to walk only at the extreme edges.

In the dining-hall, the lighting was more restrained, although it was noticed that several iron braziers had been fixed to the walls. Would they hold flaming torches? And would the important visitors be served by firelight?

Even the friendliest dinner ladies were becoming short-tempered. The extra workload was wearing them out. At

all times of day they were to be seen hurrying down corridors with trays of silverware that hadn't seen the light of day for years.

Porcelain dinner-plates, crystal glasses and golden dishes were unearthed from the cellars and carried up to the kitchens for a sparkling wash.

Fairy lights had been strung along the dark corridor that led from the hall to the canteens and dining-hall, and Charlie noticed that some of the portraits had been decorated with gold ribbon. Not all of them, however. Perhaps only those characters who were directly related to the honoured visitors.

Charlie and Billy sat in the dormitory watching the others pack their bags. Charlie felt strangely elated. He tried to look suitably glum when Bragger Braine and Rupe Small walked to the door, with their bags slung nonchalantly over their shoulders, but he couldn't prevent a grin from curling one corner of his mouth.

'What are you smirking at?' asked Bragger.

'Rupe's bag is so heavy he looks as if he's sinking. How many cans of Sweet Petal have you got in there, Rupe?'

Some of the others giggled and Rupe cried, 'Shut up!'

'Have a bad weekend, Charlie Bone,' said Bragger, swaggering out with Rupe in tow.

Gabriel and Fidelio were the last to leave. They wished Charlie good luck and promised to meet up on Sunday.

'I'll bring extra gerbils,' said Gabriel, giving a final wave.

Not long after the last pupil had left the school, Lucretia Yewbeam looked into the dormitory and told Charlie and Billy they would be having an early supper. 'I want you both back in here by six o'clock,' she said. 'Lights out at seven, and neither of you are to leave this room until breakfast-time.'

'Lights out at *seven*!' Charlie complained. 'Why?'

'Why d'you think? It's a punishment. Now clean yourselves up. Supper's in the canteen at half-past five.' With a grim smile the matron swept out.

When the boys went looking for Cook, they found her in the kitchen, in quite a state. Frantic assistants kept moving round her while she rushed from the giant ovens to the cold room and back again, mumbling, 'A hundred this, a hundred that, turtle soup, pigeon pies, boeuf this and that. No meat for him, no cream for her . . .' Without looking up, she went on, 'Hello, boys. It's only baked beans on toast for you, I'm afraid. Here it comes.'

Cook shared a saucepan of beans between two plates of buttered toast, and put them on a tray with two bowls of custard.

'What time does the dinner begin?' Charlie asked.

'Half-past seven and I'll never be ready.'

A cluster of frantic assistants ran up to Cook and she waved the boys away. 'Sorry, my loves, got to keep going.'

Charlie carried the tray into the canteen and put it on a table furthest from the counter. The noise from the kichen was so loud the boys couldn't even hear their own thoughts. They wolfed down their suppers and left the canteen as soon as they could.

Back in the dormitory they changed into their pyjamas and crept along to the landing above the hall. Lying flat on their stomachs, they peered between the banisters down into the great hall. It was a place they barely recognised.

Brilliantly illumined by the thousand lanterns, a sea of people moved slowly round the hall. Most of the visitors wore evening dress but there were also men in turbans, some in gold-encrusted capes and others in rainbow-coloured jackets. There were a few white robes to be seen, and one man was dressed from head to toe in purple silk, with a jewelled scabbard attached to his belt. Women in saris chatted to others in kimonos, and people in bright national costumes leant eagerly forward, trying to understand each other's language.

Mr Ezekiel, in a black velvet coat and a red skullcap,

wheeled himself through the throng, while everlasting sparklers hissed and crackled from the back of his chair, causing some of the guests to leap away, sucking their burnt arms and knuckles.

Waitresses in short black dresses and white caps and aprons threaded their way through the crowd, bearing large dishes of bite-sized snacks, while waiters in red and gold waistcoats carefully balanced trays of bubbling champagne.

At the bottom of the staircase, a harpist in a flowing pink robe ran her fingers across the strings of a giant gold harp. The gentle sound rose and fell at intervals between the buzz of conversation.

Billy put his head close to Charlie's and whispered, 'Only the wicked ones stayed here.'

'What are you talking about?' Charlie whispered back.

'The Red King. His good children left their father's castle forever. Some even left the country. So the people down there, well, maybe the ones from abroad, are descended from the good children.'

It hadn't occurred to Charlie, but now he watched the faces below more intently. Was it his imagination, or did most of the people in evening dress wear guarded expressions? And surely they looked more grim and

determined than the others. The majority of the foreigners looked friendly and relaxed. They smiled more readily and even laughed.

Charlie suddenly remembered to look at his watch. It was five minutes to seven. He nudged Billy's arm. 'Matron'll be in the dorm in five minutes. As soon as she's gone we'll nip down to the dining-hall and find somewhere to hide before the meal begins.'

They crawled away from the landing and tore back to the dormitory. A minute after they had leapt into bed, the door opened and Matron looked in. She was quite a sight in her long emerald green evening dress, with green earrings that practically touched her shoulders. Her grey-white hair had been pulled on top of her head and decorated with an enormous green bow. 'Lights out,' she said coldly. 'And in case either of you takes it into his head to go wandering, please remember your next punishment will be far worse than this one.'

'Yes, Matron,' Charlie replied meekly. He thought it rather unfair that Billy should be included in his punishment, but decided not to mention it.

The matron turned out the light, but before she closed the door, she said, 'Don't tell your aunt how lovely she looks, will you?'

'No, Aunt,' said Charlie. 'I mean –'

She slammed the door.

Charlie listened to her receding footfalls. 'She won't be back,' he said, 'not looking like that.'

'I bet she's out to catch a nice rich headmaster,' Billy giggled.

They waited another five minutes and then jumped into their slippers, crept along to the back staircase and down to the ground floor. Now they were in the passage that ran past the canteens and down into the underground dining-hall. Keeping to the shadows, they had almost reached the dining-hall when one of the waitresses backed out of the green kitchen. She was pulling a trolley laden with dinner plates.

The boys shrank against the wall but she had seen them. 'Hello, boys,' she said, eyeing their pyjamas. 'What are you doing here?'

'We came down for some water,' Charlie said quickly. 'We were so thirsty and we're not supposed to drink from the taps upstairs, because the pipes are rusty – or something.'

'Poor lads. Pop in and help yourselves.' She nodded at the canteen door.

'Thanks!' Charlie gave her his best smile. But no way was he going into the green kitchen where Mrs Weedon

177

held sway. She was mean, short-tempered and a terrible cook, and she would probably get her husband to drag the boys back to their dormitory.

The waitress wheeled her trolley past them and up to the blue canteen. 'Wrong plates,' she grumbled. 'What a palaver.'

As soon as her back was turned the boys dashed along to the dining-hall. They were about to slip through the doors when Billy said, 'Where are we going to hide?'

'Under a table,' Charlie said.

'But – they might see us.'

Charlie didn't want to think about that. He opened the door a fraction and peeped inside. What a piece of luck. Every table was covered with a huge white cloth that hung almost to the floor.

A waitress was busily arranging the glasses on Dr Bloor's top table, but the other three tables were already laid. Silver cards, printed with names, sat on red velvet place-mats, and each mat was surrounded by more knives, forks, spoons and glasses than Charlie had time to count.

The fiery braziers gave every shining surface a dangerous orange glow and, even from the door, Charlie could feel waves of heat from the leaping flames.

Choosing a moment when the waitress's back was

turned, Charlie whispered, 'Let's go. Now!'

Bending low the boys half-ran, half-crept towards the middle table and slithered under the cloth. A terrible smell hit Charlie's nostrils and he saw, to his horror, that Blessed had chosen the same hiding place.

It was too late to change tables. A door beside the platform opened and two waiters bustled in with trolleys of hot food.

Under the table, Blessed ran up to Billy, whining softly.

'Tell him to be quiet,' whispered Charlie, 'or he'll give us away.'

Billy gave several soft grunts, and Blessed lay beside him, thumping his hairless tail.

'What's that?' said one of the waiters.

Billy puffed, almost soundlessly, into Blessed's ear and the thumping stopped.

'Probably a rat,' said the other waiter.

The first one laughed. 'Hope it nips someone's ankle. I'm fed up with this job. I've been here since six o'clock this morning, and the pay's rotten.'

'They're a mean bunch,' his companion agreed.

The two waiters made so much noise transferring food from their trolleys on to the tables, Charlie and Billy were able to crawl, undetected, towards the platform. Charlie

wanted to be in a good position to hear what was said on the top table.

Two more trolleys were wheeled in and, not long after that, the boys heard a great babble of voices that drew closer and closer until it spilled into the dining-hall. A hundred pairs of feet shuffled, marched, stamped and pattered round the room, as the visitors searched for their places.

Crouched in the dark, Charlie and Billy listened to the chomping, slurping and gulping that was going on above them. Charlie was trapped between two pairs of very long black-trousered legs. He decided to move and backed into Billy who, unfortunately, put his hand on a foot in a silver shoe.

'Do you mind?' said a woman's voice.

'Pardon?' said the man opposite her.

'You kicked me.'

'You're mistaken. It was someone else.'

Pushing Blessed before them, the boys crawled away from the silver shoe as fast as they could. Just in time. The tablecloth was lifted and the woman in silver shoes looked under the table. The boys held their breath until, with a grunt of annoyance, the woman let the cloth fall back into place.

The dinner went on and on and on. Blessed fell asleep and Billy started yawning, and then a hush fell over the room as Dr Bloor began to speak.

After he had welcomed his guests, the names of all the academies were read out: Loth, Oranga, Morhan, Derivere, Somphammer, Festyet, Ipakuk, Altabeeta ... The list continued. Charlie's eyes began to close, and then, suddenly, he was wide awake. Dr Bloor had uttered the name Lyell Bone, and it was connected to a crime. Charlie sat bolt upright, his head just grazing the top of the table.

'Those of you who were here ten years ago will remember my grandfather, Ezekiel Bloor, as an active and agile ninety year old. Today, sadly, he is confined to a wheelchair. Lyell Bone is distantly related to us, and so the crime was doubly shocking.' Dr Bloor paused and cleared his throat.

'Please,' said a voice close to Charlie, 'can you tell us how this crime was committed?'

'He knocked me down,' shouted Ezekiel. 'Tried to kill me. Pushed me. Head hit stone. Bingo! Couldn't move. Done for. The SCOUNDREL!'

A gasp rippled round the room.

'But why?' asked another voice, a woman this time. 'Why did he do this terrible thing?'

'Some of you,' said Dr Bloor, avoiding the question, 'will run your establishments in a different way from us. But all of you will be acting in the interests of our wider family. Like you, we draw the Children of the Red King towards us. We offer them scholarships, first-class teaching and equipment. We protect them, nurture them, prepare them for the difficulties they may face when they are adults . . . Occasionally it becomes necessary, for the child's own good, you understand, to remove it from its parents.'

'Do you mean that you steal them?' asked an indignant voice.

'He said "remove",' screeched Ezekiel. 'Stealing doesn't come into it. For the greater good we must control these children, and if their parents seem likely to resist, then, yes, we must take them by any means.'

A murmur of agreement ran along the table above him, but Charlie noticed a few sounds of dissent.

'However,' Ezekiel continued, 'in the case of a certain child who could fly, her father, Dr Tolly, was happy to hand her over. It was Lyell Bone who tried to prevent it, by striking me to the ground. His protest was unsuccessful and he was duly punished.'

'And did the punishment fit the crime?' someone asked in a gruff voice.

'Yes, Dr Loth. Thanks to my great-grandson Manfred Bloor. Manfred, stand up!'

The distant scrape of a chair seemed to indicate that Manfred was sitting at the top table. Someone clapped and others joined in. Charlie couldn't imagine why.

'Manfred may be the greatest hypnotist who ever lived,' Ezekiel proudly announced. 'At only nine years of age, he erased Lyell Bone's memory with a single glance. The man is now utterly helpless. He doesn't even know who he is.'

A profound silence followed this remark and, for some reason, this made Ezekiel laugh. He laughed so much he almost choked. Charlie found the sound unbearable. He could hardly contain his anger and had to clasp his arms tight around his body to stop himself from leaping out.

In a stirring voice, Dr Bloor continued, 'Manfred also put the baby "under". She was two at the time. It lasted until she was ten and then Lyell Bone's confounded son woke her up.'

There was a mutter of surprise. Snatches of conversation reached Charlie. 'Who?' 'How was this done?' 'Do you . . .?' 'Could it be . . .?'

'Ladies and gentlemen,' boomed Dr Bloor. 'Do not be concerned. The girl is still here, and so is Lyell's son, Charlie. These endowed children stick together like glue.

Charlie is a picture-traveller – a priceless gift, as you will know. He has proved difficult, probably because he is his father's son, but he is well-guarded. These charming ladies on my right are his grandmother, Grizelda Bone, and his three great-aunts, Lucretia, Eustacia and Venetia Yewbeam. They all keep an eye on Charlie Bone –'

'And one day,' Ezekiel broke in, 'Charlie will take me with him into the past, where I can rearrange history.' He began to cackle again.

Dr Loth called, 'Bravo!' and others took up the call. But some remained silent.

Billy, who had been lying asleep on top of Blessed, suddenly woke up and gave a tiny sneeze. The cloth was lifted right in front of Charlie and an upside-down face appeared. It had a beard and wore a blue turban.

Charlie stared straight into the man's dark brown eyes. He didn't know what to do. The man stared right back at him. Charlie waited for something to happen. The man with the turban seemed to be waiting too. So Charlie did the only thing he could think of. He put a finger to his lips.

The man gave him a broad smile and dropped the cloth back in place.

Charlie had only just begun to breathe again when a thin, petulant voice cried, 'I smell boy!'

'Boy?' said several voices.

'Smells are my thing,' went on the thin, male voice. 'I can smell a boy, maybe two – or three.'

Charlie and Billy looked at each other in terror. It was all over. They were about to be found out. And then Charlie had an idea. He pointed at Blessed.

Billy grunted into the old dog's ear and Blessed scrambled to his feet. With a little shove from Billy, he tottered under the tablecloth and out into the dining-hall. As he went he let out the worst stink Charlie had ever smelled. It was so bad and so strong he nearly keeled over. Billy had told Blessed to give the biggest fart of his whole life.

Cries of horror and disgust reverberated round the room. 'Uuuurrgh!' 'Pooooh!' 'What *is* that smell?' 'It's a dog.' 'An old dog!' 'What a monster!'

'That's not the smell of boy, it's the smell of dog,' said an irritated voice.

'Your nose is growing old, Professor Morvan.' This voice belonged to a jolly-sounding woman. 'It can't tell boy from dog.'

Laughter followed, and old Ezekiel screamed, 'Don't be so rude about my doggie. He can't help it.'

'I think we should let him out, Dr Bloor,' someone

suggested. 'I'm sure he wants to go – that is – leave.'

'A good idea,' Dr Bloor agreed. 'Would someone kindly . . .'

'And be quick about it,' added another female voice.

A chair scraped. Someone ran and opened the door. Blessed gave a bark of thanks and padded out. More laughter.

Fortunately, the old dog had left such a bad smell behind him, Professor Morvan's nose was thoroughly confused and he said nothing more about the smell of boys.

When the laughter had subsided, Dr Bloor coughed loudly and said, 'I apologise for the distraction but now I would like to get back to the momentous development that we hinted at when we welcomed you here tonight.'

'We're all ears,' said Dr Loth.

'Thank you.' Dr Bloor waited for complete silence and then continued with barely suppressed excitement, 'First I must give you a brief history of someone whom even *I* had never heard of, until last week. Count Harken Badlock.'

Silence. Obviously no one knew about Count Harken Badlock. Charlie listened intently, aware that he was about to learn something of immense importance.

'Count Harken was eighteen years old when he arrived in Spain. He began to court the beautiful Berenice,

daughter of a knight of Toledo. The young count was an enchanter and very soon Berenice fell under his spell. They were to be married, and then –'

'Surely Berenice married the Red King,' a voice interrupted.

'Indeed, she did,' agreed Dr Bloor. 'But there was a duel between the two men and Count Harken lost. For all his sorcery, all his charm, he could not compete with the Red King's magic, and so he lost the fair Berenice.'

Dr Bloor's audience waited in wordless suspense for the story to continue, as surely it must.

'As you know, Queen Berenice died when her tenth child, Amoret, was born. The King, as was the custom of his people, went into the forest to grieve for his wife. His children were left in the care of servants – until Count Harken appeared. Yes, my friends, he came to protect the children of his beloved Berenice. He taught them all he knew, guarded them against marauding strangers, and married the King's eldest daughter, Lilith.'

'How has all this suddenly come to light, Dr Bloor?' someone asked.

There was a dramatic pause. Charlie's scalp prickled and he imagined Dr Bloor leaning forward in an attitude of triumph. 'Because I have heard it from the count himself.'

There was a collective gasp of disbelief before Dr Bloor continued, 'I know it's hard to believe that a man who lived nine hundred years ago is with us again. But it's the truth. I am utterly convinced of it.'

Above a chorus of questions and protests, old Ezekiel cried, 'He was a mere shadow in the Red King's portrait, but someone has let him out.'

Charlie grabbed Billy's arm so tightly he gave a little gasp of pain. In the dim light beneath the table, Charlie could see that Billy's eyes were as wide as his own. *The shadow*, he mouthed. Charlie nodded.

The noise that greeted Ezekiel's revelation almost amounted to an uproar.

'Who let him out?'

'Where is he now?'

These two questions could be heard above all the others. Dr Bloor begged for silence and when the commotion had subsided he answered. 'Where is he? He is safe. He has acclimatised to this century in the most remarkable way. It took him ten minutes to learn our language, and once that was accomplished he was able to acquaint himself with our politics, our finances, our mode of dress, our habits, in short –'

'But then, he is an enchanter,' Ezekiel put in.

'Indeed, yes,' said Dr Bloor. 'Unfortunately he had to be a little ruthless when it came to finding a home and an income, but these things cannot always be avoided.' He gave an awkward laugh. 'At this point, I must ask you, dear guests, not to repeat a word of what I have told you outside this building. We are used to keeping secrets, are we not? We have to, or the world would take against us.'

There was a rumble of agreement and then Dr Loth's voice drowned out the others. 'Who was it?' he demanded. 'Who let the shadow out, and how?'

'Ah.' Dr Bloor paused. 'The count is not sure. He claims it was done with a mirror – some called it the Mirror of Amoret. We found him in the hall, during a snowstorm. The person who released him had slipped away.'

'We thought it was Venetia here,' said Ezekiel. 'She's the cleverest of us. The wickedest.' He chuckled.

'Well, it wasn't,' said Venetia sullenly.

'So you see –' began Dr Bloor.

'It was me,' said a voice. 'I did it.'

'*You?*' The headmaster sounded utterly astonished.

'Yes, me. I found the Mirror of Amoret.'

Charlie froze. Every nerve in his body began to tingle. He knew that voice. It came from one of the last people in the world he would have expected.

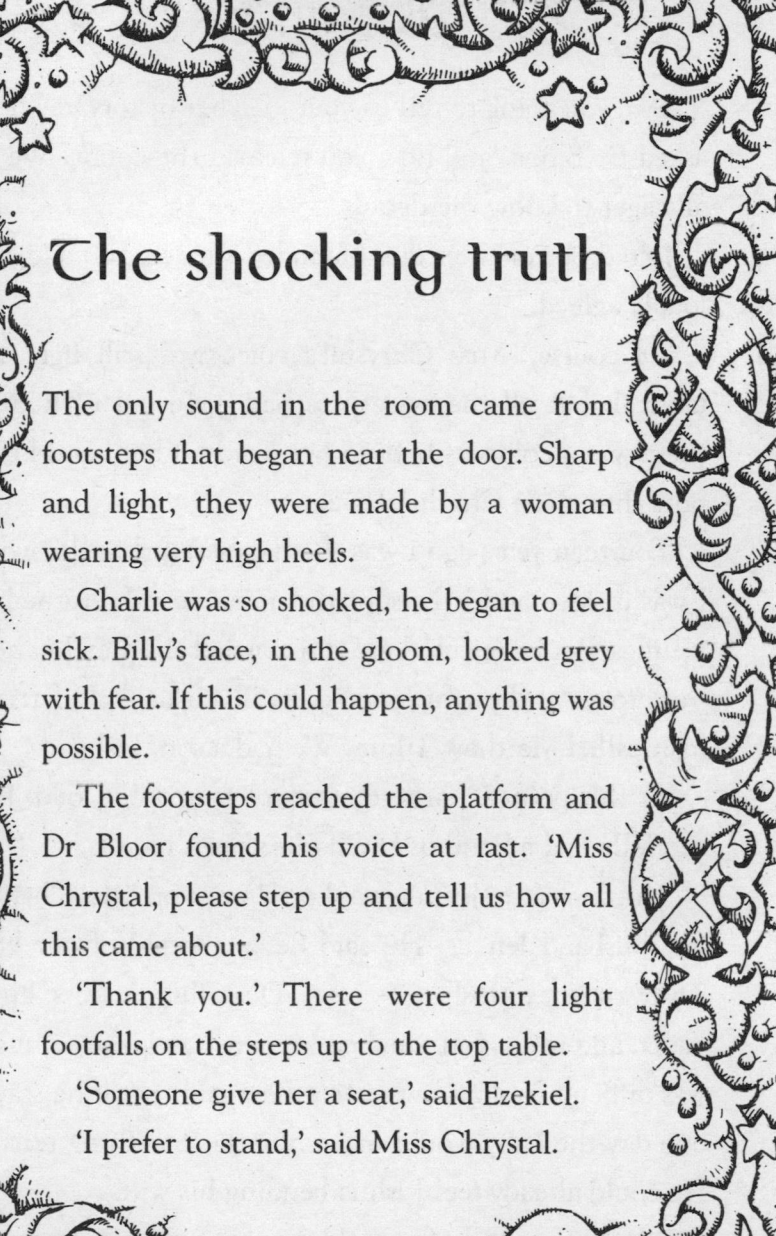

The shocking truth

The only sound in the room came from footsteps that began near the door. Sharp and light, they were made by a woman wearing very high heels.

Charlie was so shocked, he began to feel sick. Billy's face, in the gloom, looked grey with fear. If this could happen, anything was possible.

The footsteps reached the platform and Dr Bloor found his voice at last. 'Miss Chrystal, please step up and tell us how all this came about.'

'Thank you.' There were four light footfalls on the steps up to the top table.

'Someone give her a seat,' said Ezekiel.

'I prefer to stand,' said Miss Chrystal.

'Are you going to tell us your . . . your history, my dear,' asked Dr Bloor, 'and how you released the count? We are all eager to know the details.'

Jolted out of their dumbfounded silence, the audience loudly agreed.

'Of course.' Miss Chrystal's voice was still light and musical, but all the sweetness had gone out of it. Now there was a coldness behind her words; a hard and brittle note that made Charlie shiver.

'Fourteen years ago I was the happiest girl in the world. I was in love and I thought the man I loved returned my feelings. But he rejected me and married another. My heart was broken. I thought I would die. Eventually, I married a man called Matthew Tilpin. We had a son, Joshua.'

At this point Charlie almost spluttered out loud. Billy carefully laid a hand over Charlie's open mouth.

'Not long after Joshua was born,' went on Miss Chrystal, 'my husband left us. He said he was afraid of our baby. Things stuck to Joshua, you see. Dust, fluff, insects, bits of paper, and when you touched his tiny hands they clung. It was difficult to draw away. Matthew said that if he stayed, one day the baby would make him do something terrible. He could already feel Joshua bending his will.

'My mother had often told me that we were descended

from the Red King,' Miss Chrystal continued, 'and I had some success with magic when I was a child. But it is useless in affairs of the heart, so I rather gave it up. And then, last Christmas, my great-uncle died and left me a chest full of papers. Some had been in the family for nine hundred years. A lot of it was impossible to read. Much was useless scribbling, but I did discover that we were descended from Lilith, the Red King's eldest daughter, and her husband, Count Harken Badlock.'

The hundred heads all gasped at once, but Miss Chrystal ploughed on, almost without taking breath, 'Among the papers was a map, in perfect condition, but very, very small. You wouldn't believe how small it was – is. It must have been overlooked for generations. I have no idea who made it – perhaps the count drew it himself. I must ask him.' She gave a small laugh. 'It told me where I could find the Mirror of Amoret. The mirror that would bring the count back into the world. I merely had to hold it before the Red King's portrait, so that reflected light fell over the shadow behind him and,' she paused, 'and so I did – and it worked. The count is back!' When she said the last four words Miss Chrystal's voice crackled with rapturous excitement.

'A glass of water,' said Dr Bloor.

'Here, a chair.' Someone pushed a chair across the floor.

A babble of conversation broke out among the guests. If Charlie and Billy had wanted to change their positions, now would have been the time, but Charlie was too stunned to move.

Miss Chrystal hadn't finished with her audience. 'I have something more to say,' she announced. 'My son, Joshua, is very powerful. Like Charlie Bone, he has the blood of two magicians running in his veins. If Charlie is to be controlled, then Joshua can do it. As for the matter of Charlie's father, the count will make sure that he never wakes.' She gave a brittle laugh. 'Oh yes, the count will make sure that Lyell Bone is lost, lost, lost forever.'

After a brief silence, a voice above Charlie said, 'Miss Chrystal, I would like to ask you a question.' Charlie had a feeling that the voice belonged to the man in the turban. 'Will you tell us the name of the man who rejected you?'

'Who d'you think?' she said coldly. 'It was Lyell Bone.'

Charlie shuddered so violently Billy had to hold his arm.

'Let's get out of here,' Charlie whispered.

There was now such a hubbub in the dining-hall, the boys' frantic scramble to the end of the table couldn't be heard. Chairs began to squeak. People got up and moved

about. Trolleys were wheeled in and the boys could hear the clink of china.

'Coffee, everyone!' Dr Bloor announced. 'Coffee and Turkish delight. Please take your seats for a few more minutes.'

'How are we going to get out of here?' Billy whispered.

Charlie shrugged hopelessly. The doors were at least two metres from the table. Even if they crawled, someone was bound to see them. He had an idea. Hoping that the waiters would wheel their trolleys right to the end of the table, he waited, just out of reach of the last pair of legs.

The trolleys rolled closer, one each side of the table. As best he could, Charlie mimed climbing on to the lower shelf of the trolley. Billy understood and nodded.

At last the two waiters reached the very end of the table. With a last look at Billy's anxious face, Charlie grinned encouragingly and scrambled under the red cloth that covered one of the trolleys. The lower shelf was now empty, and the waiter distracted by serving coffee. Huddled uncomfortably on the shelf, Charlie realised that the red cloth didn't entirely cover him. Crossing his fingers, he remained perfectly still while the trolley was wheeled slowly to the other end of the dining-hall. As soon as they were safely through the swing doors, the

waiter came to a stop and began to swear. 'What the . . .?' He looked under the cloth and found Charlie.

'Blimey, a kid!' said the waiter, a young man with a slightly spotty face. 'What are you doing here?'

'I got detention and I was bored,' said Charlie, hoping the young man was a sympathetic type.

The young man laughed. 'I'll bet you were bored. Now, do you mind getting off my trolley? My back's been playing up something awful.'

'Please, couldn't you take me a bit further,' Charlie begged, 'just through the kitchens?'

'You're joking. I've been working since six o'clock a.m.'

'Just through the green kitchen, then,' Charlie pleaded. 'I don't want Mrs Weedon to catch me.'

'I get your point. All right, hold tight.'

Charlie gritted his teeth as they passed through Mrs Weedon's domain. He could see the lower half of her wide body, stomping along in a cloud of steam beside the vast sinks. And then they were in the next part of the kitchens, behind the Drama canteen. The waiter wheeled Charlie through the canteen and into the passage.

'Now, scarper,' said the waiter, 'or I'll be in for it as well as you.'

Charlie rolled off the trolley, thanking the waiter

profusely. 'I've got a friend who's –' he began, but the waiter had gone.

Hoping that Billy was also in sympathetic hands, Charlie nipped up the back stairs and along the dark passages until he reached his dormitory.

Billy didn't appear. Charlie waited and waited. The cathedral clock struck ten. The voices of departing guests could be heard in the courtyard. What had happened to Billy? Charlie chewed his nails with anxiety. If Billy was caught, would he tell the Bloors that Charlie had been with him?

When the clock struck eleven Charlie made a body-shaped bundle out of his clothes and pushed it under the covers of Billy's bed. A few minutes later, the matron looked in. Charlie closed his eyes and lay very still. The matron left.

Charlie couldn't sleep. He went over to the window and looked out across the courtyard. No lights showed in the windows of the west wing. The whole building was in darkness. Charlie had just decided to go looking for Billy when a small figure crept in.

'Billy, where've you been?' cried Charlie.

'I got locked in a storeroom,' Billy said wearily.

'How?'

'The waiter just shoved my trolley into this cupboard

sort of place and locked the door.' As Billy crossed the pitch-dark room his face was suddenly lit from below by a tiny, flickering light. Charlie saw that he was carrying a slim candle that had, apparently, burst into flame by itself.

'How did that happen?' asked Charlie.

Having reached his bed, Billy blew out the candle and scrambled under the covers, flinging out the bundle of clothes as he did so. 'Neat trick,' he said with a yawn.

'Billy, I'm wide awake,' said Charlie. 'Before you go to sleep, please tell me how you got out of the storeroom, and how that candle lit itself.'

'Well,' Billy yawned again, 'I waited till it was quiet, then I found a bit of paper and pushed it under the door. I poked a pencil into the keyhole and knocked the key on to it, then I pulled it through to my side. It was dark and I was so, so scared. I always carry my candles with me, the ones my guardian, Mr Crowquill, gave me before he died. I didn't know what they could do until tonight. I took one out and . . . and . . .' Billy's next yawn was almost a groan.

'And,' pressed Charlie.

'I tried to find a match, but it was so, so dark, and I was so, so scared, and . . . and. . .'

'And?' cried Charlie, who was now past caring if the matron heard him.

'And . . . and I cried,' Billy confessed, 'and I said, "Oh, I wish I could see," and the candle just – came alight.'

'Wow!' Charlie lay back at last. 'Amazing. You've had those candles for ages and you never knew what they could do. Poor Christopher Crowquill.'

'I've got five candles, now, because your uncle gave me the one Mr Crowquill sent to him. I wish my guardian was still alive.' Billy snuffled and turned over.

Charlie allowed himself to feel tired, but before he went to sleep he asked Billy if he'd like to come home with him on Saturday night.

'No thanks,' mumbled Billy. 'I think I'll stay here. I've never seen a Grand Ball.'

Charlie hadn't seen a Grand Ball either, but nothing could have persuaded him to spend another night in Bloor's Academy.

The following morning, the boys' breakfast was interrupted by a tall man with a bald head and a large ginger moustache. Putting his head round the door of the blue canteen, he said, 'Ah. Not in here, then?'

'What were you looking for, sir?' asked Charlie through a mouthful of cornflakes.

'Don't speak with your mouth full,' snapped Ginger Whiskers.

Cook emerged from the kitchen and the stranger said, 'You look a reasonably sensible woman. Where is the meeting hall?'

Cook glared at the man, indignantly puffing out her chest, 'I've no doubt at all that I'm a lot more sensible than you. You should have turned right, not left.'

Ginger Whiskers withdrew his head and closed the door with an irritable click.

'Headmasters!' muttered Cook. 'No manners at all. Think they're gods. And some of them just can't resist showing off. I've had enough of shape-shifters, vanishers and hocus-pocusers. They vanish the food, send it into the air, change it into chocolate or whatever takes their fancy and some even tinker with the china, just because they've got a preference for gold or silver. Well, they'll have to restrain themselves tonight. The mayor can't stand that sort of thing.'

The boys had been unaware of the enchantments going on while they had been under the table, and were very sorry to have missed them. But they hadn't missed everything.

'Cook,' Charlie lowered his voice, 'Miss Chrystal is –'

'I know, Charlie. I heard. I can't talk about it now! They'll all be here in a minute. All the heads. They'll start

in the theatre and then there'll be meetings all over the place; some in the classrooms, some in the gym. I don't know where you two are going to go.'

The boys soon found out. They were on their way back to the dormitory when they walked straight into Manfred Bloor.

'What are you two doing here?' barked Manfred.

'We don't know where else to go,' said Billy.

'Out!' Manfred pointed to the main staircase.

'Out?' said Charlie. 'Till when?'

'Until I come and get you,' said Manfred.

There was no point in arguing. Charlie and Billy reluctantly walked back to the stairs where they looked down on a great crowd of headmasters and headmistresses. Some were still showing off. Charlie spotted a donkey and a bear, and watched an ostrich change into a yellow-robed woman. A man in a black coat vanished into thin air, and there was a giant lizard hanging from a beam.

Charlie and Billy cautiously descended into the hall. Once there, they had to push their way through the gabbling mass. No rule of silence for them, Charlie noted. No one paid any attention to the two boys fighting their way towards the cloakrooms, until they came face to face with the man in the blue turban.

'Aha, we meet again,' said Blue Turban, smiling broadly. He put a finger to his lips and winked at Charlie. 'Good luck!'

A large woman pushed Charlie sideways and before he knew it, the man in the blue turban had disappeared into the crowd.

'Who was that?' asked Billy, when they were safe inside the blue cloakroom.

'He saw me under the table last night. But he didn't give me away.' Charlie pulled on his coat and boots.

'So they really aren't *all* bad. He didn't look like a head-master, did he?' Billy sat on a bench to untie his shoes.

'He's foreign,' Charlie pointed out. 'Maybe headmasters look like that wherever he comes from.'

As soon as they were outside, Charlie headed for the ruin. The frosty grass crunched under their feet and a freezing mist lay over the grounds. The great red arch of the ruined castle could hardly be seen.

Billy trudged along behind Charlie, hoping it would be warmer inside the ruins. He didn't realise that Charlie had a different purpose.

'What's happened?' Billy stepped into the wrecked courtyard and gazed at the broken flagstones.

'She was looking for the mirror, and that's where she

found it,' Charlie pointed to the dark square of earth. 'Miss Chrystal, the teacher we all thought was the best and kindest in the whole school.'

'And she's the worst,' said Billy.

'A witch,' added Charlie. 'I must warn the others, but we don't want her to know we're on to her.'

'We'll just be on our guard,' said Billy.

They scrambled down one of the five dark passages that led out of the courtyard. At the end of the passage there was a wide, grassy area, surrounded by trees and thick, broken walls. The boys sat on a wall and Charlie rubbed his cold hands together, thinking of Bartholomew Bloor. 'The Red King is still in his castle,' the explorer had said. 'But he's hidden.'

'So where is he?' Charlie said, almost to himself.

'Where's who?' asked Billy.

'The Red King. We need him, Billy.'

A cold breeze blew into their faces and the leafless branches crackled above them. A twig snapped, and then another. Charlie turned, half-expecting Asa in his beast form to come leaping out of the bushes. But it wasn't Asa. Standing very still, beneath one of the trees, Charlie saw a white horse.

'It's the queen,' said Charlie softly.

The boys slid off the wall and the queen came trotting towards them.

'It's you, it's really you,' said Charlie, stroking the silky white neck.

Billy grunted and whinnied, and then the queen lowered her head to hear better the odd little hums and snorts that burst out of Billy like sneezes. She replied in her own way, with several long whinnies.

Charlie, burning with impatience, demanded to know what the queen was saying.

'I asked her if the king was here,' said Billy, 'and she said that he was deep, deep inside his castle. I asked her how we could reach him, and she told me that when the time came, he would be found.'

'That's all?' Charlie was disappointed. 'But when will the time come?'

The white horse nuzzled Charlie's ear, and he laid his arm over her long mane. She caressed both their heads and their faces and then, suddenly, she looked into the sky.

There was a rumble in the air that was too sinister to be thunder. The sound was followed by a darkening sky; it was as though a heavy curtain had been pulled over the land.

In the sombre light the queen's eyes shone white with

fear. She gave a scream, reared up and galloped away, her pounding hooves becoming ever more distant as the sound in the air turned to a deafening roar.

Charlie and Billy tore out of the ruin. They raced across the grounds, tripping over their own feet in their hurry to reach the shelter of the school.

'What's that noise?' panted Billy. 'Is it an earthquake?'

'P'raps it's the end of the world,' yelled Charlie.

They got to the school door and found it locked. Charlie banged insistently on the hard oak panels until, at last, the door opened and Manfred looked down on them.

'Scared of a bit of thunder, were you?' Manfred said scornfully.

'That's not thunder,' said Charlie. 'It's . . . it's . . . Please, can we come in?'

'You're a nuisance, Charlie Bone, but, all right, go to your dormitory.' Manfred stood aside and the boys leapt into the hall. It was now deserted, the heads having all dispersed to various classrooms.

'It wasn't thunder, sir,' said Billy.

'I wonder what it was, then.' Manfred seemed to know the answer but he wasn't about to tell them.

'When is the Grand Ball, sir?' asked Billy, feeling more courgeous now that he was inside the building.

'The guests will arrive at half past seven, and you'd better keep out of the way, Billy Raven. There'll be five hundred people coming through our doors tonight.'

'Five hundred!' Charlie exclaimed.

'It's *the* occasion of the decade,' Manfred boasted. 'The mayor will be here, and the entire town council. There will be three judges, a duke and a duchess, the owner of every large business in the city, a bishop, several chairmen, directors and presidents . . . no, not American presidents,' said Manfred as Charlie's mouth dropped open, 'I mean company presidents.'

'Phew!' Charlie was grudgingly impressed.

Manfred smiled with satisfaction. 'Would you like to see the ballroom?' he offered.

The two boys wondered what had come over him. Manfred wasn't usually this friendly. Perhaps he just couldn't resist the temptation to impress.

Billy said, 'Yes, please,' before Manfred could change his mind.

'Follow me.' Manfred unlocked the small door that led to the Music Tower. When the door opened Charlie was amazed to see the usually dim passage transformed by thick carpeting and a ceiling strung with sparkling stars.

He had never noticed the doors into the ballroom. Now,

restored to their former splendour, the arched doors gleamed with polish. Manfred gave them a little push and they opened into a room whose magnificence quite took Charlie's breath away.

'What do you think, boys?' Manfred seemed a little breathless himself. He pressed a switch and four chandeliers hung with crystals came alive with a glittering burst of light. They were suspended from a ceiling decorated with plaster creatures. Not real, everyday creatures, but monsters: goblins, gnomes, trolls, bats with fangs, devils with forked tails, demons and wicked-looking dragons.

Charlie struggled for words, and at length Billy came up with 'Awesome!'

The shining floor swept up to a stage with a grand piano in one corner and several music stands in the other. Charlie imagined the ballroom crowded with swaying figures in long dresses that sparkled in the chandelier-light.

'Good, isn't it?' Manfred switched off the lights and hauled the boys out.

'Yes,' they agreed. 'Great.'

As they walked away from the ballroom, a light footstep made them all turn to look back. The piano teacher, Mr Pilgrim, appeared at the other end of the passage. Charlie

was surprised to see him. He thought Mr Pilgrim had left the school.

'Hello, Mr Pilgrim,' he said.

'Hello. Who . . .' The teacher looked puzzled.

'I suggest you return to the music room, Mr Pilgrim,' Manfred said imperiously.

'I thought –'

'Cook will bring you some lunch.'

'I'm not hungry.' Mr Pilgrim nervously pushed a lock of black hair away from his pale face.

'Suit yourself. Come on, boys.' Manfred herded the boys down the passage. When they were in the hall he locked the ancient door behind him.

'You've locked Mr Pilgrim out,' said Charlie.

'In,' said Manfred. 'I've locked him in for his own good. He can't deal with crowds.' He stuck out his skinny neck and stared at Charlie. 'Take off your coats and get back to the dormitory.'

Charlie wasn't afraid of Manfred's black hypnotic eyes. He stared right back and it was Manfred who looked away. He's losing his old power, Charlie thought. But now there's something else. What is it?

Manfred shoved his hands in his pockets and strode away.

Back in the dormitory, Charlie and Billy sat on their beds and waited. Their stomachs began to rumble. A whole hour to go until lunchtime. Charlie didn't think he could last much longer without a snack. He had just decided to go and see Cook when her messenger arrived.

Several loud barks outside the door announced Blessed's arrival.

'Food!' Billy leapt off the bed. 'Blessed says there's food in the canteen.' He opened the door and patted the old dog's wrinkled head. 'Thanks, Blessed.'

In the canteen they found a pile of sandwiches sitting on a table. They could hear Cook shouting orders in the kitchen. The place seemed to be in an uproar all over again, with more than a hundred smart lunches to prepare in the dining-hall.

When Charlie and Billy had finished their sandwiches, they looked into the kitchen, hoping for a chocolate biscuit at the very least.

'In that cupboard,' said Cook, pointing. She was very red in the face and her apron was covered in big splodges of yellow and brown. 'And, Charlie, you're to get your bag and go to the main doors before half-past twelve. Your uncle will pick you up.'

'Uncle Paton? But he can't. He never . . .'

'He'll have to,' puffed Cook. 'No one else is available. I'm told it's all been arranged. Now, off you go!'

Grabbing their chocolate bars, the two boys backed out. Charlie looked at his watch. It was twenty minutes past twelve. He had ten minutes to pack his bag and get to the main doors.

'Are you sure you don't want to come with me?' asked Charlie, as they raced up to the dormitory.

'I want to see the ladies in their ballgowns,' said Billy. 'Then I can tell you all about it.' He didn't add that he wanted to imagine one of the beautiful dancing figures was his mother.

Mr Weedon was waiting in the hall when Charlie came clattering downstairs with his bag. There was one minute to go.

'Nearly didn't make it, did you, Charlie Bone?' Mr Weedon had the sort of sneery tone that always made Charlie want to say something rude. But he was a little afraid of the bald, muscle-bound porter. If he said the wrong thing now, Mr Weedon was quite capable of locking him in a storeroom, or worse.

'Thank you,' Charlie managed to say, as the burly porter slid back the bolts and unlocked the door.

'Haven't opened it yet, have I?' mocked Mr Weedon.

'No, sir.'

Mr Weedon opened one of the doors a fraction. Charlie squeezed through the gap and ran across the courtyard. He bounded down the steps into the cobbled square, almost falling off the last one, he was so happy to see Uncle Paton's car parked at the end of the square.

Uncle Paton didn't hear Charlie's joyful shouts. He was wearing his dark glasses and appeared to be completely engrossed in the newspaper on his lap.

'Uncle Paton!' Charlie wrenched open the car door and slid into the passenger seat. 'I'm here.'

Uncle Paton looked up. 'So you are.' He gave Charlie a faint smile.

'Is everything all right? I mean Maisie. Has she . . . Is she . . .?'

'No change there, I'm afraid,' Uncle Paton sighed.

'I'm sorry you had to come out in daylight. Did you have any accidents?'

'None so far.' Paton started the engine. He seemed distracted.

'Are you OK, Uncle P?' asked Charlie.

'Me? Yes, I'm fine. It's just . . . well, I'm worried about your mother, Charlie.'

'Why?' asked Charlie in alarm.

'She's going to the Grand Ball.'

'Mum?' Charlie couldn't believe it. 'How on earth? They'd never let her. Who's she going with? My mum? She can't be.'

'Well, she is.' Paton put his foot down and they bumped over the cobbles and out of the square.

Bartholomew's diaries

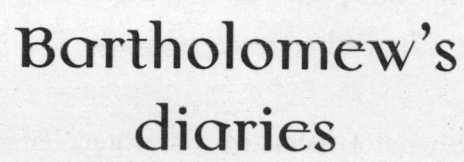

Uncle Paton insisted on taking a route that would avoid any traffic lights. There had been instances when one glance at a red light had resulted in a shower of glass.

Charlie found it difficult to be patient. He kept throwing questions at his uncle, who seemed to have no answers, though he did know that Amy's invitation had come from Kingdom's, the store that had provided the fatal prawns.

'Maybe they're trying to make it up to her, for Maisie's accident,' said Charlie.

Uncle Paton shook his head. 'Maisie's trouble was no accident. It was meant to put me out of action. And your mother's

behaviour these last few days leads me to believe that this invitation means a great deal more to her than mere compensation. She's positively glowing.'

'Glowing?' Charlie had never heard the word applied to his mother.

'You'll see what I mean in a minute.' Paton drew up outside number nine. 'Your mother's not at work today.'

Charlie was out of the car and up the steps before his uncle could reach for his key. As soon as he was in the hall, Charlie cried, 'Mum! Mum!' at the top of his voice.

Grandma Bone stepped smartly out of the kitchen and barked, 'Quiet! You're too old to be calling for your mother like that.'

'I want her to know that I'm back,' said Charlie, leaping up the stairs before his grandmother could stop him.

He found his mum in her little room at the top of the house. The ballgown was the first thing he saw when he opened the door. It hung on the wardrobe, a deep, gleaming blue, with thin straps, a tight waist and a long flaring skirt.

'D'you like it, Charlie?' Amy Bone looked up from her dressing table. Her hair was different. It was glossy and smooth with streaks of a lighter blonde.

'Mum, why are you going to this ball?' asked Charlie.

'Charlie, don't look so solemn.' Amy Bone's new

glowing face smiled at him from her mirror. 'I want to have some fun. I want to go out and sparkle again.' She was gleamy and glittery and not her old self at all.

Charlie swallowed hard and asked, 'Who are you going with?'

'Mr Noble. He's the new owner at Kingdom's. Such a nice man. You'd like him, Charlie.'

'Like him? Why should I?'

'He's good to me, Charlie. Doesn't that mean anything to you? He makes me feel special.' Her voice took on a dreamy quality. 'He uses such wonderful words.'

Charlie went up to the blue dress and touched the slippery material. It felt bewitched. 'Has Aunt Venetia been at this dress?'

'Oh, Charlie, of course not. I bought it at Kingdom's. I watched the girl pack it myself.'

'Must have cost a bomb,' Charlie muttered.

'It was a gift,' his mother said shyly.

A trap more like, thought Charlie. 'You can't leave Maisie,' he blurted out. 'Not all frozen. You said you couldn't.'

'Don't be stupid, Charlie. Uncle Paton will be here if Maisie – unfreezes. If you can't say anything nice, you'd better go.'

Charlie's hands fell to his sides. He felt that he was losing a battle. He didn't know what weapons to use against the man who was stealing his mother with wonderful words. He crept out of her room and closed the door.

On his way downstairs, Charlie looked in on Maisie. She was still lying in the bath. Someone had put a sleeping mask over her eyes, and it made her look more like a burglar than a frozen granny. Except for the pink sweater.

'I suppose you're hungry,' said Grandma Bone when Charlie entered the kitchen.

'No thanks, I've just had lunch,' said Charlie.

'I wasn't offering, I was asking,' said his grandmother, without looking up from her newspaper.

Charlie sighed. 'Did the hamper come?' he asked.

'Of course. Paton wouldn't touch a thing, silly man. It was all quite delicious.' Grandma Bone smacked her lips.

'So there's none left?'

'Not a crumb.'

Charlie sighed again. He went upstairs and tapped on his uncle's door.

'Come in, dear boy, come in,' called Uncle Paton.

Charlie went in and sat on the edge of his uncle's horribly untidy bed, while Paton pushed some papers into a drawer in his desk.

'You're right, Uncle P,' Charlie said miserably. 'Mum's more than glowing. I think she's been kind of enchanted.'

'Me too!' Paton whizzed round on his swivel chair and stared hard at Charlie. 'But look here, dear boy, it's not all gloom and doom. We've got news for you.'

'Good news?' said Charlie hopefully.

'Interesting, at least,' his uncle told him. 'When our good ladies have left for the ball, Miss Ingledew will join us here for supper. Emma is staying with the Vertigos apparently. Julia has a most intriguing-looking package for you, and we are both dying to know what's in it.'

'For me?' Charlie was puzzled. His uncle could tell him no more, so he went to his room and unpacked his bag. The white moth flew down from the curtain and settled on his shoulder. Charlie sensed that it was her way of greeting him.

Time passed very slowly. Charlie thought of visiting Benjamin, but he felt uncomfortable in number twelve, knowing that the Browns were spies. Benjamin would have to come over to him.

At seven o'clock, Grandma Bone's door opened and she rustled downstairs. The front door slammed and Charlie looked out of his window. Below him, Grandma Bone and his two great-aunts, Eustacia and Venetia, stood in a

huddle, talking in low voices. They all wore long dark cloaks, but Venetia's had a particularly slimy look. It glistened like the track of a slug.

The three sisters got into Eustacia's car, and the next minute it was hooting its way, irritably, up Filbert Street. A few seconds later there was a swish of silk outside Charlie's room. The door opened and a woman stepped in. Charlie barely recognised her. Was this beautiful woman in a blue gown really his mother?

'How do I look?' she asked.

Charlie's gaze travelled down her pale, bare arms. A wide silver bracelet encircled her left wrist, but her diamond ring had gone. Charlie shivered. He had never seen his mother without her ring. Never.

'Your ring!' He looked into her face.

'My ring? Oh, I took it off. I don't want to sparkle too much, do I?' She gave a funny little laugh.

'But, Mum . . .'

'Goodnight, Charlie.' She suddenly bent forward and kissed him on the cheek, and Charlie was enveloped in a scent that was utterly unfamiliar. For a few minutes, he stood in a daze, and then he rushed downstairs after his mother. Someone was already ringing the bell, and Amy Bone left the house without a backward glance. A man

in a black uniform closed the door behind her.

'Mum!' Charlie wrenched open the door, just in time to see his mother get into the back of a long, gold limousine. It had dark smoked windows that he couldn't see through. The man in black, a chauffeur no doubt, gave Charlie a nasty look, and then got into the driver's seat. The gold limousine glided away, as silently as a serpent.

'Don't stand in the cold, dear boy.' Uncle Paton came up behind Charlie.

'Uncle P, did you see Mum?'

'No. Sorry. I missed that. Did she look good?' Uncle Paton drew Charlie aside and closed the door.

'Yes,' Charlie said slowly. 'But she'd taken off her ring.'

'Hmm. What does that signify, I wonder? Come on, help me to lay the table for Julia. She'll be here any minute.'

They went into the kitchen where Uncle Paton had already set candles on every available surface. Charlie laid the knives, forks and spoons, while Uncle Paton dealt with the glasses. There was a delicious smell coming from the oven and by the time Miss Ingledew arrived, Charlie was feeling so hungry, he had eaten three of Grandma Bone's favourite cookies.

The brown-paper parcel that Miss Ingledew carried certainly looked interesting. It was tied up with string and

stamped with so much sealing wax, Charlie didn't know where to start untying it. His name was printed in large capital letters above Miss Ingledew's address.

'It was delivered by hand,' Miss Ingledew told Charlie, 'by a rather nervous-looking Chinese woman. Quite elderly.'

'Meng!' Charlie nearly dropped the parcel.

'Meng?' said his uncle. 'Do you know this Chinese person?'

Charlie hesitated. In uttering Meng's name, he had already half-broken his promise to Bartholomew. But surely, of all the people in the world, Uncle Paton and Miss Ingledew were the most trustworthy. So he sat down with the parcel on his lap and told them everything about his visit to the wilderness and, for good measure, added an account of what he'd heard during the Bloors' Hundred Heads Dinner.

'I don't like the sound of it,' said Miss Ingledew. 'I worry about you all in the hands of those dreadful people.'

Uncle Paton didn't seem so concerned. 'So, Dr Bloor's father is back,' he exclaimed. 'Well I never.'

'I promised him I wouldn't tell,' said Charlie, tearing at the brown paper. 'He doesn't want anyone to know.'

'I don't blame him. He had a bad time with Ezekiel, his father, and never got on with his son. And then Mary

died.' Paton shook his head. 'Poor Barty.'

'He knew my father,' Charlie said.

'He did indeed.' Paton handed Charlie a steak knife. 'They went climbing together, just a year before Lyell – disappeared.'

Charlie used the knife on the last piece of string and the brown paper slipped to the floor, along with several small books. Charlie picked them up. Battered and weather-stained, they were each bound with a thin strip of leather to keep the loose and slightly dog-eared pages together.

'Diaries,' Miss Ingledew declared. 'See, they all have the years printed on the cover. Five years in each book. How fascinating.'

'Diaries?' said Charlie. 'Why has he sent them to me?'

Uncle Paton advised eating his specially prepared meal before examining Bartholomew's diaries. Roast duck, roast parsnips, potatoes, carrots and peas quickly appeared on the table, followed by a pineapple pudding that melted in their mouths. Uncle Paton was obviously trying hard to impress his guest.

As soon as the dishes had been cleared away, Charlie put the diaries on the table and undid the first leather string. When he opened the book he found a letter tucked inside.

'*Dear Charlie,*' he read, '*I thought you should know what*

you are up against. You talked of "the shadow" and I have remembered his name at last. In these diaries I have marked the places where he is mentioned. As you will see, I travelled extensively before settling in China. In almost every country I visited, I came across stories of the Red King. I wrote them down and, one day, you will have time to read them all. But now you must concentrate on those that concern "the shadow". He is known by many different names but here, in Europe, he is Count Harken Badlock.

'When you have pieced together the true accounts of the shadow, you will know that he is a hunter and a murderer. He steals souls and breaks hearts. Every creature that crossed his path has suffered for it. Somewhere in these books there is a spell that may defeat him. I wrote it down in the language of its creator, and I believe it will lead you to the Red King. But you may need help to understand it.

'Be safe, my friend, and don't be afraid.

Bartholomew.'

Miss Ingledew caught the letter as it fluttered out of Charlie's hands. 'He shouldn't have written those things,' she said crossly, 'scaring Charlie half to death.'

'I had to know,' said Charlie.

Uncle Paton scratched his head. 'Let's have a look.' He picked up the diaries. Each one had several slim leather

markers hanging out of it. 'Let's begin with 1965.'

A flurry of sleet whirled past the window and Miss Ingledew closed the curtains. Uncle Paton brought another candle to the table and they pulled their chairs close together, so that they could all read Bartholomew Bloor's spidery, travel-stained writing.

Hardly a word was said. They only spoke to tell each other when to turn a page, or to exclaim over some unbelievable atrocity. The night grew colder and the candles wore down until they were flickering stubs of wax. Uncle Paton got up and fetched new candles from a drawer.

They read on. All three were now caught up in the adventures that had led Bartholomew to uncover the stories of 'the shadow'. It seemed that he had passed through almost every country in Europe, Asia and Africa. But it was on his Italian journey that he found the true origin of the Red King's portrait.

A certain Luigi Salutati had inherited the king's red cloak from his ancestor the Princess Guanhamara. Luigi was a painter and sometime in the fifteenth century he had travelled to Venice to study with the great painter, Jacopo Bellini. One night, alone in the studio, Luigi had thrown the cloak over his shoulders to keep warm. As soon as he did this he had been overwhelmed by a desire

to paint a portrait of a man who had been visiting him in dreams. The face had now become so clear to him, it was as if they were in the same room. Realising that this must be his ancestor, the legendary Red King, Luigi began to paint him. But while he worked, Luigi was aware of a hostile presence in the room, a shadow that persisted in entering the portrait. Try as he might, Luigi could not prevent his brush from drifting sideways, where a dark shadow began to form behind the figure of the king. Luigi accepted that he was in the power of some malevolent enchanter who was determined to haunt the Red King's memory.

The painting had remained in Venice until Luigi's descendants brought it to Britain in the sixteenth century. It was at this time that they changed their name to Silk.

'Gabriel!' cried Charlie. 'Gabriel's family owns the Red King's portrait.'

'Not any more.' Uncle Paton ran his finger down the page. 'It says here that the painting was bought from the Silks by trickery and now hangs in Bloor's Academy.'

Charlie rubbed his eyes. Reading by candlelight wasn't easy, especially when he was half asleep. 'It was all lies,' he said, 'all that stuff I heard about Count Harken when I was under the table. They said he had come to protect the

king's children, but he only wanted to cause trouble. He taught them to murder and torture; to hunt animals to extinction, just like Bartholomew said.'

'So much for our books, Julia,' Uncle Paton remarked. 'I have never found a single reference to such a person in my library.'

'Nor I,' said Julia, 'but there must have come a time when people didn't look favourably upon men like the Count. The descendants of the five children who had so slavishly followed him probably decided to cut him out of their histories.'

'Not Miss Chrystal,' Charlie mumbled through a yawn. 'She *would* choose a name that makes you think of something good and beautiful. Her real name's Tilpin.' He gave another huge yawn. 'I wonder what it was before that.'

'Time for bed, Charlie Bone,' said his uncle. 'We've read everything that Bartholomew marked for us, now let's sleep on it. There's nothing more we can do tonight.'

Charlie was relieved to be sent to bed. His eyes were already closing. Leaving the diaries with his uncle and Miss Ingledew, he bid them goodnight and went up to bed.

As he passed the bathroom, he saw the white moth fluttering outside the closed door. How thoughtless he'd been! The moth was his wand. It could help him. Opening

the door, he stepped inside. Was it his imagination, or had Maisie slipped a little further into her frozen stage? Charlie pulled the mask up to her forehead and saw that her eyes had closed.

'Stay with us, Maisie,' he whispered. 'Cling on. Tight. We'll help you!'

The moth swung wildly round the light and Charlie quickly turned it off. Now the only light came from the moth's shining silver-white wings. The little creature settled on Maisie's feet and crawled slowly towards her face. When it reached her chin it lifted into the air and hovered above Maisie's closed eyes. Suddenly they flew open.

'Maisie!' cried Charlie. 'Maisie, Maisie, come back. It's me, Charlie!'

She seemed to see him and her lips moved the tiniest fraction. The moth flew down and perched on her grey curls. A flush spread across Maisie's cheeks and then, all at once, her eyes clouded over and a look of panic appeared on her face. Her eyelids drooped and she looked more frozen than ever. Whoever had frozen Maisie wanted to prove that they were more powerful than Charlie and his wand together.

Charlie trudged back to bed with the moth on his shoulder. Tired as he was, he knew he wouldn't sleep.

*

Billy Raven was kneeling on the landing above the great hall. Blessed crouched beside him. The main doors were open and flurries of sleet blew in with the guests. Billy had never seen so many fine people all at once. The women, in particular, looked as if they had stepped out of fairytales. The colours of their ballgowns were breathtaking. Even Charlie's great-aunts looked reasonable.

There was a sudden lull in the conversation. Heads turned towards the doors and a couple walked in. Billy clutched the banisters. The woman was Charlie's mother, Mrs Bone. Mrs Bone as Billy had never seen her. Dressed in a floating blue gown, she looked like a dazzling angel.

A low growl throbbed in Blessed's throat. He backed away, whining and trembling.

'Blessed, what is it?' Billy grunted softly.

'Green – man – shadow,' whined Blessed.

'Green man?' Billy looked down into the hall. Charlie's mother was holding the arm of a man in a green velvet suit. He had thick brown hair that was touched with gold, and a nose like a hawk.

Billy shuffled away from the light. 'The shadow!' he breathed. 'I must tell Charlie.'

Blessed grunted, 'Come away, quick.'

'Yes, yes, I must.'

As Billy scrambled to his feet, a voice said, 'What are you doing here?' Manfred stepped out of the passage.

'I–I was only looking, sir,' Billy stuttered.

'Spying more like,' said Manfred, coldly.

'No. Not spying. Honestly.'

'It's a shame you can't spy for me any more.' Manfred's pitiless black eyes found Billy's and glared into them.

Billy's red, albino eyes had always managed to withstand Manfred's hypnotising glare, but tonight Billy felt there was something different about Manfred. His gaze had lost the power it used to have. Something had changed.

'Don't stand there gawping,' snarled Manfred. 'Get to bed. And send that mangy dog down to the kitchens.'

But Billy continued to look at Manfred, trying to guess what had happened to him.

'What did I say?' Manfred grabbed Billy's wrist, and there was a bright flash as his long fingers pressed into Billy's flesh. The small boy felt that his whole arm was on fire.

'Owwwwww!' yelled Billy.

Several of the guests looked up, but Manfred dragged Billy away from the landing and deep into the passage. 'Get to bed,' he hissed.

Billy's arm was released, and the headmaster's son whirled away. Moments later the tap of footsteps could be heard descending the stairs.

Sobbing with pain, Billy rushed back to the dormitory. He held his arm under the cold water tap but the pain persisted. There were four deep red welts above his wrist and one beneath it where a thumb had squeezed his flesh. Manfred's hypnotising power had been replaced by something even worse.

Billy lay on his bed, holding his injured arm across his body. Blessed jumped up and attempted to lick it, but Billy pushed him away. 'It's no good,' he grunted. 'Sorry, Blessed.'

'Sorry, sorry, sorry,' howled the old dog.

The harsh light in the dormitory was beginning to give Billy a headache. He needed comfort. Scrambling off the bed, he turned out the light and put all five of his guardian's candles on the windowsill. A tiny flame appeared at the top of each one, and they all burned with a clear, steady light.

Billy began to breathe more easily. His head cleared and his arm stopped throbbing. In a few moments the angry red marks had completely faded.

Charlie heard the soft purr of an engine in the street. He

rolled out of bed and went to the window.

The gold limousine was parked outside number nine. A man in a green velvet suit walked round the back and opened the door nearest the kerb. Charlie's mother stepped out: her blue dress gleamed in the street light. They walked towards the house, the man's arm round Amy Bone's shoulders.

Mum, don't let him kiss you, Charlie silently prayed.

When the couple reached the steps, the man bent his head and kissed Amy Bone on the lips. Charlie felt as though all the breath had been knocked out of him. As his mother climbed to the front door, the man looked up and saw Charlie at the window. He smiled. And, in that instant, Charlie knew that his mother had been kissed by an enchanter.

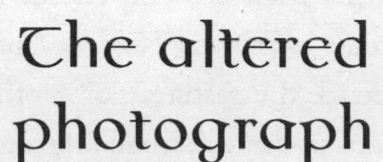

The altered photograph

A Warm Welcome to all our Customers

said a sign on the door of the Pets' Café. Below the sign there was a list of all the extra treats on the Sunday menu. Mrs Onimous had evidently been cooking some very special food for the returning animals.

When Charlie went in he was met by Norton, the bouncer, in a pink T-shirt adorned with sparkling elephants.

'Come in, Charlie. Your mates are over there with an extra gerbil for you.' Norton pointed at Gabriel, who waved and held up a small bundle of black-and-white fur.

The café had been decorated with

coloured streamers and fairylights, just as if it were Christmas.

'We wanted the place to look festive now that the animals have come back,' said Norton, 'but I'm not sure that they appreciate the gesture. Some of them are still very nervous. Look at that cat, trembling something awful. And the birds aren't singing as much. Whatever it was that made them all run away is still around, if you ask me.'

'I think so, too,' said Charlie. He made his way over to the table where Gabriel was sitting with Olivia, Emma and Fidelio.

Olivia's rabbit had tucked its head under her chin and Nancy duck was sitting under Emma's chair.

'Nancy's still in a state,' said Emma. 'It's great to have her back, though.'

'Mum let me bring Wilfred's hutch into the hall,' said Olivia. 'Look at him. He's just a bundle of nerves.'

Fidelio's deaf cat was fast asleep in a cat basket under the table. Deafness and old age seemed to have made her immune to the atmosphere that was troubling the younger animals.

Fidelio advised Charlie to get some Green Heavenlys before they all went. 'They're fabulous,' he said. 'Dripping with green icing and chocolate and stuff.'

Charlie joined the queue at the counter. Lysander and Homer were two places ahead of him and Charlie noticed that the grey parrot looked very depressed. His head drooped and he kept repeating, 'Retreat! Retreat! Watch the dogs!'

Did he mean the Looms' Rottweilers? Charlie wondered. He looked round the café but there was no sign of them. Perhaps Homer was remembering something that had happened to him in the army.

By the time Charlie reached the counter all the Green Heavenlys had gone. 'Sorry, mate,' said Mr Onimous. 'Lysander took the last two. Should have rationed them, shouldn't I? The Nut-Pom sticks are good. Try some.'

'Aren't they for animals?' asked Charlie.

'They're uni-food,' said Mr Onimous with a chuckle. 'Get it? One for all.'

'Uni? Oh, yes, OK. Just one, please,' Charlie said cautiously, 'and a jam and ginger ring.'

Charlie had just sat down when Tancred swept in. Norton was being rather fussy. 'No animal, no entry,' he told Tancred.

'Look,' said Tancred, pointing at Gabriel. 'He's got my entry ticket.'

'Animals aren't tickets, young man,' growled Norton.

Tancred stamped his foot and a wild wind blew through the room. Plates, tumblers and cutlery were sent flying, not to mention Nut-Pom sticks, Green Heavenlys, ginger rings and other goodies. Luckily, Mr Onimous had taken to providing plastic instead of glass and china, so there were no breakages. But the commotion sent some of the more nervous animals over the edge. A terrible wailing, howling and squealing started up.

Gabriel rushed over to Tancred with a white gerbil. 'It's all right, Mr Norton. Here's Tancred's gerbil. Calm down, Tanc, everything's OK.'

Once Tancred was in a mood it took him ages to calm down. Charlie and the others, having just retrieved their food, clung to their plates as Tancred came storming over. He took the empty seat next to Lysander and then realised he had nothing to eat.

'Here,' Lysander pushed his second Green Heavenly over to Tancred.

Charlie watched sadly as the storm boy bit into the delicious-looking cookie. It *did* drip with icing and honey. But at least it soothed Tancred's temper. The wind died to a little breeze that occasionally flipped over a nut-stick or a thin biscuit.

'So,' said Lysander, when things had calmed down,

'I heard you got detention, Charlie. Did you see the hundred heads?'

'*Did* I?' Charlie said emphatically. 'I'll say I did. You'll never believe what I heard.'

'WHAT?' said his friends in unison.

Charlie swallowed his last piece of ginger ring, washed it down with cherry juice and then told his friends everything he could remember about his night under the table. When it came to Miss Chrystal's revelation, he built the tension by describing his prickling scalp and by the time he had finished, everyone was scratching their heads.

Fidelio looked completely stunned. 'What am I going to do?' His voice was quiet and scared. 'She's my violin teacher.'

There was a dramatic silence. No one knew what to suggest.

'She's got nothing against you,' Lysander said at last. 'So I'd just carry on as normal.'

'But I can't, can I?' Fidelio looked wildly round the table. 'I mean I know what she is – how can I forget it?'

'And what about this count she's let loose?' Emma hugged Nancy so hard she let out a startled quack. 'Where is he? What's he going to do?'

'I can tell you where he is,' Charlie said grimly. 'He's the

new owner at Kingdom's and he calls himself Mr Noble.'

'How d'you know that?' asked Tancred.

'Because . . .' Charlie hesitated. He hadn't wanted to mention his mother, but he'd gone too far to stop. 'Because my mum went to the Grand Ball with him.'

'Charlie, no!' Emma's hand flew to her mouth.

The others gasped and spluttered and Fidelio said, 'What are you going to do?'

'I don't know. I need a bit of help, don't I?' Charlie said wretchedly.

His friends murmured in agreement, and then fell silent again. A wordless gloom settled on the group, until, without any warning, Olivia decided to do something rash.

One minute the table was empty but for a few crumbs, the next it was covered by a huge, fat, yellow-and-black spotted caterpillar.

Tancred yelled and leapt away from the table. A terrified gerbil flew several feet into the air, and Homer swooped eagerly, only to see his meal disappear before his eyes.

'Who did *that*?' Tancred demanded.

'Who *did* that?' Lysander looked furious.

'*Why* did whoever did that, do it?' Gabriel asked shakily.

The others, who knew about Olivia's endowment, looked uncomfortable.

'It was me,' said Olivia. 'You all looked so gloomy, I thought you needed a bit of a jolt.'

'*You*,' said Lysander. 'Since when have you been able to do stuff like that?'

Olivia glanced at Charlie. 'Since last term. Charlie was there, and Fidelio and Emma. But no one else knows.'

'And we want to keep it that way,' said Charlie. 'So there's at least one endowed person the Bloors don't know about.'

Lysander looked over his shoulder. 'You'll have to be more careful,' he said gravely. 'Anyone in this café could have seen that yellow monster.'

'There are enough monsters in here already. No one would have guessed it was an illusion.' Olivia gave Lysander a smug grin.

'They would if they'd seen it disappear,' he retorted.

Charlie was still hungry. His mother had been fast asleep when he left the house, and without Maisie to cook one of her big Sunday roasts, he'd had to make do with a lump of cheese and a stale bun. He was about to go up to get another Nut-Pom stick, when he saw Mr Onimous making his way towards their table. His hand was placed on the shoulder of a very small girl with bouncing brown curls and large hazelnut eyes. The little girl was carrying

a plate piled high with pink and blue balls.

'I want to introduce you to Una,' said Mr Onimous when he reached the children's table. 'She's brought an extra treat for you all. Marshmallow globes.'

The little girl beamed round at everyone.

'Hullo, Una!' They all returned her bright smile.

Mr Onimous leaned closer to the table and confided, 'She's my brother's daughter. Twins we are, and with Onoria and me not having been blessed with children, Una here is like our own little daughter. Also,' he lowered his voice, 'she is endowed.'

When he said this, the little girl suddenly vanished, leaving the plate of marshmallows hanging in the air.

'No. Not now, darling,' Mr Onimous said sharply.

Una reappeared, still holding the plate which she carefully placed on the table, saying, 'Grub's up!'

Everyone grabbed a marshmallow globe and Una cried gaily, 'That's right. Stuff yourselves.'

'She's very forward,' Mr Onimous said ruefully. 'It's her mother's fault. She spoils her.' Before leading the little girl away, he added, 'Una's only five but, like some of you, she's special. So remember her when the time comes.'

'What time, Mr Onimous?' said Charlie.

'Who knows what lies around the corner?' Mr

Onimous's smiling, whiskery face all at once became very grave. He clasped Una's hand and they made their way back to the kichen.

'I hope that count thingy isn't lying round the corner,' said Gabriel, through a mouthful of marshmallow.

'He's bound to be, isn't he?' said Emma. 'I mean if he's not round this corner, he'll be round another one, until –'

'Em, don't be so pessimistic.' Olivia wiped her mouth and stood up. 'We can take him on. We've got powers.'

'I think they need our table.' Lysander pointed at an elderly couple with trays of food and four white cats, one perched on each of their shoulders.

Homer settled the argument over who should have the last marshmallow by spearing it with his beak. The group collected their pets and moved to the door. Charlie was the first out and to his surprise, he walked straight into Benjamin and Runner Bean.

The big dog leapt up at Charlie with a welcoming bark, and Charlie realised how much he'd missed him.

'You didn't tell me what time you were coming here,' Benjamin said accusingly. 'You're not leaving already, are you?'

The others were coming out of the café and Charlie stood aside to let them pass. 'Sorry, Ben,' he said.

'Are you going to come for a walk, then?' asked Benjamin.

'Um – I don't think so,' Charlie said uncomfortably. He'd promised to meet his uncle at the bookshop, but he didn't want Benjamin tagging along.

Gabriel waved at Charlie and followed the two older boys out of Frog Street. All three lived on the hill outside the city, and Gabriel's mother usually gave him a lift. Fidelio and the girls waited for Charlie.

'Why are you being like this?' Benjamin said, with a sob in his voice.

Charlie felt bad. 'I'm not being anything,' he said as gently as he could. 'I'm just busy.'

'No one will be my friend.' Benjamin stared gloomily at his feet.

'We will.' Frowning at Charlie, Emma put her arm round Benjamin's skimpy shoulders. 'We're going to the bookshop. You can come if you like.'

'The bookshop?' Benjamin seemed uncertain. 'No, I don't think so, thank you. Runner needs a walk.' He threw Charlie a reproachful look. 'Maybe I'll see you next weekend.'

'It's a deal,' said Charlie. 'Friday night. Soon as I get back from school.'

'OK.' Benjamin trudged away from them, while Runner Bean did his best to cheer him up, bouncing round his

woeful figure with squeaky barks of encouragement.

'Why are you being so mean to Ben?' asked Emma.

Charlie gave a guilty shrug. 'His parents are spies, Em. There's too much to lose. Other people's lives depend on our secrecy.'

'Oooh!' Olivia mockingly wiped her brow. 'We *are* being serious today. Charlie, you can carry my rabbit. Now, let's all go and bother Emma's auntie.'

Handing her pet-carrier to Charlie, she skipped ahead, while the others struggled along with baskets of duck, cat and rabbit. Charlie and Fidelio exchanged looks. They wished Olivia hadn't dressed quite so flamboyantly. In a long faux-fur white coat, red boots and a black hat with silver tassels, she was attracting far too much attention. The boys were relieved when they left the High Street for the quiet alley that led to the bookshop.

Halfway up the alley, Fidelio suddenly stopped and said, 'Charlie, I forgot to tell you. Tolly Twelve Bells has been stolen.'

'What?' Charlie put down the rabbit-carrier.

Gently lowering Nancy's basket on to the cobbles, Emma exclaimed, 'The knight that woke me up!'

'That's the one,' said Fidelio. 'Remember, Charlie. You gave me the case to keep safe. There was a mechanical

knight inside it, that stood up while bells rang and a choir chanted.'

Charlie remembered it very well. How could he forget Tolly Twelve Bells? Emma's father, Dr Tolly, had made the knight before he died. It was intended to wake Emma from her deep hypnosis, and it had worked. Charlie had hoped that, one day, it would wake his father. But now that chance had been lost.

'I can't believe it. How can it have been stolen?' Charlie demanded.

Fidelio shrugged. 'Sorry, Charlie. There are so many people in our house – children coming for music lessons and stuff. No one noticed.'

Olivia had reached the bookshop and began to shout at the others. 'Come on, you lot. What are you doing?'

They picked up their animals and trudged towards her.

Ingledew's was closed on Sundays and Emma had to ring the bell. Uncle Paton opened the door and gasped, 'Who's the pop star?'

'Don't be silly, Mr Yewbeam.' Olivia grinned with pleasure.

'Silly, am I?' Paton raised an eyebrow.

They followed him into the shop and put their baskets and coats beside the counter. Luckily, the duck, the cat and the rabbit were all asleep.

Miss Ingledew called them into the back room, and they found her sitting at her desk with Bartholomew Bloor's diaries in front of her. One was open, and the others were stacked in a neat pile.

'Charlie, I hope you don't mind,' she said. 'But we couldn't resist reading through them all.'

'Hey. What are they?' asked Fidelio, peering at the open diary.

'Just diaries,' Charlie said awkwardly. 'Well, not just diaries. They were sent to me by someone who collected stories about the Red King.'

'Cool!' Olivia grabbed a diary from the top of the pile and plonked herself down on the sofa. 'Not so cool,' she declared, leafing through the book. 'It's a real mess.'

Uncle Paton took the diary out of her hands. 'Olivia, dear girl, you must understand that real treasures never advertise themselves. This book has been where you can never hope to go; its contents are priceless and may, one day, save your life.'

Olivia looked into Uncle Paton's solemn face and blushed. She had a deep respect for Charlie's uncle. In fact he was one of the few people whose criticism she took to heart. 'Sorry,' she mumbled.

'I should think so.' Uncle Paton replaced the diary. 'Now,

I am sure Charlie has already told you about his night under the table, so you might as well know what Miss Ingledew and I have discovered while reading through these books.' He tapped the pile and said impatiently, 'Do sit down, the rest of you. You look most uncomfortable, hovering like that.'

Emma and Fidelio moved several files from the sofa and squeezed themselves either side of Olivia. Charlie sat on the floor and Uncle Paton dropped into an armchair.

'Much has been said of a certain mirror.' Paton looked at his audience, but no one said a word. 'Charlie heard that it was called the Mirror of Amoret. And it was, indeed, made for the baby who was born nine days before Queen Berenice died. The Red King made it himself. He gave it to his second son, Amadis, to keep for the baby until she was old enough to use it. The mirror has many magical properties; most important of all, it can give its owner the power to travel . . .'

'D'you mean . . .?' said Charlie.

'Yes, Charlie. Your sort of travelling. Look into the mirror and the person you wish to see will appear. If you want to find that person, look again, and the mirror will take you to them, wherever they are.'

'Awesome. I'd like to have a go at that,' said Fidelio. 'Hey, I could meet Mozart.'

'I'm afraid you couldn't', said Miss Ingledew. 'The mirror will only work for the Children of the Red King.'

'But it worked for the count,' Fidelio argued.

'He is an enchanter,' Uncle Paton said flatly. 'We believe he stole the mirror, partly to prevent others from using it. Though when he buried it, naturally, he hoped that one of his endowed descendants would find it, and use it to help him travel out of the king's portrait.'

Miss Ingledew gave an involuntary gasp. 'Paton, it has just occurred to me that if the count has the mirror, he can travel again.' She gripped the arms of her chair and leaned forward. 'In and out of paintings and photos and – oh dear, I hope he doesn't.'

Miss Ingledew had conjured up such a frightening picture, the loud ringing of the doorbell had everyone jumping out of their seats.

Uncle Paton went to answer the door and returned a minute later with an extremely glamorous woman. She was wearing an identical version of Olivia's outfit, except that her hat was red and her boots silver.

'Mum!' cried Olivia. 'You're early.'

'It's getting so dark,' said Mrs Vertigo. 'Unnaturally dark. I'm sorry if I've broken up a meeting, or whatever you clever folk were getting up to.'

'You're very wise, Mrs Vertigo,' said Paton. 'I don't like the look of it at all. Very unpleasant weather. Perhaps you could give this young man a lift.'

Fidelio was about to protest, but Olivia and her mother swept him out of the room. As soon as the pets were retrieved the three of them left the shop. Fidelio shot Charlie a look of bemused surrender before the door closed and the Vertigos bore him away.

'It's time for us to be going,' said Uncle Paton, a little reluctantly. 'Come on, Charlie.'

Emma followed Charlie into the shop while Paton and Miss Ingledew said a private farewell. When Paton emerged his face was pink and there was lipstick on his cheek. Emma raised her eyebrows and grinned at Charlie, who decided not to mention the lipstick.

'We decided the diaries will be safer here,' said Uncle Paton, putting on his dark coat, 'rather than at number nine.'

Charlie agreed. As soon as his coat was on, he and his uncle set off. They were almost home when Uncle Paton gave Charlie some incredible news. He had found a photo of Charlie's father.

'I didn't mention it before because I didn't want to raise your hopes,' Paton explained. 'It's not a good likeness, you see.

I remembered it when you told me about Bartholomew. There were several photos taken on that climbing holiday. I knew I had one. I've got an old leather case under my bed that I always keep locked. The photo was right at the bottom.'

Charlie couldn't walk another step. 'Have you got it with you, Uncle P?'

'Well, no. I gave it to your mother. Told her not to say a word to Grandma Bone, knowing that she'd destroyed every other photo of Lyell that existed.'

Charlie began to run.

'Not so fast,' called Paton, striding after Charlie. 'It won't disappear.'

'I can't wait, Uncle P. I just can't,' cried Charlie, leaping ahead.

Amy Bone was alone in the kitchen when they walked in. Charlie ran straight up to her. 'Can I see the photo, Mum, now? Uncle Paton said he'd found one. A photo of my dad.'

'Goodness, Charlie, you are in a hurry.' His mother unwound a silk scarf from her neck. 'I've only just got in.'

'Where is it?' Charlie begged.

His mother picked up her handbag from the table. 'In here, somewhere.' She rummaged around in the bag and took out a small square photograph. 'Here.' She held it out.

Charlie took the photo. A man dressed for climbing

smiled out at him. The man was Bartholomew Bloor. There was someone else, standing in the corner, but he had his back to the camera. Only his head and shoulders could be seen.

'Mum, this isn't . . . it can't be.' Charlie voice was thick with disappointment.

Uncle Paton came up behind him and took the photo. 'Amy, what's happened?' he demanded. 'This isn't what I gave you.'

'Of course it is,' said Amy. 'What's wrong?'

'This isn't your husband.' He pointed at Bartholomew.

Amy peered at the photograph. 'Isn't it? Oh dear. D'you know, I've completely forgotten Lyell's face. I just can't . . .' she frowned, 'just can't seem to picture it.'

'Mum!' said Charlie in a stricken voice. 'You must remember. You MUST!'

'But why, Charlie? I'm sure it'll be better for everyone if your father is forgotten.' His mother smiled at him.

'NO!' cried Charlie. 'We can't. Don't you understand? If we let go of his memory, he won't be able to come back. EVER!'

The shadow attacks

'It has begun,' said Uncle Paton.

'Begun?' asked Charlie.

They were sitting at the kitchen table. A single candle burned in the centre and beside it lay the photograph: the image of a man who had been moved by sorcery, so that no one should see his face.

'Count Harken has the mirror.' Paton stared moodily at the candle flame. 'Who knows what evil he has in mind for us.'

To Charlie it seemed that the count had already done his worst. 'Uncle Paton, do you think that if a person is forgotten they ... they die a little?'

'Charlie!' His uncle looked shocked,

almost angry. 'Your father is not forgotten, and never will be. He was a good friend to so many.'

'But Mum . . .' said Charlie. 'If she forgets . . .'

'She *hasn't*, Charlie. She hasn't.' Uncle Paton began to pace round the kitchen. 'She's been bewitched, I grant you that, but it's temporary. Somehow we must find a way to undo what's been done, though, at the moment, I confess I am a little out of ideas.'

'I must get the Mirror of Amoret,' Charlie stated.

His uncle stopped pacing and looked at him. 'A near impossible task, Charlie, but yes, it would be a start.'

'Then I'll go and think about it. Goodnight, Uncle.' Charlie picked up the photo.

''Night, Charlie. And don't let your thoughts keep you awake. It's school tomorrow.' Uncle Paton blew out the candle and followed Charlie upstairs.

As soon as he was in his room, Charlie opened his curtains and sat on the bed. Foggy clouds swirled over the moon, but it was still bright enough to send a beam of light across the wall. Charlie didn't have to wait long for Naren's message. She must have been thinking of him.

The thin, spidery forms came tumbling over the sill as though they were running from something. They piled on to Charlie's bed and raced up the wall, wriggling and

churning in a kind of frenzy. Already the message had begun to form.

'*Charlie, when Meng came into the city, she thinks she was being watched. If she was seen at the bookshop the owner . . . may . . . be . . . in danger. The diaries tell the truth. The . . . shadow . . . will . . . not like this.*'

'I'll try and warn her,' Charlie whispered. But he had more important things on his mind just then. 'Naren, my mum is beginning to forget my dad. She *wants* to forget him. What shall I do?'

'*Find him,*' said the small, twisting words.

'The shadow has gone into a photo and turned him around,' Charlie told the wall of letters. 'I can't see his face.'

'*Find . . .*' the words seemed to be having trouble in reaching their places. They began to swirl in a great kaleidoscope, a single word popping out of the circle every now and then. '. . . *the king . . . I must . . . go . . . Father . . . says danger . . . message . . . caught . . .*'

For a while, no more words came. Charlie whispered to the fading letters, begging them to form a word, anything to let him know that Naren could hear him. But only one word made itself clear before the moon was swamped by a black cloud.

'*Go . . .*' said the letters.

Charlie lay back on his bed, defeated and afraid. Could the shadow see Naren's message? Could he feel it speeding through the air, like radio waves? Was he everywhere, then, even inside people's heads?

Charlie put the photo on his bedside table and got into bed. Before he closed his eyes he saw the white moth sitting on the photo; its silvery wings shed a gentle light on the man with no face, as though it were trying to keep him alive.

As he drifted off to sleep, Charlie had a vague feeling that there was something he should have done. Something important. Whatever it was, he was too tired to remember it now.

Julia Ingledew had been working late. There were books to unpack before Monday morning. There were accounts to be done and labels to be marked. At ten o'clock she finished her work and went up to bed. The stairs creaked and the windows rattled more than usual, but she thought nothing of it. The house was very old, and time had warped the ancient beams and window frames.

When Julia got into bed, the rattling grew louder, until it became a heavy, insistant banging. She realised that someone was shaking the shop door.

Flinging on her dressing gown, Julia ran down into the shop. By the light of the street lamp, she could make out two dark forms standing motionless outside her window. Grasping the edge of the counter, Julia froze.

And then the voice came. 'Give me the books.' It was hardly more than a whisper, but the words reached into her very soul. Deep and dark and terrible.

She mouthed the words 'What books?' but, of course, she knew the books he wanted. Bartholomew's diaries were lying on the counter; she had meant to take them upstairs with her, but had been too busy to remember. Gathering them up, she backed away from the light.

'The books of lies.' This time the words were roared at her. 'Give me those lies.'

Clasping the diaries even tighter, Julia ran through her sitting room and began to climb the stairs. The awful voice followed her. 'Give them to me. Give them, give them. Lies, lies, lies, all lies.'

'They tell the truth,' she muttered. 'And you shan't have them.'

There was a deafening crack, as though the door was being torn off its hinges.

'Auntie, what's happening?' A terrified Emma stood outside her door.

'They want the diaries.' Miss Ingledew bundled Emma back into her room. 'Stay there, darling. I'm going to get my mobile.' She put the diaries into Emma's arms and ran to fetch her phone; on her way back to Emma, she dialled 999 but the voice at the other end wasn't reassuring.

The police had been called to every part of the city. There had never been a night like it. A power failure had caused five traffic accidents, there had been nine robberies and eleven fights in public places. Footsteps had been heard in empty rooms. Basements had been flooded and a fire had broken out in the council offices. 'So I don't know when we'll be able to get to you,' the police receptionist told Miss Ingledew. 'I suggest you –'

Julia was already re-dialling. She sat beside Emma on her bed, as a familiar voice said, 'Hello, Julia.'

'Paton, we're being broken into. It's – well, I think it's –'

'Grief!' came Paton's voice. She could hear him running down the stairs with his mobile still pressed to his ear. The door of number nine slammed shut. Footsteps pounded up the street. 'Hold on, my dear. Hold on! I'm coming!'

'Oh, Paton,' cried Julia. 'Hurry, please. They're . . . oh, Paton, I can smell burning.'

Paton Yewbeam's legs were probably the longest in the city, but that night they must have stretched another six

inches. Everyone who saw him storming through the streets swore that he was seven feet tall. And did he care about exploding lamps? Not a bit of it. One by one, they broke into a thousand pieces as he raced beneath them.

A police car, responding to yet another robbery, drove past Paton as his tenth light shattered.

'Did you see that?' asked PC Singh, the driver. 'Bloke just knocked a lamp out.'

'I saw it,' PC Wood confirmed. 'Better make a left, soon as you can. That maniac's going to do some damage.'

When Paton burst into the cathedral square he saw flames leaping round the door of Ingledew's. In front of the shop a violent fight was taking place. An unfair fight by the look of it. Paton ran up to the group and recognised Manfred Bloor. The street lamp exploded just as Manfred lifted his head. He gave a shriek of pain and retreated into the square, holding his face.

The other character wasn't such an easy target. He was kneeling over his victim with his hands round the man's throat. His long, hooded cloak covered both himself and the man on the ground. With the street lamp gone, all that could be seen in the gloom was a mop of silver hair.

Bending over the hooded man, Paton seized him by the shoulders. The bones he grasped felt like iron, and try as he

might, he couldn't loosen the man's grip. The silver-haired victim gave a stifled groan as the iron fingers continued to choke the life out of him.

Paton swung round frantically. 'Sorry, Julia,' he muttered, staring at the soft lights that hung above the books in Ingledew's window. With an explosive crack, the shatterproof glass broke into pieces and fell on the pavement. 'I bet you couldn't do that, Enchanter,' said Paton as he reached in and lifted out the heaviest book Julia had ever displayed.

Lifting the book as high as he could, Paton brought it down with all his strength on to the head of the hooded man.

There was a muffled growl of fury as the man loosened his grip and fell sideways. He began to roll over the cobbles of the square, wrapping himself in his cloak until only a pair of shining eyes could be seen, glaring out from the dark hump of his body.

Paton was deciding whether to pursue his quarry when he heard an approaching police siren. The next minute, a police car roared into the square and when Paton looked for the hooded figure, it had vanished.

Two policemen jumped out of the vehicle and raced towards Paton, yelling, 'Don't move! You're under arrest.'

Flinging open her smouldering door, Julia Ingledew cried, 'That man saved our lives. The villains are getting away.'

'Who's this, then?' PC Singh pointed to the man on the ground.

'I've no idea,' said Paton.

'By the look of it, you've killed him.' PC Wood grabbed Paton's arm.

'He didn't,' cried Julia. 'He saved his life.'

'Seems to me you've got it all wrong, madam,' PC Singh sighed irritably. 'We witnessed this man,' he pointed at Paton, 'breaking a street lamp. And who broke the window, I'd like to know?'

'Ah. I did that,' Paton confessed.

'You did?' PC Singh frowned. 'Wait a minute. This glass is supposed to be shatterproof, bulletproof, unbreakable. It's in a hundred pieces.'

'That's as may be,' Paton said nonchalantly. 'But I broke it.'

'And saved our lives,' said Julia. 'I saw it all. Oh, Paton!' She flung her arms round his neck.

Paton, smiling shyly, said, 'Ah well.'

'So where are these other villains?' asked PC Singh suspiciously.

'I told you, they ran off,' said Julia. 'You won't catch them

now. But could you help to stop my door burning down?'

'It's all right, Auntie!' Emma emerged with a bucket of water, which she flung at the door.

'Well done, Emma. You've saved the day,' said Paton.

PC Singh had just opened his mouth when a voice from the ground said, 'Good Lord, Paton Yewbeam.'

Paton peered down at the man on the ground. 'Bartholomew?' he said in disbelief.

'It's not like you to stick your neck out,' Bartholomew grunted, as Paton helped him to his feet.

'I've changed,' said Paton gruffly.

The two constables began to make notes. They took phone numbers and wrote down addresses, but Bartholomew Bloor refused to give them any information. The constables decided that the incident was not as serious as many others in the city that night, and drove away. PC Singh even gave the group a friendly wave.

The four survivors retreated into the shop. To Julia's relief, the thick oak door had survived the fire. It was scarred and scorched and its creak was worse, but the bolts and hinges still worked perfectly.

'I'll make some tea,' Emma suggested. Her long blonde hair and red dressing gown were soaked from a giant splash, but she was flushed with excitement.

Bartholomew refused to stay another moment. 'I never meant to come into the city, but I was anxious,' he explained. 'My wife was watched; the shadow's spies are everywhere. I knew he'd want the diaries and I realised that I'd put you in danger, Miss Ingledew.'

'Just stay a moment . . .' Julia began.

'I must be gone,' Bartholomew insisted. 'Where are my diaries?'

'I'll get them.' Miss Ingledew ran upstairs and Emma went to put the kettle on.

When the two men were alone, Bartholomew asked, 'What made you change, Paton? You were always such a ninny.'

Paton winced. 'The boy,' he said simply. 'I had to help him.'

'Ah, Charlie.' Bartholomew smiled at last. 'His father was the best and bravest man I ever knew. You were a poor friend to him, Paton.'

'Here they are.' Miss Ingledew returned with the diaries. 'I'll put them in a book bag.'

'Good,' said Bartholomew. 'Paton, you must give them to Charlie. Tell him to take them into the past.'

'What?' Paton took the bag from Julia and stared at Bartholomew in perplexity.

'He's the only one who can put them out of harm's way.' Bartholomew's tone was cold and commanding. 'Don't you understand? He has the gift. Tell him to take them where the shadow can never reach them.'

'But where . . .?'

'How do I know?' Barthlomew said roughly. 'He must decide. Charlie's a clever lad. He knows that my diaries hold a secret that will help to rescue his father. I'll bid you all goodnight.' He turned to the door.

'Wait,' Paton begged. 'Can't we talk? It's been so long. Once you saved my life.'

'And you have just saved mine. It changes nothing. Goodnight, Miss Ingledew.' Bartholomew gave a curt nod and swept out.

'What a strange man,' Miss Ingledew remarked. 'So unfriendly. Come into the back room, Paton, and have some tea before you go.'

Paton shook his head. 'No, I must leave. It's all my fault, Julia. On Saturday night, after you'd gone, I left the diaries on the kitchen table. My sister must have seen them when she came home from the ball. What a fool I am.'

'That's not true. You weren't to know.'

Paton opened the heavy door. 'Good night, my dear. Take care.'

Across the square, the great cathedral clock began to strike midnight. Paton closed the shop door and stood for a moment, staring into the moonlit square – the place where his greatest friend had been lost.

'Yes, Lyell, I was a poor friend,' Paton murmured. He strode down the cobbled alleys, heedless of the danger that would surely follow the diaries he carried. He was not even aware of the great cold that threatened to turn the tears in his eyes to crystal.

Charlie woke up to see the moth sitting on his pillow. He sensed that it wanted something. Yawning sleepily, Charlie got out of bed and crept on to the landing. The house was in darkness but he could see a thin trickle of light coming from under the kitchen door. It could only have been Uncle Paton. Anyone else would have put the hall light on.

It was freezing cold. Charlie wrapped his dressing gown tightly round him before he went downstairs. He found his uncle sitting at the table with the diaries lying before him. The single candle had almost burnt out, but Charlie could see Paton's face. He wore an expression that Charlie had never seen before. It troubled him.

'Uncle Paton?'

His uncle looked up. 'Ah, Charlie, I've just come from the bookshop. It's been an extraordinary night.'

'I heard police sirens,' said Charlie.

'Yes. Someone tried to break into Ingledew's. They were after the diaries. We think it was the shadow.'

'Oh, wow! Was anyone hurt? Is Emma OK? Are you . . .?'

'Charlie,' Paton said solemnly. 'Bartholomew was there. He wants you to take the diaries into the past.'

'The past?' Charlie didn't understand.

'I'm sorry I have to ask you to do this now. You're tired and it's very late. But Bartholomew was most insistent, and I think he's right. You can travel into paintings, photographs, pictures. Is there anywhere you can think of, where the diaries would be safe? Where the shadow couldn't find them.'

Charlie scratched his head. 'Yes,' he said slowly. 'I could take them to Skarpo.'

'The sorcerer? A dangerous journey, Charlie. But if the old man could be persuaded to guard them, the diaries would certainly be safe.'

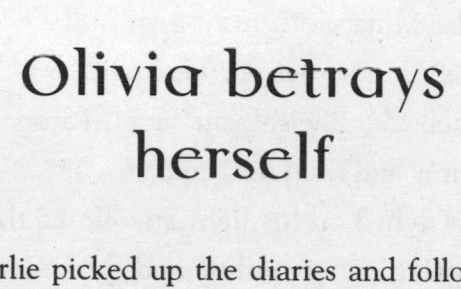

Olivia betrays herself

Charlie picked up the diaries and followed his uncle upstairs. The candle Paton held aloft flickered and smoked in the draughty stairwell, and Charlie had to tread carefully in order to avoid missing a step.

When he got to his room Charlie put the books on his side table and pulled a small painting out from under the bed.

'I imagine you will need a good light, Charlie.' Uncle Paton hovered by the door.

In the meagre light from the candle, Charlie could hardly see the painting. 'It'd probably be better if I put my bedside light on,' he agreed.

'I'll leave you, then,' said his uncle. 'But,

Charlie, how will you get back? Do you need my help?'

Charlie shook his head. 'I'll take her with me.' He nodded at the white moth resting on his bed. 'She'll help me back. She's done it before, you know.'

'I see. Well ... I wish you luck.' Paton shifted his feet uncertainly and then retreated.

Charlie switched on his light and closed the door. He put the painting on his pillow and sat beside it on the bed. In his arms he held Bartholomew's ten leather-bound books.

The small painting was centuries old. The paint had darkened and cracked, and its very age added menace to an already sinister scene. The title 'The Sorcerer' had been scrawled in black paint at the bottom. And there he stood, the black-robed sorcerer in his cell-like room, with magical effects strewn across the table behind him. The sorcerer's dark hair and beard were threaded with silver and his eyes held a yellowish gleam. It was the eyes that Charlie focused on.

He had visited Skarpo the sorcerer several times before. Once, he had been afraid of the old man, but not any more. He had become accustomed to the fiery eyes and deep, lilting speech.

'*Charlie Bone?*'

Although Charlie had expected it, the voice still took him by surprise and a shiver ran down his spine. The white moth flew on to his shoulder, prepared for the journey ahead.

As the familiar objects in his room began to fade, Charlie caught a whiff of the sorcerer's damp cell, mixed with the scent of burning herbs and candle grease. His head whirled and his feet became as light as air. Clutching the books even tighter, he fixed his gaze on Skarpo's burning yellow eyes. Now he could hear the drag of the sorcerer's robes, the rattle of iron and the hiss of flames. Charlie felt himself tumbling through the centuries, his body buffeted like paper in the wind.

When his feet hit cold stone he opened his eyes. The sorcerer stood before him.

'What's this? I see Charlie Bone entirely.' Skarpo rubbed his hairy chin. 'Time was when only your head appeared. Your power has strengthened.'

'Has it?' Charlie looked at his arms, clasped round the diaries. 'Oh.'

'You have a gift for me?' The sorcerer eyed the leather-bound books.

'Not exactly,' said Charlie. 'I've come to ask you a favour.'

'Ah!' The sorcerer rubbed his bony hands together. 'I like favours. It means I can ask one of you.'

'I suppose it does,' said Charlie nervously.

'Let us be seated.' Lifting the red cloth that hung over his table, Skarpo drew out two rough wooden stools. One he pushed towards Charlie, the other he placed behind him, pulling his heavy robes to one side as he sat upon it. 'Are you going to tell me about those books?'

Charlie placed the ten books in the sorcerer's outstretched arms. 'They're diaries, sir, Very special diaries. They were written by a man called Bartholomew Bloor, a distant relative of mine. He's been all over the world and whenever he heard a story about the Red King, he wrote it down. They're precious because they've got secrets in them – things about the Red King that we've never known before.'

'If they're precious why give them to me?' Skarpo gave a light chuckle. 'Do you trust me, Charlie Bone?'

'I have to,' said Charlie. 'There's a man – a thing – that people call the shadow. He's in the Red King's portrait and he . . .'

'The shadow?' Skarpo stood up, his swirling black robes sending an icy draught across Charlie's slippered feet. 'Say no more. I know of this shadow. Magicians try not to speak of him, for he brought our powers into great disrepute. A fleeting whisper of his name and my brother

sorcerers will raise their hands in protest.'

'Well, I'm going to have to say a bit more about him,' said Charlie, 'because he's the reason for me bringing those diaries to you.'

'Ah, now we have it.' Skarpo turned and put the books in two neat piles on his table. 'Tell me, then.' With a swish of his robes, he sat down.

The sorcerer's cave-like room was a fitting place for Charlie's story. He told Skarpo all that had happened since the snowy night when the animals had left the city. He told him about frozen Maisie and his mother's ring, about Miss Chrystal and the Mirror of Amoret. And, as he spoke, the five candles in their tall iron holder burnt lower and lower, and soon the only light in the room seemed to come from the sorcerer's yellow eyes.

When Charlie had said all there was to say, Skarpo got to his feet again and went to the table. He lit a thick candle in the centre and by the light of its leaping flame, he began to leaf through each book. Charlie watched him, hoping for a remark or a word of advice, but the sorcerer said nothing until he had scanned every page. When he had replaced the last book he turned to Charlie and said, 'Fine stories, my boy. Revelations! I'll keep them safe, but the spell, the Welsh spell, you must take that back with

you. I'll translate it, for I have the Welsh, you know, and you'll need it.'

Charlie waited, wondering if this was the spell Bartholomew had mentioned. The sorcerer snatched a scrap of parchment from a leather folder and, dipping a fancy-looking quill into a jar of ink, he began to scratch across the surface of the parchment. Now and again he would glance at one of the diaries lying open on his table, scratch his head, look into the distance, smile and then continue writing.

When the last line had been scrawled, Skarpo laid down his quill and looked at Charlie with a grin of triumph. 'A wonderful spell,' he declared. 'Not mine, oh no. Your relative must have got it from one of Mathonwy's descendants, Mathonwy being the friend of your Red King, of course.' He gave another of his light chuckles. 'It was from him that I stole that wand of yours, Charlie Bone. Not stole, no – he was old then, and would have given it to me before he died. How they love to pass on their names, those Welsh.' He paused and cocked his head. 'Speaking of wands, where is it?'

'As a matter of fact it's a moth now,' said Charlie.

'Ah, *that* moth. I see it.' Skarpo put out his hand to catch the white moth that was fluttering between them.

'DON'T!' shouted Charlie. 'She's mine!'

'Just a joke, Charlie Bone! I'll not hurt your wee moth.' The sorcerer blew on the parchment and held it out. 'Take your spell and leave this place. It doesn't do to linger in distant worlds.'

'Yes, I'd better go,' said Charlie, taking the spell, 'and thank you. You will keep the diaries safe, won't you?'

'Do you doubt it?' The sorcerer tilted his head and gave a crooked smile.

'No. No, of course not.' Charlie held out his free hand and the moth flew on to his finger. 'She helps me to travel,' he explained.

The sorcerer nodded. 'Ah.'

Before Charlie left, he glanced through a small window at the back of the shadowy room. A dark forest could be seen, fringing a sea of glittering moonlit water. Once, Charlie had accidentally made a visit to that forest, and it had always lain at the back of his mind, a memory that puzzled and yet comforted him. 'Sir, did the Red King ever live near here?' he asked.

'Aye, he did that,' said Skarpo, turning to the window. 'And when the king was gone, Mathonwy, the magician, came to live here. He took me in when I was very young; a homeless orphan, my people murdered by the soldiers of the

English king. He was a great magician and he taught me much, but I was never as good as he, in any sense of the word.' A shadow crossed the sorcerer's face, a fleeting hint of regret, and then the wicked grin returned and he waved his hand at Charlie. 'Go, boy, go. And may luck accompany you.'

'Goodbye then, sir, and thank you.' Charlie looked at the moth and gently asked, 'Can we go now, Claerwen?'

The sorcerer's face was the last thing Charlie saw before the mist of time drifted between them and he began to travel home. Skarpo's yellow eyes were wide with surprise, for Charlie had spoken in Welsh. The unfamiliar word had come to him out of the blue, and yet he knew that it belonged to the moth. Claerwen – Snow-white.

A moment later he was sitting on his bed with the painting beside him and the moth on his arm. Charlie yawned and kicked off his slippers. He had never felt so drowsy. In a few hours he would have to get up and pack his bag, ready for school. But not yet. He put the painting under his bed, lay back on the pillow and fell asleep.

He awoke to find his uncle anxiously peering at him from the doorway.

'Far be it from me to remind you of school,' said Uncle Paton, 'but I thought I should at least alert you to the time. No one else seems to be awake.'

As Charlie rolled out of bed a scrap of stiff, yellowish paper floated to the floor. Frowning, Uncle Paton stepped into the room and picked it up. 'What's this?'

'Don't know,' mumbled Charlie, rubbing his eyes.

'A poem? No, more a . . . a sort of charm.' Paton turned the paper and studied the large, slanting script. 'Good Lord, where did you get this, Charlie?'

'Oh, I forgot. From Skarpo.' Charlie brushed past his uncle on the way to the bathroom.

'From Skarpo?' called his uncle in astonishment. 'Charlie, I'm going to keep this in my room. It's quite remarkable. It could change everything.'

Charlie wasn't paying attention to his uncle. Once again he had to brush his teeth while Maisie lay frozen in the bath beside him. There she was, the one person in the whole house who might have been able to keep his mother safe from Count Harken.

By the time Charlie had washed his face, Uncle Paton had disappeared into his own room and all Charlie could hear was a low, foreign-sounding mumble.

Charlie dressed, packed his bags and went down to the kitchen. The stove was out and the table was bare. There was no evidence that anyone else had eaten breakfast. Where was his mother? Out or asleep? Charlie was afraid

to find out. The house smelt of a cold slumbering emptiness. He quickly made himself a piece of toast and left.

Bloor's Academy had still not recovered from the weekend festivities. The staff were, if anything, even more bad-tempered than they had been before the hundred heads' arrival. Pine needles, tinsel, broken plastic and bits of food littered the hall floor. Items of clothing were missing from the cloakrooms and it was no use complaining.

'You shouldn't have left it there,' was Manfred Bloor's surly response to any timid suggestion that a visiting headmaster might have stolen a scarf, or a shoe, or a fur-lined glove.

Manfred himself looked a real mess; his face was pitted with tiny wounds which could only have been made by splinters of glass. There was no doubt in Emma Tolly's mind that Manfred had been with the shadow, banging on the bookshop door the previous night.

Fidelio was due to have a violin lesson after Assembly, but he wasn't inclined to see Miss Chrystal. 'I don't see how I can pretend I don't know what she is,' he whispered to Charlie as they left Assembly. 'I mean, I'm not an actor like Liv.'

'You've got to,' said Charlie. 'If she even guesses that we know, her claws will really be out.'

'I'll say I'm feeling –'

'Fidelio Gunn,' said Dr Saltweather, emerging from Assembly, 'remember the rules.'

'Yes, sir,' said Fidelio, grateful that it wasn't Manfred who had caught him.

Charlie rushed off to a Maths lesson, leaving Fidelio to get in the right frame of mind for his dreaded visit to Miss Chrystal.

At first break there was no sign of Fidelio. Charlie wondered what had happened to him. The school grounds were cold and misty. Children huddled together in little groups, stamping their feet and muttering disconsolately. Charlie had to peer at each group as he searched for Fidelio's familiar curly head. But none of his friends appeared to be outside.

As he wandered up to the castle, Charlie was vaguely aware that a crowd of children were following him. Rather than be trapped in the ruin, he turned off into the woods. The crowd drew closer. Charlie began to run. And then, suddenly, he was surrounded. Every tree was veiled in mist, and he could no longer distinguish their thin trunks from the drifting forms of his pursuers.

'What do you want?' cried Charlie. 'Why are you following me?'

One of the children stepped closer. Charlie might have guessed it would be Joshua Tilpin.

'Your friends are pretty useless, Charlie Bone,' sneered Joshua. 'You might as well give them up.'

'What are you talking about? Why should I?' Charlie said defiantly.

Joshua gave his cold, crooked smile. 'We've come to teach you a lesson, Charlie. We'll teach you over and over again, won't we, guys?'

'YESSSS!' roared the crowd.

And now it was Dorcas Loom's turn to slink out from behind a tree and jeer at Charlie. 'You're pathetic, Bone. You don't stand a chance. You've lost your father, and now your mother. You can't keep anything, can you? If you join us we can help you. We're so-o-o much stronger than your miserable friends.'

Charlie had been steadily retreating from the crowd, and now his back was against part of the ancient wall. Without thinking, he turned and found a foothold. He pulled himself up, higher and higher, reaching for gaps in the stones, while his feet desperately sought another foothold. At last he was standing twelve feet above the crowd.

They laughed at him.

And then the Branko twins appeared. Standing close together, they stared at the stones in the wall, stared and stared. A huge boulder dropped out and the whole wall shuddered.

Can they do that? thought Charlie. Can they bring down a wall that's lasted nine hundred years?

They could. Two huge stones tumbled from the top of the wall, and then one of the twins began to talk. They so rarely spoke it was quite a shock.

'What a tragic accident,' said the black-haired, doll-faced girl. 'Charlie Bone climbed an old wall, and down it came, rumble, tumble, with Charlie on top . . .'

'And then underneath,' continued the other twin in a deeper, more sinister tone.

With a jarring thud another huge stone hit the hard earth, and this time the wall trembled so violently, Charlie fell to his knees. He clung to the mossy surface as it rocked and shook, trying to imagine what it would be like to be buried alive.

When the sound came, Charlie thought it was from another part of the wall. But then it grew louder – an angry, swelling buzz.

The children on the ground were looking up. They began

to back away. Some of them screamed. Following their gaze, Charlie saw a black cloud falling through the trees. The buzz became a roar and the whole crowd scattered, howling and screaming. Joshua Tilpin was the last to go. 'You're going to be stung to death, Charlie Bone,' he shouted as he ran off.

Bees? Swarming in winter? Who had sent them? The shadow? Charlie closed his eyes. Which was worse, he wondered, being stung to death or buried by a wall?

The buzzing stopped. Charlie kept his eyes closed, waiting for the tickle of bees' feet on his bare face and hands. Waiting for the first angry sting. Nothing happened. Charlie opened one eye. Nothing on the wall. Nothing in the air.

'Charlie!'

Charlie opened his other eye. He saw Emma and Olivia looking up at him from the base of the wall. They were both smiling.

'What on earth . . .?' said Charlie.

'An illusion!' cried Olivia, leaping in the air. 'It was a good one, wasn't it?'

'Certainly was.' Charlie gingerly let himself down from the wall.

None of them noticed a woman approaching through the mist. She stopped a few metres away from them, and hid behind a tree.

'We saw them following you,' said Emma, 'so we followed them, but we didn't know what to do. There were so many of them. Joshua's magnetism is definitely having an effect.'

'And then I thought of bees.' Olivia gave another joyful leap. 'I'm so proud of myself.'

'You saved me!' Charlie gave her a hug. 'Phew! I'm so glad to be . . .'

There was a sudden rustle in the trees behind them, and they all turned to see a figure making off, rather fast, into the mist. There was no mistaking the neat grey suit and short trim haircut.

'Mrs Brown,' Charlie whispered. 'She must have heard you, Liv.'

'And now she knows about your endowment. Oh, no!' Emma wrung her hands. 'What are we going to do?'

'There's nothing we can do,' said Charlie. 'We'll just have to wait and see what happens.'

Apparently, Mrs Brown was biding her time. Olivia wasn't summoned to the headmaster's study and no one dragged her away for questioning or locked her in a classroom. Wondering when the Bloors would make a move against Olivia was almost worse than knowing what they would do. At bedtime, when Charlie crept up to the

girls' dormitory, Olivia came prancing down the passage in her black and gold pyjamas, as chirpy as ever.

'I'm OK,' she said, waving Charlie away. 'Don't get detention on my account.'

'Good luck then, Liv.' Charlie backed down the stairs. He intended to keep an ear open for any unusual sounds in the night, but just in case he fell asleep, he passed on the word to Billy, Fidelio and Gabriel.

'Blessed will let us know if anything happens,' Billy whispered before he closed his eyes.

Charlie didn't have much faith in Blessed. He was a bit deaf for a start. But if he was the best they could do for a guard dog, they'd have to trust that it was one of his better days – or nights.

Paton Yewbeam was eating a cold supper. Candles shone from every corner of the kitchen, and there were four more on the table. Paton told himself that he needed the light to read the small print of a particularly engaging book, but truthfully he had lit the extra candles to keep at bay the dark thoughts that had begun to creep into his mind. Was it his imagination, or were some of the people walking down Filbert Street *really strange*? Men and women who peered into windows, who ran their hands over gates and

railings, who squinted at door numbers and wrote hurried notes in small black books.

Spies, thought Paton. Bought by the count. Won over, hypnotised, coerced or whatever. They belong to him. What's to become of us all?

Paton shivered and quickly tossed back a glass of white wine. He shivered again and took a bite of his cold salmon sandwich.

He was not inclined to answer the sudden loud knock on the front door. One of *them*, he thought. Well, they won't catch me like that.

But the knocking continued and, detecting a rather frantic note in the sound, Paton reluctantly went into the hall.

'Who's there?' he called through the door.

'Oh, Mr Yewbeam, please, *please, I must* speak to you.'

Recognising the voice, Paton opened the front door and Mrs Brown practically fell into the hall.

'I must to talk to you, I must,' pleaded Mrs Brown. 'I don't know who to turn to. I don't know what to do.'

'Please calm yourself, Mrs Brown,' said Paton. 'Would you care for a salmon sandwich?'

'No, no, not unless, that is . . . well, I am rather hungry. My husband won't speak to me.'

'Good Lord! How uncivil.' Paton led the way into the candlelit kitchen. 'Forgive the lack of electricity. You're probably aware of my little weakness.'

'Oh, I wouldn't call it a weakness, Mr Yewbeam.' Mrs Brown took the chair that Paton drew out for her.

'Paton,' he said. 'Do call me Paton.'

'Thank you.' Mrs Brown looked startled. 'I'm Trish.'

'Trish. How nice.' Paton poured Mrs Brown a large glass of white wine. 'Do go on.'

'Yes, well, I don't know if Charlie told you, I expect he did, but I've been working for Mr Ezekiel Bloor. Both of us have. Mr Brown and me.' Mrs Brown paused to get her breath. 'He offered us a very great deal of money to find out certain things about the children at Bloor's Academy.'

'To spy on them, Mrs Brown?' There was a note of accusation in Paton's tone.

'Well – yes!' Mrs Brown quite suddenly burst into tears.

Paton handed her a handkerchief and then went to the counter where he placed a piece of smoked salmon between two slices of bread, cut it in half and brought it to the table on a small plate.

'Th-thank you,' sobbed Mrs Brown, wiping her nose on Paton's hanky. 'It's all been too much.'

'Go on,' said Paton.

'What?' Mrs Brown seemed confused. 'Yes, well, I did discover something about one of the children, Olivia Vertigo as a matter of fact, but I just couldn't bring myself to – to betray her. My husband knows I'm on to something, but I refused to tell him. And now I just don't know what to do.'

'Patricia!' (Paton disliked shortened names.)

Mrs Brown looked up in alarm. 'Yes?'

'How can you possibly be in any doubt?' Paton said gravely. 'You must on no account breathe a word of what you have discovered to anyone. Think what your betrayal would do to Benjamin. Charlie would never speak to him again, never visit your house, never dog-sit your dog. At the risk of causing a divorce, I absolutely forbid you to tell your husband. He is obviously not as principled as you.'

'I don't think it would actually come to a divorce,' Mrs Brown said timidly. 'It's just that we need the money. You see we've just bought a new car and the bills –'

'If you need money, there's plenty of work about for highly skilled detectives like yourselves,' said Paton. 'There's been a spate of robberies in the city, not to mention suspicious fires, questionable accidents and unsolved murders. Go and tell your husband that working at Bloor's is making you ill, that you know absolutely

nothing, and that you'll have a nervous breakdown if you don't have a rest.'

Mrs Brown smiled. 'Yes,' she sighed. 'I'll do that. Thank you, Mr Yewbeam. You've made me feel so much better.'

The Mirror of Amoret

It was a good thing that no one had to rely on Blessed to wake them up. The old dog slept very soundly in Cook's underground room. But Olivia was not dragged away in the middle of the night, and Charlie had an exceptionally long and peaceful sleep. His uncle, on the other hand, had a very bad time.

Not long after Mrs Brown left, Paton's four sisters arrived. He was in his room when he heard the front door bang and a babble of voices in the hall. He was in two minds as to whether to go down and confront them. In the end he told himself he had to go. They might ignore him, but he had to try and get

them to listen, if only for Charlie's sake.

When Paton walked into the kitchen, he found his sisters seated at the table, drinking an unusual-looking soup – octopus by the look of it. They were all talking at once and not one of them looked up when their brother appeared. He quickly switched off the light.

'Oh, no, it's him.' 'Go away.' 'Put the light on!' Paton's sisters growled and grunted at him.

'If I put the light on, you'll get glass in your soup,' said Paton.

'Then go away,' said Grandma Bone.

'No.' Paton crossed to the dresser and lit two candles.

'I can't see what I'm eating,' whined Venetia.

'All the better if you ask me,' said Paton, putting the candles on the table. 'It looks disgusting.'

There were four large sighs of irritation.

'I want to talk to you.' Paton pulled out a chair at the end of the table.

'About what?' asked Grandma Bone impatiently.

'About your daughter-in-law.'

'Huh!' She continued to gulp down her soup.

'For heaven's sake, Grizelda, you must be aware of what's happening. The arrival of this count – the enchanter – must have taken you all by surprise. You surely can't

approve of what he's doing – turning the city upside down, twisting people's minds, stealing Charlie's mother.'

'He's very powerful, Count Harken,' said Venetia, fingering the green silk rose pinned in her black hair.

'Very powerful,' Eustacia agreed, patting a green enamel brooch on her lapel.

'Very,' Lucretia touched a green glass earring dangling above her shoulder.

Paton's attention was drawn to the bracelet with large green stones that glinted on Grandma Bone's wrist as she lifted the soup spoon to her mouth. He got up from the table. 'You appal me, all of you,' he said.

'The feeling's mutual,' grunted Venetia.

Paton seized his eldest sister's shoulder. 'Grizelda, where's your son?'

'Dead!' she said, shaking him off. 'Now leave us alone.'

'No!' roared Paton. 'We all know that Lyell's not dead. But where is he? Don't you realise that your great enchanter, your count, is making Amy forget her husband?'

'When Amy thinks of Lyell, she keeps him clinging to this world,' Eustacia the clairvoyant informed him. 'But if she forgets him, for a day, a week and then a month, he'll be lost forever. Never get back.'

'She's taken off her rings,' Venetia said happily.

'That's the first step,' said Eustacia. 'It's only the boy who can keep him alive now.'

'And he can't even remember his father's face.' Venetia smiled spitefully.

'It'll be better for everyone if Lyell Bone is forgotten,' said Lucretia, glancing at her eldest sister.

Grandma Bone's face was like a stone.

Paton stared at them all in horror. 'I can't believe I'm hearing this. The count will carry Amy into the past, the future, who knows where. Oh, yes, I know about the Mirror of Amoret. Do you really want Charlie to lose both his parents?'

'We've given up on Charlie,' Grandma Bone said in a flat voice. 'Once we thought he'd join us, put his endowment to good use. But he's too much like his father. I realise that now. Neither of them wants to be like us, to be part of Ezekiel's great plan to control things. *They will not toe the line!*'

'Don't you think that's something to be proud of?' asked Paton quietly.

'It's stupid!' Grandma Bone said bitterly. 'There's no future in swimming against the tide. You have to join in if you want to have power.'

'Join in? Destroy people's lives? Steal their children?

That's what you call power, is it?' Paton turned on his heel and left the room, shaking with disgust.

Where will all this end? he wondered gloomily as he climbed the dark stairs. His fingers closed over the scrap of parchment in his pocket and he remembered that there might be hope, if the king could be found.

At Bloor's Academy a whole day passed in which neither Mr nor Mrs Brown was seen. Charlie began to hope that Benjamin's parents had changed their minds. Perhaps, after all, they couldn't bring themselves to spy on children.

In the King's Room that evening no one said a word. They all worked with heads down, never meeting anyone else's eye. It was as though a silent truce had been declared, though Charlie knew it wouldn't last long. Joshua, Dorcas and the twins were merely biding their time, gathering their strength. As for Manfred, someone was going to have to pay for his horribly scarred face.

Asa was not in his usual seat beside Manfred. He was sitting slightly apart from the others. Ever since the shadow had arrived Asa had seemed nervous and ill-at-ease – just like some of the animals, thought Charlie.

After homework, Charlie caught up with Tancred and Lysander before they went up to their dormitory. 'Could we

meet somewhere tomorrow?' Charlie asked in a whisper. 'I need your advice – well, your help really.'

'Art room, before supper.' Lysander glanced down the passage. 'Manfred's coming,' he said in a low voice.

Charlie stepped back. ''Night, 'Sander! 'Night, Tanc!' he called as the two older boys strode away.

Charlie knew he wasn't going to escape that easily. The next moment he felt a heavy hand on his shoulder. It was so hot, Charlie winced with pain. 'Ow!' He looked up into Manfred's pitted face.

'Go on, take a good look,' said Manfred. 'Pretty, isn't it? Your uncle's responsible for these.' Manfred touched two of the larger scars with his finger.

Given the tricky situation, Charlie should have sympathised, but instead he blundered, 'It was your own fault.'

'My fault?' Manfred dug his fist into Charlie's shoulder.

Charlie twisted away. The pain was agonising. It felt as though a hot poker had been plunged into his shoulder blade. 'Ouch! What *is* that?'

'I've told you before, call me sir.' Manfred raised his hands, palms outward. '*That* is pain, Charlie Bone. Two hands full of pain. Don't tempt me to use them again.'

Charlie stared at Manfred's back as the tall, bony youth

walked away. So Manfred had a new endowment. He was becoming like Borlath, the Red King's eldest son who killed with fire. Better pass the news along, thought Charlie.

The following evening Fidelio offered to keep Billy distracted while the others met in the Art room. It wasn't that they didn't trust Billy. If too many of the endowed were missing someone might become suspicious. As it was, they were a little wary of using the Art room for a meeting. It was possible that Dorcas and Joshua might come barging in. Both were in Art, although neither of them appeared to be very enthusiastic about it.

Charlie was the last one to get to the meeting. He had just managed to slip out of the dormitory while Fidelio and Billy were arguing with Bragger Braine about the superiority of rats over hamsters.

He found the others sitting on the floor beside the long windows that overlooked the garden. They were hidden from view by one of Emma's large bird paintings – a particularly fine one, Charlie observed in the light of Lysander's new hurricane lamp.

'Olivia told us about the wall,' said Lysander, as Charlie knelt beside him.

'And the bees,' added Tancred with a grin.

'I reckon they saved my life,' said Charlie.

'We'll keep an eye on you from now on, Charlie,' said Gabriel. 'That little Tilpin has certainly got it in for you.'

Lysander had brought a notebook with him. He suggested they should work out a rota, so that Charlie would never be left alone during break. 'We'll begin with first break tomorrow, Thursday.' He laid the open book on the floor and wrote 'Thursday' at the top of the first page.

' 'Sander,' Charlie said tentatively. 'It's not me I'm worried about.'

'Well, you should be,' said Tancred.

'I know and, of course, I am a bit scared, but it's my mum I'm really worried about. Somehow I have to get the Mirror of Amoret. If I don't, I . . . I . . .'

'If you don't?' Emma asked gently.

'I think the shadow will take her out of the world. He can travel with the mirror, like me. My mum's already under his spell; she's forgotten my father's face, she's never at home; last time I saw her, she looked right through me, as if I didn't exist.'

Charlie's friends looked so appalled he almost wished he could take back his words. Horror seemed to have robbed them all of speech, until Olivia said, 'I'll do it!'

They all looked at her and Lysander asked, 'Do what?'

'I'll get the mirror,' Olivia said brightly.

'You don't even know where it is,' said Tancred.

'It'll be wherever *he* is, won't it?' Olivia said in a practical voice. 'Charlie says Count Harken is the new owner of Kingdom's. Well, I know for a fact that the old owner lived in a fabulous penthouse at the top of the store. So that's probably where the count lives.'

'So what are you going to do? Snaffle the mirror from under his very nose?' said Tancred. 'That is, if you can get into his very exclusive penthouse, which is probably guarded night and day by two heavy henchmen.'

'Don't scoff, Tancred Torsson,' Olivia said hotly. 'Obviously I'll wait until the count is out of the way. He's bound to take Charlie's mum for a weekend jaunt in that fancy limo.'

'You're going to look a bit out of place in Kingdom's, Liv,' Charlie remarked. 'I'm not saying you're not smart or anything, but –'

'That's where Mum comes in.' Olivia's grey eyes glittered with excitement. 'She's been dying to do something like this. She's had such rotten stage parts lately. We'll have a ball. Trust me. She can look incredibly glamorous. The assistants at Kingdom's will be falling over themselves to make her happy. I'll just slip away while they're all bowing and scraping.'

There was a pause while they all digested Olivia's plan.

'I think it's a brilliant idea,' Emma said at last.

Everyone agreed.

'There's just one more thing,' said Lysander. 'Where are you going to take the mirror when, and if, you get it?'

'Home,' said Olivia. 'Charlie can meet me there.'

'I think we'll stick around, too.' Lysander looked at Tancred and Gabriel.

'You're on,' said Tancred.

Gabriel nodded vehemently.

They all got to their feet, stretching their arms and shaking their cramped legs. But Lysander wouldn't let them go before he had organised a rota for watching Charlie. Every minute of every break was accounted for. Fidelio would be told about his part in the scheme as soon as they could get him alone.

Charlie was a little uncomfortable about the whole arrangement. It was embarrassing to think he couldn't take care of himself. Nevertheless, it was good to know that every time he stepped outside he wouldn't be alone.

Olivia's plan was fraught with danger. There were so many ways in which it could go wrong and yet, as the weekened drew closer, Charlie's spirits rose ever higher. It had to work. To fail was unthinkable.

No one knew what to do about Billy. He didn't want to spend yet another weekend alone at Bloor's, but Charlie's house was not a pleasant place to be, with a frozen granny in the bath and a mother in thrall to an enchanter. Besides, no one could think how Billy's endowment could help in such a dangerous enterprise. He would only get in the way.

'Billy can stay with me,' said Emma. 'I don't think I'm going to be much use either.'

Billy was very excited at the prospect of spending the weekend at Ingledew's. There were no dogs to chase Rembrandt, only a friendly duck to talk to. And Emma's aunt was an excellent cook.

At eleven-thirty on Saturday morning, Amy Bone emerged from her room at the top of the house. Charlie wouldn't have heard her light footsteps if he hadn't been waiting for them. When she reached the bottom of the first staircase, Charlie stepped out on to the landing.

Amy's appearance left Charlie speechless. She wore a glistening fur coat and her hair was as smooth as yellow silk. Two large pearls hung from her ears and her nails were a vivid green. Charlie's heart missed a beat when he saw that her wedding ring had gone. In its place a huge emerald sparkled on her finger.

'Where are you going, Mum?' he asked in a strangled voice.

'Just out.' She descended the second flight of stairs in high heels that made her bounce like a wave.

Charlie followed her but she left the house without a word, without a backward glance. Charlie ran into the kitchen and stared dismally out of the window, as the gold limousine pulled away from the kerb. For a moment he was too dismayed to move, then, remembering that this was the moment he'd been waiting for, he ran into the hall and phoned Olivia.

'Hi!' came her cheery voice.

'Mum's gone out,' said Charlie. 'She was with . . .' He paused, with his mouth open, as Grandma Bone walked out of the sitting room. 'I didn't know you were in, Grandma!'

'Didn't you? Who are you phoning?'

'Hello! Hello!' Olivia's voice came bubbling out of the phone. All those drama lessons had given her a very clear, ringing voice. 'Who's she gone out with, the –'

Charlie put his hand over the earpiece. 'It's my friend Olivia,' he told Grandma Bone. 'I was just asking her if I could go to lunch, because Mum's gone out, and I don't suppose there'll be much food around here.'

'You suppose right,' said his grandmother. 'Go on, ask her then.'

Charlie lifted the receiver closer to his mouth. 'Um, as I said, Mum's gone out – in a very smart car.' He grinned at Grandma Bone, 'So could I come round for lunch? My grandma, who's *here*, says it's OK.'

'Got it,' said Olivia in an excited undertone. 'Mum and me are ready to go. See you, Charlie.'

'You'd better get your coat,' said Grandma Bone, as she drifted back into the sitting room. 'It looks like snow.'

Uncle Paton had already been told of the plan and, although he worried about the danger if things should go wrong, he agreed that it would have to be attempted, if Charlie were not to lose his mother altogether.

Charlie snatched his coat from his room and popped his head round Uncle Paton's door. 'Mum's gone out with you-know-who, so it's all systems go,' he told his uncle.

Paton looked up from his desk. 'Good luck!' he said. 'I'll be waiting.'

Mrs Vertigo decided to wear a tight red leather coat and high-heeled black boots. A red velvet beret and large gold bag completed her outfit. She looked stunning. Olivia, however, didn't want to be too conspicuous. Today she

would play the shy young daughter. Casually dressed in jeans and a navy duffel coat, and with her hair restored to its natural light brown, she looked the picture of innocence.

'You've got your mobile, haven't you?' Mrs Vertigo asked her daughter as they approached Kingdom's.

'In my pocket,' said Olivia.

'Promise to contact me if you're in trouble.'

'Course.'

'This is so exciting.' Olivia's mother gave the two doormen a radiant smile and they sprang into action, pulling open the door as wide as they could.

Olivia and Mrs Vertigo stepped into the sweetly scented, velvety shadowed and incredibly crowded store.

'The sales!' Mrs Vertigo exclaimed. 'Oh, Liv, what fun! Let's start with scarves, shall we?'

Olivia followed her mother across to the colourful display of scarves. Mrs Vertigo began to enjoy herself. She had brought four lipsticks in shades varying from palest pink to deepest red. 'I want a scarf to match each of these colours,' she told the assistant. 'They must be silk, naturally, not too square and not too long and, hopefully, half price.' She fluttered her false eyelashes.

As a group of smartly dressed shoppers pressed around her mother, grumbling impatiently, Olivia slipped away. Pushing

through the crowds of bargain hunters, she reached the lift and jumped in, just before the door closed. An elderly couple smiled at her from the other side of the lift. They were both dressed in brown check coats and trilby hats.

'Two?' enquired the man in a foreign accent.

'Two?' said Olivia.

'Second,' explained the elderly woman, nudging her husband. 'He get it wrong always. My English better.'

'No, thank you. Not second,' said Olivia.

The man tried again. 'Tree, four?' His finger hovered over the display panel.

'Toys,' said Olivia.

'Ah, toys,' sighed the man. 'I wish.'

'Quick, Herman. We go. Bye bye.'

The lift door opened and the couple tottered out, the woman waving feebly and Herman still muttering forlornly about toys.

Alone at last, Olivia pressed a button with no number and the lift sailed to the top of the building. When the door opened she peeped out. A few yards away a large man sat reading a newspaper, his feet lost in a sea of black fur that extended all the way to the end of a long passage. Beside the man a white-panelled door bore an inscription in bronze. 'Noble.'

Olivia thought fast. The lift door began to close. She pressed the button again. As the door slid open a loud tweeting could be heard. The man grunted, flung down his newspaper and ran to the end of the passage, where a bird flapped round the light fitting.

Olivia leapt out of the lift and raced to the door marked 'Noble'. It was not locked. She slipped inside and closed it softly behind her.

Ankle-deep in white fur, Olivia gazed around the extraordinary apartment. 'No time for gawping, Liv,' she whispered to herself, as she took in the pony-skin sofa, the ivory tables and horribly real-looking stuffed birds.

There were two doors leading out of the fur-carpeted sitting room. Olivia tried the nearest. It opened into a vast walk-in wardrobe. Every garment was either green or furry. There was a long mirror on the wall, but no sign of a small, ancient one. Olivia backed out.

The second door led into a room that was far more promising. A huge four-poster bed stood in the centre. It was curtained in thick tapestries and looked hundreds of years old.

How on earth did they get that up here? Olivia wondered. The great bed had the look of an illusion, something Olivia herself might have conjured up. All at

once, she had her answer. The bed *was* conjured up. So was the blackened chest of drawers standing against the wall, and the small table by the window. They were not illusions but ancient objects brought here by magic.

A large wooden chair stood in the corner. It looked immensely old with its high curved back and thick, worm-eaten arms. Olivia had seen such a chair in the local museum.

Where did the count keep the mirror? Perhaps he never let it out of his sight. The table was bare and the chair didn't even have a cushion in it. Olivia approached the bed. There was nothing under the pillows or between the starched white sheets. She went to the chest of drawers. Starting at the top she pulled out the drawers, one by one.

Empty, empty, empty. Olivia's heart sank. She had to kneel on the floor to pull out the last drawer. It squeaked and shivered as she tugged at the handles, but it would only open a few inches. Olivia thrust in her arm and felt about. Her fingers touched something smooth and flat, right at the back. Slowly, she eased it forward and pulled it out of the drawer.

It shouldn't come as a surprise when something you hope to find turns up in a place where you half-expect it to be. But Olivia was so stunned by her discovery, she had to

sit back on her heels and take several deep breaths before she could bring herself to examine the object on her lap.

It was a mirror – very ancient, by the look of it. The circle of glass, if you could call it glass, was set in a delicate golden frame. Intricate patterns had been worked into the gold: leaves and birds and tiny dancing creatures with jewelled eyes. The handle was a long oval of twisted gold and silver, and when Olivia held it she felt a throbbing warmth travel through her body. Slowly, she brought the mirror up to her face. There was no reflection. Am I a vampire, then? Olivia asked herself, squinting into the glass. Where am I?

A fine mist swirled across the surface of the glass but, try as she might, Olivia could see nothing behind the mist. Remembering the danger of her mission, she quickly pushed back the drawer and slipped the mirror into her duffel-coat pocket. She had forgotten to make her bird disappear and wondered if the guard had discovered by now that it was merely an illusion. She would have to create something more dramatic if she was to distract him a second time. Closing her eyes, she thought of smoke rising out of the black carpet. She didn't forget to add the smell of burning fur, which she had to imagine, never having smelt it before.

Tiptoeing through the apartment, she put her ear to the main door. A distant sound of swearing and stamping reached her ears. Holding her breath, Olivia eased open the door, slipped out and closed it softly. The smoke illusion had worked a treat. At the far end of the passage the terrified guard was jumping on the smouldering carpet with both feet. As soon as one smoking patch vanished, another appeared.

Olivia rushed to the lift and pressed the button. The lift was busy. She pressed again, again and again. The guard took a break from his attack on the carpet. He rubbed his head and looked down the passage. Olivia shrank against the lift door. With a loud ping it slid open and she tumbled in, quickly pressing the ground floor button as she lurched against the back wall.

'Oi!' called the guard.

But Olivia was on her way down and, happily, the lift didn't stop once until she reached the ground floor. Trying to look as casual as possible, Olivia hurried over to her mother. In spite of the crowds she had no trouble in locating Mrs Vertigo's bright red coat. She was now busy at the make-up counter. When Olivia reached her mother, she found the counter littered with creams, powders, sticks of mascara, brushes and bottles.

'Mum, we've got to go,' said Olivia.

Mrs Vertigo turned and saw her daughter's anxious face. 'Oh, right.' She gave the assistant a rueful smile. 'Sorry, it's not what I want. None of it. Thank you so much.'

The assistant glared at the mess on her counter as Olivia tugged her mother away.

'Mission accomplished?' asked Mrs Vertigo.

Olivia nodded.

When they emerged into the street, they walked straight into Miss Chrystal who was, unbelievably, holding Joshua Tilpin by the hand.

'Miss Chrystal, isn't it?' said Mrs Vertigo in a flamboyant tone. 'Aren't the sales brilliant? And who is this?' She smiled at Joshua.

'One of the pupils,' Miss Chrystal said lightly. 'His name's Joshua. The school asked me to get him a new shirt.'

'An expensive shirt for a little boy!' Mrs Vertigo remarked, cocking her head at Kingdom's marble pillars.

Miss Chrystal ignored this and hurriedly pulled Joshua into the store.

'Poor little fellow,' said Mrs Vertigo. 'He looks so pathetic.'

'Don't you believe it, Mum.' Olivia linked arms with her mother. 'And *please* hurry.'

Charlie was standing on the Vertigos' step when Olivia

and her mother arrived at the house. He knew the mission had been successful as soon as he saw Olivia's smiling but anxious face.

'We bumped into Joshua and Miss Chrystal,' Olivia told Charlie as they stepped into the Vertigos' large hallway. 'They might be suspicious, and I think the guard saw me.'

'Let's hope he didn't,' said Charlie. 'Can I see the mirror, Liv?'

'Yes, do let's. I can hardly wait.' Mrs Vertigo flung her coat on a peg and pushed the children into the sitting room.

As Olivia drew out the mirror, there was a loud bang on the front door. Immediately two figures appeared outside the French windows.

Mrs Vertigo screamed.

'It's all right, Mum,' said Olivia. 'It's Tancred and Lysander. They're here to help.'

'And we're going to need them,' said Charlie as another loud bang echoed through the house. 'It sounds as if you were followed, Liv.'

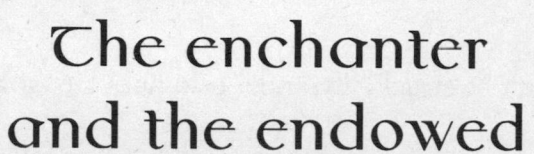

The enchanter and the endowed

Tancred and Lysander liked nothing better than a challenge. They didn't have to see Mrs Vertigo's unwelcome visitors to know who they were. The furious barking gave them away.

'Rottweilers,' said Lysander.

'Looms!' Tancred grinned in anticipation. Looking into the sky, he raised his arms. The next moment a torrent of water fell from above, as though a floodgate had opened in the clouds.

Olivia unlocked the French windows and Lysander ran inside. The rain continued to pour upon Tancred like a waterfall. In seconds he was standing in an inch of water, while lightning zipped across the Vertigos'

smooth lawn in sheets of blinding light.

'He'll be struck,' cried Mrs Vertigo. 'Someone bring him in.'

'He can't be struck,' Lysander told her. 'He's a weather-monger.'

Olivia ran into the kitchen where a small window overlooked the street. Huddled on the step, the Loom brothers were having a hard time controlling their dogs. The frantic creatures were biting their leads in an effort to escape from the storm.

Cursing their predicament, the brothers finally left the house and stumbled away through the rain, dragged by their hysterical dogs.

Olivia ran back to the sitting room and announced, 'They've gone!'

'Oh, good,' said Mrs Vertigo, who always bounced back from trouble as though it had never happened. 'You can call the blond boy in now, and we'll all have some muffins.'

'I'm afraid it's not over, Mrs Vertigo,' said Lysander. 'The Looms are harmless compared to what might happen next.'

'If you're talking about that enchanter thing, he's not going to put me off my tea,' said Mrs Vertigo with remarkable composure. 'Come to think of it, we haven't had lunch, have we?'

'If you don't mind,' said Charlie quietly. 'I couldn't eat anything at the moment. I just want to see the mirror.'

Olivia pulled the mirror out of her pocket with a flourish. 'There!'

'Heavens!' exclaimed her mother. 'It's utterly, utterly beautiful.'

'Awesome,' Lysander peered into the glass. 'But it's not a mirror. I can't see anything.'

'What a relief,' said Olivia. 'I thought I was a vampire.'

'Can I?' Charlie held out his hand.

Olivia gave him the mirror. 'What are you going to do with it, Charlie?'

'I hadn't really thought about it, I just wanted to get it away from the count. But now . . .' Charlie looked at the mist that clouded the surface of the glass. 'I'd like to be alone with it for a while.'

'Course, Charlie.' Olivia led the way up to her room. She left Charlie sitting on her bed and whispered, 'Good luck,' before she closed the door on him.

For several seconds Charlie was almost too afraid to look at the mirror again. He closed his eyes and Uncle Paton's words came back to him. 'Look into the mirror and the person you wish to see will appear. If you want to find that person, look again, and the mirror

will take you to them, wherever they are.'

'But I can't remember his face,' sighed Charlie. 'Help me, someone.'

He felt something lightly brush his wrist, and the white moth crawled out of his sleeve. She flew on to the mirror's gold frame and gently beat her silvery wings. The mist on the glassy surface began to clear.

'How am I to remember?' Charlie silently asked the moth.

'Remember what you can,' came the answer.

Charlie thought back to a time before he had lived in the house on Filbert Street. He remembered a bright kitchen; he was very small because the swirling hem of his mother's skirt came very close to his face. She was humming to the music that came from another room. Charlie left the kitchen and walked across a hallway. He pushed open a door and moved towards the elegant legs of a grand piano. White curtains billowed in a breeze from the window. The man sitting at the piano had his back to Charlie. He wore a brown jacket and his thick, black hair touched the top of his collar. His fingers flew over the piano keys, but when Charlie walked round the piano stool, the man stopped playing and looked down. 'Hello, Charlie!' he said.

The shock of recognition almost made Charlie lose

consciousness. He had seen the man before. Many times. He'd spoken to him only a week ago, never knowing he was his father. Clinging even tighter to the mirror, he stared into the dark, smiling eyes until he felt himself drifting closer. When his father's face began to recede Charlie cried, 'Take me to him.' And the mirror obeyed.

Now he was in another room: it was the music room at Bloor's Academy. But here the piano was silent. For the pianist had folded his arms over the keys and laid his head on them.

'Dad!' Charlie tapped the man's shoulder. 'It's me, Charlie!'

The dark eyes were no longer smiling. They looked blank and heavy.

'Are you still asleep? You must remember me. I've never stopped thinking of you. Never. Please try and remember. Please say something. Please . . .' Charlie shook his father's shoulder, this time with some vigour.

Without moving the man said faintly, 'There's nothing left. Go away.'

A cry escaped Charlie. A cry that was like no sound he had ever heard. And then he was being dragged away. His father's face began to fade and Charlie spun through the air, now twisting upside down, now floating on his back.

He began to see the mirror again, glinting out of a fog, but the glass was empty. The face that had looked out at Charlie was gone.

With a sudden bump, Charlie landed on a bed. Olivia was standing in front of him, holding the mirror.

'Charlie, you made a dreadful sound.' She peered into his face. 'I thought the mirror had frightened you. So I took it out of your hands.'

Charlie blinked. 'I wasn't frightened exactly.'

'Did you see your father?'

'Yes. Liv, I think he's almost dead.'

Charlie's voice was so weak Olivia couldn't be sure that she'd heard him. 'Dead?' she asked. 'Did you say dead?'

'Almost.'

At that moment a deafening roar caused the whole house to shudder.

'He's here!' Suddenly alert, Charlie rushed to the window.

Tancred was not alone. On the other side of the garden stood a tall stranger in a shimmering green robe. The man's abundant hair was touched with gold and his nose was curved like the beak of a hawk.

'He doesn't look like a shadow,' Olivia remarked, 'but certainly an enchanter.'

Before Charlie could reply, Tancred swung his arm

forward and an arc of lightning flew from his hand towards the man in green. The enchanter caught the band of light and, in a flash, sent it back across the few yards that separated him from the weather-monger. But Tancred had already produced a sheet of pure white light that enveloped the enchanter like a shroud.

Olivia and Charlie watched helplessly as the count stepped out of his shroud and sent a ribbon of fire snaking over the grass. It began to wind itself round Tancred's body, and he fell to his knees, unable to move his hands or defend himself.

The enchanter advanced, smiling.

Charlie turned away from the window, crying, 'I can't let this happen.'

But Olivia held him back. 'Look! Look out there!' she commanded.

A figure had darted between Tancred and the enchanter. He stood shielding Tancred as the enchanter strode towards them.

'It's Gabriel,' said Charlie in disbelief.

'What's he wearing?' Olivia pressed her head against the windowpane. 'Some old cloak.'

'The Red King's cloak,' breathed Charlie. 'It belongs to his family, the Salutatis.'

'The enchanter can't touch him. Look at the fire, Charlie.'

Every streak of lightning, every ribbon of fire that the enchanter hurled at Gabriel slid round the cloak and then burnt out.

With a roar of fury, the count rushed at Gabriel, only to be stopped by an invisible wall, his mouth agape, his hands reaching for the cloak, but unable to touch it.

'He's beaten,' Olivia cheered, a little prematurely.

The enchanter glared up at her and, abandoning his attack on Gabriel, rushed at the house. The crash of broken glass sent Charlie and Olivia tearing downstairs. They burst into the sitting room, where Mrs Vertigo stood in a trance before the shattered window. From the other side, the enchanter gazed at her with treacherous green eyes.

'Excuse me, Mrs Vertigo,' said Lysander, swinging her away from the window. Giving her no time to protest, he swept her off her feet and carried her, bodily, into the kitchen. 'It's better you stay here.' He lowered her to the ground with a bashful smile. 'And lock the door, perhaps.'

'I've no intention of locking myself away from the action,' Mrs Vertigo protested breathlessly.

There came a second, even louder, crash from the sitting room.

'Then please keep the door closed.' Lysander seized Olivia's wrist and thrust her in with her mother.

'Hey! Do you mind?' Olivia cried indignantly.

'You'll be safer in here, Liv,' said Charlie. 'Safer still without that mirror.' He grabbed the mirror as footsteps advanced, crunching over the broken glass.

Charlie could already feel the enchanter's green glare on his back, and the hand that held the mirror trembled violently. 'I'm not afraid,' he told himself. 'I won't let go.'

'*You are afraid. You will let go.*' It felt as though the awful voice was deep inside Charlie's head.

'I won't.' He turned to face the enchanter.

A dark figure stood at the end of the long tiled hallway. Charlie squinted into the gloom. Was it him? Or had he turned into a shadow again?

'Give it to me and there's no harm done.' This was a different voice, gentle and persuasive. 'You have no need of it, Charlie. You can travel whenever you wish.'

Charlie took a step towards the shadowy figure.

'Don't!' hissed Lysander. 'It's a trick.' He leapt into the centre of the hall and began to spin, faster and faster, while he chanted in a strange, musical language. When he came to rest, Charlie could hear a distant drumming that grew louder every second.

'My spirit ancestors,' said Lysander.

I don't need help, thought Charlie. I'm strong. I can send this feeble ghost away.

As Charlie stepped closer to the shadow, the drums grew louder until the hall was filled with the sound.

'What's this?' said the enchanter. 'A merry tune to make me dance. You fools!'

A brilliant flash showed Charlie that it was no feeble shadow he was facing. Every detail of the enchanter was thrown into sharp relief: the green robe patterned in gold, the studded leather belt, the sword in its jewelled scabbard and the mantle of deeper green, edged in pearls.

'Give me the mirror,' the enchanter commanded, 'before it's too late.'

'Never.' Charlie held the mirror behind his back.

The drums stopped all at once, and in the sudden silence a troupe of dark-skinned men appeared. They wore white robes and carried gleaming weapons: swords, knives and axes.

'SO!' The enchanter lifted his sword and brought it whistling down on to the tiles. The whole floor shivered and, from between the tiles, razor-sharp spikes appeared. Lysander and Charlie tried in vain to grip the walls, but the floor heaved so violently they were forced on to their

knees. Charlie clung to the mirror, though he longed to let it go, if only for a second, so that he could pull himself upright.

'Hold on, Charlie,' croaked Lysander.

The white-robed warriors were now swinging their weapons across the ground. The floor stopped heaving and the dreadful spikes wilted like dead flowers. Charlie and Lysander got to their feet and steadied themselves against the wall.

The enchanter's second scream was so painful, Charlie had to cover his ears. The mirror slipped out of his hand but Lysander caught it, just in time. And then the battle began in earnest.

The enchanter flung fire and ice at the advancing spirits. He conjured up a storm of scorpions, a cloud of snakes, a monstrous giant, a sabre-toothed tiger and a dragon with two heads, but the spirit ancestors brushed them away as though they were made of paper.

Olivia and her mother couldn't resist opening the kitchen door a crack. The unbelievable battle scene made Mrs Vertigo wonder if her hall would ever be the same again.

At length, with a final cry of defiance, the enchanter retreated. By the time he vanished, he had become a weak

and shivering version of his former self.

'Don't be fooled, Charlie,' Lysander warned. 'I don't think he's finished.'

Their work done, Lysander's ancestors began to fade, the occasional flash of silver the only hint that, moments ago, the hallway had been bristling with weapons.

When Tancred and Gabriel came in through the broken windows, Mrs Vertigo decided they should all have spaghetti, muffins not being quite substantial enough for such a special celebration.

After the meal, the four boys helped to clean up the broken glass. Mrs Vertigo said she would get a man in to mend the window, though it might be a good idea to tell the police about the violent intruder.

'No point, Mum,' said Olivia. 'The police wouldn't know how to deal with him. Enchanters aren't on their list.'

Charlie was eager to get the mirror home, though what he would do with it, he wasn't sure. Perhaps he could take it to Skarpo. As long as the count didn't have it, his mother couldn't be taken out of the world.

Charlie thought the mirror was safe, at least for a while. A furious battle had been won, and his elation made him careless. As he left the Vertigos' house the last person he expected to see was Joshua Tilpin.

One minute Charlie was holding the mirror in both hands, the next a magnetic force was dragging it away.

'NO!' cried Charlie, losing his grip.

The other boys ran up behind him but the mirror had flown into the road. There was a loud crack, and Joshua Tilpin bent to retrieve it. Charlie leapt towards him but Miss Chrystal, stepping out of nowhere, barred his way. Fixing him with her cold blue eyes, she hissed, 'The Mirror of Amoret will never be yours.'

Tancred and Lysander were already chasing Joshua down the road.

'They'll get him,' Charlie cried furiously.

Miss Chrystal shook her head. 'I don't think so,' she said airily. Then she ambled away with a smile, as though it was all just a silly game.

'You're a witch!' Charlie called after her. 'The worst kind.'

Miss Chrystal had turned a corner, and now Charlie had lost sight of his friends. 'I'm stupid, stupid, stupid!' He stamped his foot on the step.

'You weren't to know,' said Olivia. 'Who would have thought that little beast would turn up?'

'I should have been on my guard.' Charlie banged his fist against his forehead. 'They saw you at Kingdom's. They were bound to follow. What am I going to do?'

'Tancred and Lysander are big boys,' Mrs Vertigo said soothingly. 'Nice long legs. They're bound to catch the puny one.'

They waited. Waited and waited, never moving from the step. Twenty minutes later, Charlie saw Lysander and Tancred tramping back up the road. They looked exhausted. Charlie knew immediately that they had lost Joshua.

'We didn't lose him,' panted Tancred. 'We chased him to the park, but before we could catch him, a green figure slipped out of the trees, grabbed the mirror and vanished.'

'I felt like teaching the little squirt a lesson,' muttered Lysander. 'But what good would it have done?'

'The count will use it as soon as he can now,' Charlie said wretchedly. 'My mum could be waiting for him. She doesn't know what she's doing. By the time I get home she could be gone.'

'Hold on, Charlie,' said Gabriel. 'The mirror cracked when it fell on to the road. I heard it. Maybe it won't work.'

'I heard it too.' Olivia grabbed Charlie's arm. 'Don't give up, Charlie. If the mirror's broken, the shadow can't travel.'

'Maybe,' Charlie said gloomily.

They agreed to meet later at the Pets' Café. Animals would have to be collected, parents contacted, and another plan devised.

As the four boys walked down the road, Charlie noticed the large plastic bag Gabriel was carrying. In all the excitement the red cloak had been forgotten.

'Gabriel!' Charlie stopped dead. 'That cloak you were wearing . . . was it. . . .?'

The others came to a halt and Tancred said, 'You didn't have time to tell Charlie, Gabe.'

'Dad gave it to me,' Gabriel said with an awkward smile. 'He said I might find it useful. It's been in the family for ages, apparently.'

'But, Gabe, did the cloak tell you anything?' Charlie demanded.

'Well, yes, as a matter of fact.' Gabriel glanced at his watch. 'Look, I've got to dash, Mum's waiting for me at the library.'

'You're not going anywhere without us,' said Tancred.

'Not with that cloak,' Lysander added.

Charlie watched his three friends cross the road, still talking. When they got to the other side, they called, 'See you later!'

Charlie raised his thumb and ran home.

Number nine was eerily quiet. Charlie went upstairs and knocked on his uncle's door.

'Come in, Charlie!'

Uncle Paton looked over his spectacles as Charlie leapt into the room. 'Did you get it?'

Charlie stumbled over to his uncle's saggy armchair and dropped into it. 'We got it,' he said, 'and then we lost it.'

'What!' Paton tore off his spectacles and swivelled round from his desk. 'Please explain.'

As clearly and steadily as he could, Charlie recounted every detail of the sensational events, but when it came to the most important detail of all, he couldn't hide his fear, and his voice shook with emotion.

'You saw your father?' Paton leapt to his feet. 'And you say that, all this time, he's been in Bloor's Academy. A piano teacher called Mr Pilgrim? Whose depraved idea can it have been to keep him almost under our very noses?'

'Manfred's, I expect,' said Charlie dismally. 'Or Ezekiel's. Imagine, I talked to my very own father without knowing who he was. I bet they got a kick out of that.'

'Don't worry, Charlie. It's all over now,' Paton said briskly. 'We'll have him out of there in no time.'

'You don't seem to understand, Uncle Paton. He still doesn't know who he is. He's so weak, so nearly dead. If he gets out and finds Mum gone, then what's the use?' Charlie gave a terrible sigh. 'It's Mum we have to save first.'

Paton clapped a hand to his pocket. 'The spell!' he

declared. 'Idiot that I am. I forgot it.' He pulled a ragged scrap of parchment from his pocket.

'Spell?' said Charlie dubiously.

'Read it.' His uncle thrust the parchment into his hands.

Charlie looked at Skarpo's sweeping black script. He read the words once, twice and then, to help him make sense of it, he read the spell aloud.

> *'Look to the forest, if ye seek the Kinge, for he is*
>   *hidden there,*
> *His robes are now but autumn leaves, his teares like*
>   *ripened fruit,*
> *Blood red they fall and ne'er shall cease*
> *Untille his children, ten of them, with lesse than*
>   *twenty yeare,*
> *Shalle meete in harmonie*
> *And thrice they must walke, their fingers twined,*
> *Around the Kinge, around, around, untille his teares*
>   *are clear again,*
> *Teares to wake the wandering souls,*
> *To keep them safe and bring them home.'*

Charlie continued to stare at the spell as he said, 'It sounds as if the king is a tree.'

'There's no doubt of it,' his uncle agreed.

'Skarpo found this in Bartholomew's diary, but where did it come from?' said Charlie.

'From the descendants of someone who helped the king become what he is now,' said Paton.

'I think it was meant for the children who had to leave the castle, because the others were so evil.' Charlie looked up at his uncle.

'It was also meant for their descendants,' said Uncle Paton.

'And do you really think it could help my father?'

'It's all we have. And look at the words:

Teares to wake the wandering souls,

To keep them safe and bringe them home.'

'There are only seven of us. It says here, ten children must meet.'

'I've been thinking about that,' said his uncle. 'There's your little Chinese friend, for a start.'

'Naren!' Charlie exclaimed. 'She hasn't sent me a message for ages. I'll have to find her.'

'You also have to find the king,' his uncle reminded him.

An owl in danger

Charlie wanted to go and find Naren that very minute, but Uncle Paton insisted they discuss things calmly and sensibly.

The enchanter thought he had won; Miss Chrystal had revealed herself as a witch, so now she would hide herself away, before deciding on her next move.

'I believe you are safe for a while,' said Uncle Paton. 'The opposition think you're beaten. They won't be suspicious unless you act hastily. Go and find Naren, by all means, but take your time. Look a bit downhearted, if you can.'

'Easy,' said Charlie.

'And when you find the girl,' his uncle continued, 'tell her to come to the Pets'

Café at four o'clock tomorrow.'

'Not today?' asked Charlie. 'Shouldn't we do something now, as soon as possible?'

'Nothing is ready,' Paton waved his hand dismissively. He reminded Charlie that first the king would have to be found. The ruin was the most likely place to look, but it was vast, crumbling and overgrown. 'His robes are autumn leaves,' said Paton, 'so they will be red and gold. Not so difficult to see when all the other trees are bare. But a bird's eye view is what we need.'

'Emma!' said Charlie. 'She'll find the tree.'

'Of course, little Emma, the bird.'

'The king is supposed to be in a forest,' Charlie pointed out.

'There are trees in the ruin,' said his uncle, 'and there are few real forests left.' He began to pace round his untidy bed, wearing a deep frown of concentration.

Uncle Paton loved to take charge, and Charlie thought it sad that his uncle's exploding endowment prevented him from taking a bigger role in worldly affairs.

'I have it!' Uncle Paton swung round with a beam of triumph. 'It's all in there, Charlie.' He tapped his forehead. 'The plan. I'm afraid Mr Onimous will have to reveal his secret door to the other children, because that's the way

you'll have to go to reach the ruin – into the passage beneath the old wall.'

'Mr Onimous will never let anyone in there,' said Charlie. 'He's terrified that the wrong people will get to know about it. Suppose the Looms are in the café?'

'Our whiskery friend will have to be persuaded,' Uncle Paton said firmly. 'He'll also have to relax the rules about animals, just for a day. I'm sorry but I just can't stand having gerbils rooting about in my pockets.'

'You're coming too, Uncle P?'

'Most certainly. And I'm hoping that all the other parents will be there, too. Protection, Charlie. The more the better.'

'Animals are allergic to Mr Torsson,' said Charlie, entering into the spirit of things. 'They find him too turbulent.'

'No pets for Mr T, then. I wonder if Judge Sage could be persuaded. Now he would be an asset, and no mistake.'

'Lysander said the judge was at home today.'

'I'll give him a buzz. And the Silks, I'm sure they'll be up for it. Plenty of animals there.' Paton rubbed his hands together.

'We could get all the Gunns,' said Charlie eagerly. 'I know Fido's not endowed, but they're always keen to

take part, even in un-musical things.'

'Indeed, the Gunns.' Paton did a sort of tap dance.

'And Mrs Vertigo? Mr Vertigo's in South America, directing a very important movie.'

'Hm. She's a bit of a glamour puss, Mrs Vertigo,' Uncle Paton said doubtfully. 'She does rather attract attention.'

'But she's an actress,' argued Charlie. 'I know she could act dowdy, if you wanted her to.' He took a breath and added tentatively, 'And then there's Bartholomew Bloor.'

'Over to you, Charlie,' Paton said abruptly. 'I've no way of contacting him. You'd better be off now. And be here by five o'clock, please, or I'll come and fetch you, explosions or not. Perish those street lights.'

When Charlie left the house he felt so optimistic, he almost forgot to look miserable. He had to abandon the effort altogether when Benjamin and Runner Bean came racing up to him. Charlie was so happy to see them he gave a whoop of joy and grabbed Benjamin's arm.

'Where are you going?' Benjamin asked. 'Can I come? Please don't say no. Mum and Dad aren't working for the Bloors any more, you know.'

'I guessed,' said Charlie. 'I'm going to find someone a bit special.'

As they walked through the town, Charlie found

himself talking almost non-stop. And, in spite of Benjamin's wide surprised eyes, his nervous little skips and exclamations of horror, no one could have imagined the sensational events that Charlie was describing to him.

The afternoon sky was already growing dark. Flurries of sleet blew in their faces and by the time they reached the iron bridge an icy fog had drifted over the gorge, completely obliterating the wilderness on the other side. In his hurry to find Naren, Charlie had forgotten the danger.

'You'd better stay here,' he told Benjamin, 'or wait for me at the café. I don't want anything to happen to you.'

'Too late,' said Benjamin, as Runner Bean tore past them. 'Looks like he knows where he's going.'

'He does.' Charlie grinned. 'Come on, then.'

It took even longer than Charlie expected. Once again, the bridge was treacherous with icy dew. They walked in single file, Benjamin stepping carefully into Charlie's footprints, and both clinging tight to the rusty rail. When they got to the other side, Runner Bean led them straight to the little house in the clearing. Naren was about to go into the house with an armful of logs when she saw them. She threw down the logs, ran to Charlie and gave him a hug.

'This is Sunflower,' Charlie told Benjamin. 'And this is

my friend, Benjamin, who's Runner Bean's real master,' he told Naren.

Naren invited them into the house, but the door opened suddenly and Bartholomew Bloor stood there, looking very annoyed. 'I thought I told you not to come here again,' he said to Charlie. 'And you've brought someone with you – that's unforgivable.'

'I'm sorry, sir,' Charlie said lightly. 'I had to come because Naren's messages –'

'I told Naren to stop,' Bartholomew said impatiently. 'The shadow was becoming aware of your nightly conversations. I didn't want Naren's messages to betray our whereabouts.'

'I thought it was something like that. But, Mr Bloor, I had to come. You see, it's the spell that was in your diaries.'

'What spell?'

Charlie pulled the scrap of parchment from his pocket and passed it to the explorer. Benjamin was, by now, hopping from foot to foot and blowing on his hands to keep them warm. But Bartholomew didn't invite them into the house. He listened to Charlie's story impassively, looked at the spell, and then said, 'I will bring Naren, of course. I would do anything for your father.'

'And will you stay?' asked Charlie. 'My uncle Paton says

that if we fill the Pets' Café with parents, it will be a kind of protection.'

Bartholomew thrust the spell into Charlie's hands. 'Your uncle is full of fine ideas. He should have put them into action years ago, or your father wouldn't be where he is.'

'Don't say things like that about my uncle,' Charlie said furiously. 'I trust him more than anyone else in the world. You're a nasty, unforgiving person, Mr Bloor, just like the rest of your family. If you don't want to help us, suit yourself. We can do without you.'

A series of curious expressions fleetingly crossed Bartholomew's face: disbelief, anger and pure shock. And last of all, a kind of terror.

Before the explorer could say another word, Charlie grabbed Benjamin's arm and dragged him away from the cottage.

'Wow, Charlie! How could you say those things?' whispered Benjamin.

'I don't know,' Charlie admitted. 'He's just so mean, that man. I hope I haven't blown it.'

When they got to the gate, Charlie looked back. The explorer had gone but Naren was standing in the porch. She gave Charlie a cheerful wave and called, 'I'll be there, Charlie. Four o'clock!'

The boys waved back and Runner Bean gave a hearty farewell bark.

They had a few scares on their second crossing of the bridge. Twice Benjamin slipped on to his knees, and then, when they were almost on the bank, Charlie lost his footing altogether. He clutched the railing with one hand, while Runner Bean grabbed his sleeve in his mouth and hauled him back again.

'Phew! I'm glad Runner came,' said Charlie, crawling on to the wet grass.

They sat on the bank for a few minutes, telling each other how lucky they were to be alive. But Runner Bean was eager to be off again. Someone had mentioned the Pets' Café and he knew that Mrs Onimous would give him a treat. She'd probably smother him in kisses as well, but it was a price worth paying for a few Nut-Pom sticks.

It was dark when Runner Bean raced the two boys down Frog Street. Norton-the-bouncer was just closing the door of the Pets' Café, but he opened it again when Charlie called out to him.

'Your friends were here,' said Norton, giving Runner Bean a pat, 'the whole ruddy lot of them. They gave up waiting for you. It's closing time, young Charlie.'

'Can we come in, just for a moment?' begged Charlie.

'Be quick about it, then.' Norton frowned over Charlie's head. 'And who's this, coming down here like the prophet of doom?'

Charlie looked back to see Uncle Paton striding towards them. He was wearing dark glasses and a large black fedora, and he kept his eyes on the ground as he paced down the cobbled alley.

'It's my uncle,' Charlie said with relief.

'The power-booster? Better turn the lights off then.' Norton reached for the light switch and the café was plunged into darkness.

'Ah, there you are, Charlie. It *is* you, isn't it?' said Uncle Paton, stepping into the café. 'I can't see a thing.'

'Just as well,' said Norton.

'Uh!' Paton jumped. He hadn't seen the bouncer standing behind the door. 'I've come to see Mr Onimous on very important business,' he said, recovering his dignity.

'I'd better warn him then.' Norton could be heard banging into tables as he made his way though the dark café. 'Ow!' he grunted as he walked into the counter. 'Mr Onimous,' he called. 'Customer to see you. Mr Yewbeam, the you-know-what.'

A whisker-thin strip of light above the kitchen door was immediately extinguished and, a few seconds later, Mr

Onimous appeared, carrying a tall candelabra with two candles flickering at the top.

'What can I do for you, Mr Paton?' asked Mr Onimous, whose whiskery face could just be seen peeping over the counter.

'Good evening, Orvil,' said Uncle Paton, removing his dark glasses. 'I – that is, we,' he glanced at Charlie, 'have something of the utmost importance to discuss with you.'

'You'd better come into the kitchen, then.' Mr Onimous held the candelabra as high as he could to light their way across the room.

'Can I come too?' asked Benjamin diffidently. Runner Bean added a plaintive whine, treats being on his mind.

'Ah, Benjamin Brown. I'd forgotten.' Uncle Paton gave the boy a cool stare.

'Please! My parents aren't spying for Mr Bloor any more,' Benjamin said in a rush. 'Mr Ezekiel wouldn't pay them, and Dad had a terrible row with him, and Mum said she'd never speak to him again. Mr Ezekiel, I mean, not Dad.'

'I'm very glad to hear it,' said Paton. 'Of course you may join us.'

A few minutes later they were all three sitting round the Onimouses' ample kitchen table, drinking tea and eating lemon curd tarts. Runner Bean was not disappointed. Mrs

Onimous gave him a whole bowl of chocolate beef bars, to make up for the ten kisses he'd endured. Though with little Una about he was having to put up with a rather rough grooming.

Uncle Paton came straight to the point. He held nothing back in his long explanation of why the endowed children must use the secret door into the castle. Charlie even produced the scrap of parchment as a further persuasion.

The Onimouses listened in spellbound silence and when all that could be said had been said, Mr Onimous shook his furry head in wonder.

'Those other kids, your friends, they were talking about the king,' said the little man, 'but we couldn't get the whole picture. This bit of parchment – this spell, or whatever it is – it explains it all, doesn't it? I've never relaxed the rules before, but this is an exception. As for the door, well, I can see we have no option. As long as all the kids keep their mouths shut about it.'

'They will,' said Charlie fervently.

'I knew our little Una would come in handy,' said Mrs Onimous, grabbing the little girl and giving her a squeeze.

'Give over,' giggled Una, 'or I'll lose me lunch.'

'Bless her,' said Mr Onimous, 'she can't help it.' He

closed his eyes and counted the number of Charlie's friends on his fingers, muttering the names of each one in turn. When he came to Una, he opened his eyes and said, 'Even with the Chinese girl, there's only nine. How are we going to find ten, Mr Paton?'

'Ah,' said Paton. 'That I wouldn't know.'

A hush fell over the room. Even Una was silenced by the look of fierce concentration on everyone's face.

All at once, Mr Onimous leaned forward and said, 'If I may be so bold, I'm not less than twenty years, but I am awful small. D'you think I would do?'

They all stared at the small, furry little man, and then Uncle Paton said, 'Orvil, I think you should give it a go. For the life of me I can't imagine where we're going to find another child of the Red King under twenty.' He rose from the table. 'Orvil, Onoria, I thank you for your hospitality. Boys, we must be on our way.'

'It's been a pleasure as always, Mr Paton,' said Mr Onimous. 'But I nearly forgot something. The bird-girl, Emma, said she was going to look for the white horse tonight.'

'The white horse?' Charlie frowned.

Mr Onimous shrugged. 'She said the horse would know where the king was.'

Charlie uttered a cry of understanding. 'The white horse

is the queen. She's bound to be close to the king.'

'I do hope the dear girl will be safe,' Paton said anxiously.

'Nothing we can do about it now.' Mr Onimous lifted the candelabra and led his visitors out of the kitchen and through the dark café.

Norton-the-bouncer had already gone home, and Mr Onimous could be heard locking and bolting his door, as Uncle Paton, the two boys and Runner Bean made their way up Frog Street.

A light was on in the sitting room at number nine. Believing that Grandma Bone was watching TV, Charlie and his uncle avoided the room. They went straight to the kitchen where they immediately lit several candles.

'Better not talk about tomorrow,' Uncle Paton warned, as he set about making a plate of ham sandwiches.

Charlie nodded. He poured himself a glass of milk and sat at the table. The figure in the doorway took him by surprise and he gave a loud yell, spilling some of the milk.

'What the –?' Uncle Paton turned to the door. 'Amy?' he said. 'Is that you?'

Charlie's mother stepped into the room. Even in candlelight her skin looked icy white. Her hair was as colourless as thistledown and only a hint of blue showed in her huge pale eyes. Her ghostly appearance was

emphasised by a long white gown with a thread of silver at the hem.

'Mum,' Charlie said, with a catch in his voice. 'I thought you were out.'

'Mr Noble was very busy today.' She gave a dreamy smile. 'But tomorrow he's going to take me somewhere wonderful.'

'Care for a sandwich, Amy?' Paton asked in a loud voice.

'No thank you.' She twisted the huge emerald ring on her finger. 'I'm not at all hungry these days.'

'You look as if you haven't eaten for weeks,' said Paton, hoping his gruff tone would drag Amy back to reality.

But Charlie's mother just smiled. 'Don't be silly,' she giggled. 'I'm going to get married. How about that?'

Charlie's mouth fell open, but he couldn't speak. Even Uncle Paton seemed lost for words. They watched Amy drift away, heard her mount the stairs and then listened to a door closing at the top of the house.

'She didn't even look in on Maisie,' Charlie said miserably.

'Bear up, dear boy,' Uncle Paton squeezed his shoulder. 'Tomorrow the Red King will have his day!'

Not far from Filbert Street, Emma and Miss Ingledew were

standing outside the bookshop. The temperature was falling fast; already the cobbles were dusted with frost. The moon was rising over the cathedral and an early star shone in the deep blue sky.

'I wish you didn't have to do this.' Miss Ingledew laid a hand on Emma's blonde head. 'You will take care.'

'I will, Auntie. Gabriel says the king is a tree. He saw it when he put on the cloak. It's all up to me now. I feel so – I don't know – excited, I suppose. I know I'll find them.' Emma gave her aunt a quick kiss. 'I'm going now. Don't worry.' She began to run down the narrow alley that led away from the square.

In a dark corner, where two trees grew close to the wall of the city library, Emma stood very still and thought of a bird. She had decided to take the form of a barn owl, a bird she considered to be the most beautiful of all night owls. Her fingers tingled as they gradually changed into feathers, and she couldn't restrain a hoot of joy when her creamy wings lifted her into the air.

The sky had looked so calm, but once Emma was flying she was hit by a wave of turbulence. Someone was sending a surge of fury through the air. Tracing the path of anger to its source, Emma found herself outside a window at the very top of Kingdom's store.

She perched on the sill and cautiously peeped inside. A man in a green robe paced across an ocean of white fur. Emma shivered. The man held a beautiful mirror; its gold frame was studded with jewels but the glass itself was scarred by a crack that ran from top to bottom. The man stopped and looked at a painting on the wall behind him. The painting showed a strange landscape of dark mountains and tall, shadowy towers. A place where nightmares begin, thought Emma. The man turned the mirror to face the painting. He chanted in a deep, toneless voice. Suddenly he cursed the mirror and swung round, flinging it against the wall.

The owl gave a hoot of surprise and flew away.

Did he see me? Emma wondered. Did he know who I was?

She flew on, tilting dangerously through the violent night air. It took all her strength to avoid being thrown against tall trees and telegraph wires, but, at last, she was flying over the garden of Bloor's Academy. Below her, she could see the walls of the ruined castle. And then, with a cry of pain, she found herself falling. A stone had hit the owl's snowy neck and she dropped to the ground, her wings spread against the earth, her head twisted to the sky.

A few metres away from her stood Joshua Tilpin and

someone in a black hooded cloak. Joshua was clutching a catapult.

'Look at the owl,' said Joshua. 'Will our ancestor be pleased, Mother?'

'Very pleased.' The woman's hood fell back.

Emma's slanting owl eyes blinked as she recognised Miss Chrystal.

'It's not dead, but it soon will be.' Joshua leapt forward and Emma closed her eyes.

But the blow she expected never came. Instead she heard a low growl, and then a soft thump as a four-footed creature landed behind her. She could feel its warm breath on her back, and then the grow turned into a threatening snarl.

'Good beast,' said Miss Chrystal in a commanding tone. 'Give us the owl.'

The beast continued to snarl, and when Joshua attempted a second move, it leapt over the owl and rushed at Joshua, who fled from the scene, screaming with fear.

When Emma opened her eyes again, the boy and the witch had gone. But the beast sat close by, beneath the tree. It was a dreadful-looking creature, with a humped back and luminous yellow eyes.

'Asa?' Emma called softly. 'Asa, is it you?'

The beast whined softly and ran into the undergrowth.

Like every frightened creature, Emma lay as still as possible, until she was sure the beast was really gone. When at last she tried to move, she found that she was not injured at all. Shock had brought her down. She stood up, lifted her wings and soared into the sky. Keeping her eyes trained on the ground, she sailed over the ruined castle until a movement caught her eye. A white horse was trotting round a large, circular glade. Emma flew down and perched on a wall close to the horse. When she saw the owl, the white horse came to a halt and stared anxiously at the bird.

'Your Majesty.' Emma bowed her head. 'I need your help.'

'Bird-child!' The queen trotted over to Emma. 'How good it is to see you. How can I help?'

'I'm looking for the king,' said Emma.

'Then you have found him.' The queen moved aside and Emma saw that a large tree grew in the centre of the glade. At first it had seemed a dark and shapeless tower but, all at once, colour seeped into it, and Emma found herself gazing at a tree of astonishing beauty. Its leaves were red and gold, and when they moved in the night air they seemed to burn with a fiery light. From its small glistening crown, the branches grew in ever-widening

waves until, close to the ground, the base of its broad trunk could be seen – a trunk that was furrowed with streams of wine-dark liquid.

'Is he wounded?' asked Emma, shivering at the sight of the shining red streams.

'He is weeping for his lost children,' said the queen. 'The five who left and never returned.'

Emma ruffled her pale owl feathers, hoping a cure for the king's sadness could be found. 'Will the king be here tomorrow?' she asked. 'A friend of mine needs his help.'

'The king will be here,' the queen replied.

'Thank you, Your Majesty.' Emma lifted into the air and hovered anxiously above the queen. 'I must go now. My aunt worries.'

'Naturally.' The queen walked closer to the tree. 'Go home, bird-child. Be safe.'

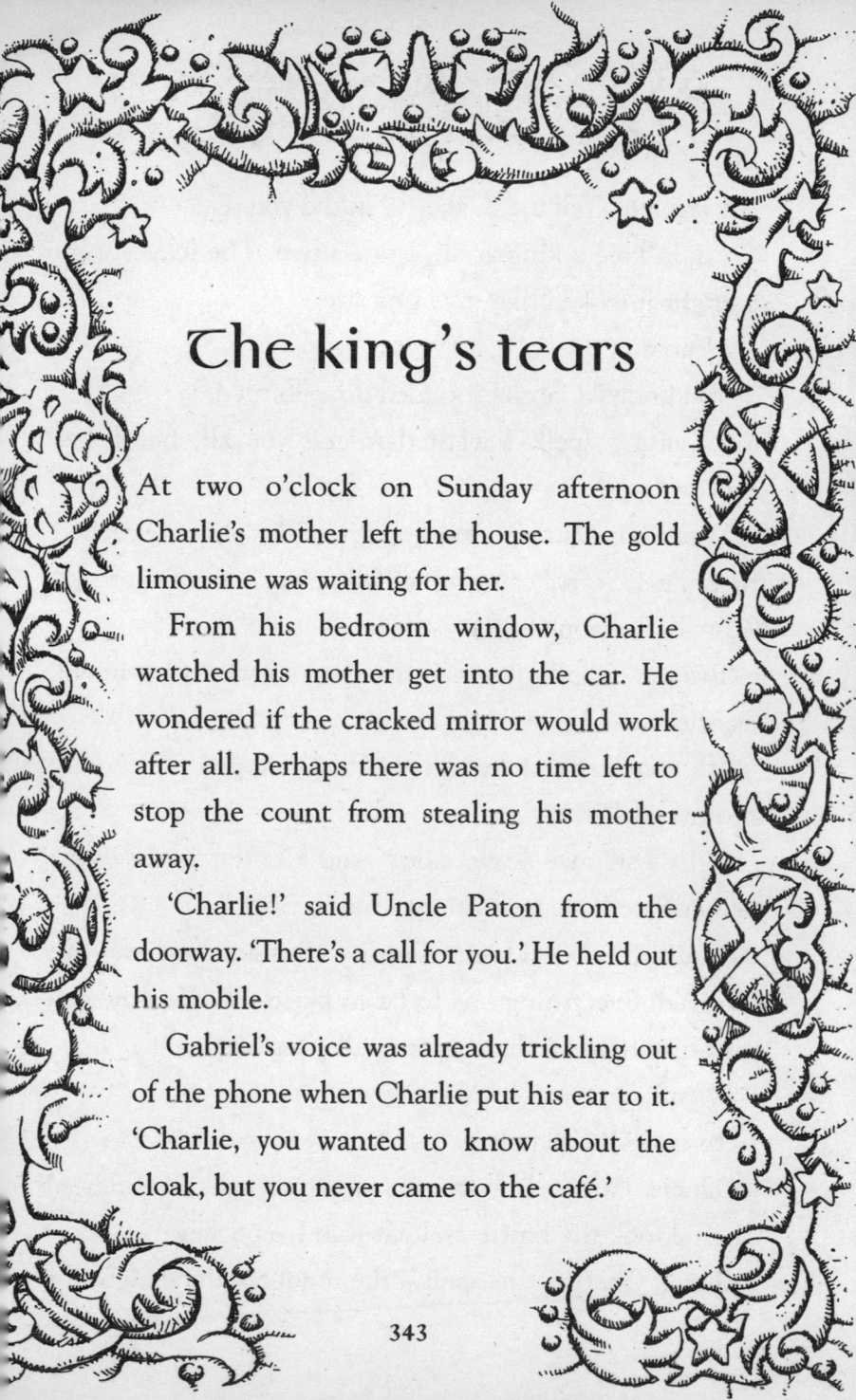

The king's tears

At two o'clock on Sunday afternoon Charlie's mother left the house. The gold limousine was waiting for her.

From his bedroom window, Charlie watched his mother get into the car. He wondered if the cracked mirror would work after all. Perhaps there was no time left to stop the count from stealing his mother away.

'Charlie!' said Uncle Paton from the doorway. 'There's a call for you.' He held out his mobile.

Gabriel's voice was already trickling out of the phone when Charlie put his ear to it. 'Charlie, you wanted to know about the cloak, but you never came to the café.'

'I was late. Tell me, Gabe, what did you see?'

'I didn't see a king at all, I saw a tree. The leaves were so bright it looked like it was on fire.'

'I know.'

'You know?' Gabriel sounded disappointed.

'I found a spell. I wanted to tell you all, but I was too late.'

There was a sudden bang and Charlie almost dropped the phone. 'Sorry,' came a muffled voice. 'Gerbil's got out. Must go. See you at four.'

'Bye . . .' Charlie handed the phone back to his uncle. 'Gabriel saw a tree.'

'It's conclusive then.' Uncle Paton slipped the mobile into his pocket.

'Why can't we leave now?' said Charlie impatiently. 'Why do we have to wait until four o'clock?'

'Sunset,' said Uncle Paton. 'Besides, others are involved. Everything has to be in place. By the way, you must take this.' He held up a small glass bottle.

'Why?'

'In case all else fails.'

'Uncle Paton, I wish you wouldn't talk in riddles.' Charlie took the bottle and put it in his pocket.

'Look, Charlie, this spell – the numbers aren't right for

a start. Mr Onimous is well over twenty years – it might not work as we hope.' Uncle Paton shrugged. 'Just keep that bottle safe. For the tears.'

Charlie spent the next hour in an agony of suspense. At last he could stand it no longer and rapped loudly on his uncle's door, shouting, 'Can't we go now, Uncle P?'

Grandma Bone leaned out of the bathroom and demanded to know what all the fuss was about. Charlie had almost forgotten his grandmother's existence and her sudden appearance gave him quite a shock.

'S-sorry, Grandma,' Charlie stuttered. 'Uncle and me were just going for a walk.'

'At this time of day? Don't be silly,' said Grandma Bone.

Uncle Paton opened his door and said, 'He's not being silly. We are going to the park.'

'More fool you,' said his sister. 'You're bound to have an accident. By the way,' she went on, 'I've arranged for Maisie to be transferred.'

'Transferred!' cried Charlie. 'Where to?'

'I can't have her cluttering up the bathroom any longer,' was all Grandma Bone would say.

'Grizelda!' roared Paton. 'How dare you speak of Maisie in that way. She's a very precious person. What have you arranged? Tell me immediately.'

'My! We are on our high horse today,' sneered Grandma Bone. 'If you must know, that nice Mr Weedon has agreed to come here tomorrow to pick Maisie up. He'll bring a body bag to prevent drips on the carpet, and then he'll whisk Maisie off to,' she paused dramatically, 'somewhere else.'

'He will do no such thing,' Paton declared. 'If Weedon so much as touches our Maisie, I'll throw him downstairs.'

'A forlorn hope,' said Grandma Bone. 'He's got muscles like iron.' She gave a mocking smile and sailed into her room.

Paton stood speechless and seething, his arms stiff at his sides and his fists working overtime.

'Come on, Uncle.' Charlie plucked at his uncle's sleeve. 'Let's go.'

Before they left the house, Charlie took the white moth to the bathroom and let it fly wherever it wanted. It came to rest on Maisie's frozen curls.

'Keep her safe,' Charlie told the moth.

As they walked through the deserted Sunday city, Charlie felt as though his whole world was tumbling down about his ears. If the spell came to nothing, then where would he be?

The mood at the Pets' Café lifted his spirits

considerably. Every table was occupied and the café was full of eager expectant chatter. The Onimouses were having a hard time getting everyone served; they whizzed along behind the counter, refilling bowls, serving pets who needed special diets, and pouring tea.

The large Gunn family had taken over a whole table. They had even brought musical instruments, Charlie observed. Fidelio beckoned him over and said, 'We thought we'd entertain everyone while you lot are doing whatever you've got to do – you know.'

'Brilliant idea!' said Charlie, looking round the café. 'I can't see any Looms.'

'I heard they were having trouble with their dogs,' said Fidelio. He turned to his youngest sister, Mimi, who'd begun to tune her violin. 'Not yet, Mimi! Wish Charlie good luck!'

When they heard this, every member of the Gunn family sang, 'Good luck, Charlie Bone!'

Several customers turned to look in Charlie's direction. He blushed, retreated from the Gunns' overcrowded table and sat down between Benjamin and Mrs Brown.

'Even Lysander's dad has come,' Benjamin told Charlie. 'Look, Homer's sitting on his head.'

Charlie was impressed, especially when the judge gave

Uncle Paton a friendly nod as he passed. If other customers were surprised by the high turnout they didn't show it, at least not until Tancred and his parents arrived. As soon as Mr Torsson set foot in the café, an icy blast sent every pet scurrying for cover.

'Sorry!' boomed Mr Torsson. 'Nothing personal. Can't help it.' He sat beside the judge, whom he knew quite well, while his wife squeezed in beside Mrs Sage. Tancred shared a chair with Lysander.

Billy had joined the Silks' table and Rembrandt, sitting in the centre, was enjoying the attention of several female gerbils.

Mrs Vertigo had almost overdone the dowdiness. In a grey wig, tatty brown mac, and with a pale scrubbed face, she would have been unrecognisable if Olivia hadn't been with her. Miss Ingledew gave a little start of surprise when she realised who was sitting next to her.

'I don't know what you told everyone,' Miss Ingledew whispered to Paton, as he took the chair on her other side, 'but it's certainly done the trick.'

Paton winked and briefly squeezed her hand.

Charlie searched the room for Naren. There was no sign of her. He darted a desperate look at his uncle and shook his head.

'What's wrong?' Mrs Vertigo asked in an elderly treble.

'I think Charlie is trying to tell me that someone we hoped might have come, hasn't,' said Paton. 'It doesn't surprise me, however.' He was looking at the door when he said this and an expression of relief and surprise crossed his face when Bartholomew Bloor walked in. He was followed by Naren and her mother.

Bartholomew saw Paton at once. You could hardly miss a man in dark glasses who was a head taller than everyone else. The explorer walked straight over to Paton and said gruffly, 'Paton, I would like to introduce my wife, Meng, and my daughter, Naren.'

Paton stood up and everyone shook hands.

'I would also like to apologise,' Bartholomew went on, a little awkwardly. 'Charlie made me take a good look at myself and I want you to know that I am *not* like the rest of my family.'

'Of course you are not,' said Paton, grasping Bartholomew's hand in both of his.

Bartholomew lowered his voice and said, 'Now then, what are we supposed to do while the children are – otherwise engaged?'

'Nothing, Bart,' said Paton. 'Just be alert. I think we should start quite soon.' He looked at his watch and then

spoke to Naren. 'My dear, would you go over to Charlie and tell him, very quietly, that it is time? Then go with him, up to the counter. He'll know what to do next.'

'Yes, Mr Yewbeam.' With an eager smile, Naren made her way over to Charlie and whispered, 'It's time.'

Charlie stood up and Benjamin said, 'Good luck, Charlie!'

As Charlie and Naren walked towards the counter, Charlie tapped Tancred and Lysander on the shoulder. The two boys gave no sign that they had felt anything, but a minute after Charlie and Naren had disappeared round the counter, they left their table and followed, Tancred poking Billy and Gabriel in the back as he walked behind them.

The Onimouses' kitchen gradually filled with endowed children. Not a word was said. Every one of them was aware that this was, perhaps, the most important day of their lives.

Mrs Onimous had given Una a cup of soothing camomile tea and the little girl was much calmer than usual, though her dark eyes sparkled with anticipation.

Charlie noticed several of the others glancing curiously at Naren and he quickly introduced her as a friend who'd been in hiding. 'She has a pretty amazing talent too,' he added.

When all nine children were assembled, Mr Onimous cleared his throat and made a small speech. 'Ahem! We all know why we are here, but before we go any further, I'd just like to say that I am now going to show you a place that has remained secret for many centuries. It is a tunnel, known only to my family, with the exception of Charlie and Billy. It leads into the Red Castle. I would ask you, please, to keep it a secret. Have I your words on this?'

Everyone earnestly murmured, 'Yes, sir.'

'Thank you. I shall lead the way, with Una. I suggest the rest of you walk in single file.' Mr Onimous picked up a lantern from the table and made for a small door at the other end of the kitchen.

'Excuse me,' called Tancred. 'But does anyone know where we're going once we're in the ruin?'

'Yes,' Emma said calmly. 'There are two old walls, with room for maybe two people between them. They go very straight for about half a mile, and then they go round and round, like a snail shell; the king is in a glade at the very end.'

At the mention of the king, everyone moved solemnly into line. Mr Onimous opened the door and Charlie, following right behind, found himself in the familiar store-room. When they reached the cavern where a sack of

potatoes hid the secret door, Mr Onimous waited until all the children had crowded into the small, musty room.

'We are about to enter the tunnel,' Mr Onimous said, almost in a whisper. 'Be prepared. It is very dark, it is damp, it is a little airless. It goes a very long way. Lysander, my man, I suggest you bring up the rear, with Tancred. You others can go anywhere in the middle. Lysander will close the door when you are all through. Are we ready?'

Everyone nodded. A few said, 'Yes, sir.'

Mr Onimous hauled a large sack away from the wall, revealing a very low and ancient door. The little man reached inside his woolly jacket and brought out a small key on a gold chain. Fitting the key to the lock, he turned it once and the door swung inwards with a loud creak. It was no higher than Mr Onimous and the taller boys had to bend their heads to get through it.

Holding the lantern as high as he could, Mr Onimous clutched Una's hand and led the way forward. Emma walked behind them, ready to give instructions once they were in the ruin. Naren followed Emma, and Billy slipped in behind Naren. Then came Charlie, followed by Olivia, Gabriel and Tancred. Lysander brought up the rear.

Everything Mr Onimous had said about the tunnel proved to be true; but it was darker, damper and stuffier

than anyone had expected. Gabriel began to cough. Charlie took deep breaths and steadied himself against the damp wall. Behind him, Olivia gave a little cry as she tripped on a stone, bumped into Charlie and tumbled to the ground.

'I can't see a thing,' Olivia moaned.

'You just couldn't resist wearing those pointy boots, could you?' said Charlie, hauling her to her feet.

The lantern light was very distant now, and those at the back began to stumble into each other. Charlie was about to change places with Olivia when Billy turned round and handed him a lighted candle.

'Pass it down,' Billy whispered. 'I've got five.'

Charlie gave the candle to Olivia, whispering, 'Pass it on.'

When all five candles were held aloft it was as though the tunnel were filled with moonlight. But more than brightness, the candles brought comfort to the anxious children; the air seemed fresher, their feet lighter and even though they had to go almost another mile, the time passed very quickly.

They emerged, at last, into a wood of thin birch trees. Straight ahead were the two walls.

'No running,' Mr Onimous commanded. 'Let's be careful now.'

The path between the walls began in the wood, but in a few paces they were out of the trees and walking beneath a blue sky streaked with evening clouds.

'Sunset,' Charlie said to himself.

Everyone had fallen silent again. The only sound came from the ground as they marched over the ancient stone pathway. When they began to round the twisting corners of the snail shell, Charlie's heart beat so wildly he had to press his hand over it. Beside him, Emma said, 'Soon.'

And then they were there.

The queen was waiting for them beside the tree. She whinnied softly and trotted towards them, tossing her head in greeting. And then she walked away and left them with the king.

They stood before the towering, fiery tree with wide eyes and upturned faces, but words failed them. They saw the dark streams coursing down the trunk and, instinctively, they moved closer.

Charlie had memorised the spell, word for word. He took Billy's hand, then Naren's and began to murmur the lines. The others linked hands but they all had to bend under the sweeping branches before they could make an unbroken ring.

'Three times,' Charlie whispered. 'Around the king, around, around until his tears are clear again.'

They circled the tree, their faces very grave now, each one of them gazing at the blood-red tears.

Once, twice, three times. Around the tree, around and around. When they had completed three circles, Charlie tugged Billy's hand and moved faster.

'We've done it three times,' said Billy.

'Keep going,' said Charlie desperately.

The king's tears were as dark as ever, but Charlie wouldn't give up. They spun round the tree until they began to feel dizzy. And then, with brimming eyes, Mr Onimous broke the ring, crying, 'It's no good, kids. It's me. I'm the trouble. How could anyone believe I was less than twenty years? Whoever made that spell meant every word to be obeyed.'

The empty space between Olivia and Emma held everyone's gaze, and yet no one else could bring themselves to break the link. They stood beneath the tree while Mr Onimous sobbed into his hands and the sky gradually filled with dark clouds. It grew so shadowy under the spreading branches they could barely see each other's faces. But something held them there.

The tall grass at the edge of the glade rustled and

shivered, although there was no wind. Something crawled out of the grass and stood up.

'The beast,' said Mr Onimous, his voice shaking with dread.

'Asa,' said Charlie under his breath.

It came towards the circle, a shadowy, humped and hideous creature. No one moved. The beast walked into the empty place between the two girls, and Emma, with her heart in her mouth, put her hand on the beast's head. Olivia, staring at Emma, speechlessly began to do the same.

The others watched in astonishment as the beast allowed the girls to curl their fingers into its long, coarse hair. The circle was complete again.

Without a word, the ring of children began to move, and the beast moved with them. Around the king, around and around.

Charlie's eyes were fixed on the scarred trunk. The blood-red tears ran faster; they splashed on to the damp earth, and then trickled away in thin, glittering strands.

The children began a second round. The grey bark was soaked in dark streams and a pool began to form at the base of the tree.

Around the king, around and around.

They began their third walk. And this time Charlie tore his gaze away from the dreadful tears. They wouldn't stop. They would flow on forever, Charlie thought, until the ring of children stood knee-deep in a crimson pond.

The tears were now falling so fast they made the air hum and the branches sigh. The breeze became a mighty wind, streaming into the children's faces, tugging their hair and blowing through their winter clothes. A cold, clean, rapturous wind that sounded like ancient music.

'Look, Charlie! Look!' cried Billy.

Charlie was too afraid to look. A cold droplet splashed on to his face.

'Look! Look! Look!' Other voices joined Billy's.

Charlie dragged his gaze back to the tree. Rain poured through the branches and ran down the grey trunk. The deep scars were now an icy white, the tears that washed them pure, clear water.

The children's hands fell to their sides. They looked up through the branches and the wind covered their faces in red and gold leaves. The washed bark shone a pearly grey as the wind carried the king's autumn robe away. Leaves sailed through the air like dancing flames, over the castle walls, over the river, over the houses – red and gold clouds that covered the city: roofs and

gardens, alleys and roads, in the depth of winter a carpet of autumn gold.

In a luxury apartment at the top of Kingdom's store, Amy Bone stared at her finger in horror. She opened the window, tore off her emerald ring and flung it at the sky.

'N-o-o-o!' roared the enchanter. But a cloud of bright leaves blew into the room and swept him through the window – a ball of green tumbleweed licked by scarlet flames.

Amy heaved a deep sigh, closed the window and left the store.

At number nine Filbert Street, Maisie Jones, fully dressed, sat up in the bath. A white moth with silver-tipped wings sat on her knees.

'My word!' Maisie said to the moth. 'Who left the window open?' For she was covered in leaves.

Leaves even found their way into Bloor's Academy. Helped by the wild wind, they forced open the great door and rushed into the hall. They whirled up the ancient stairs, and rustled down the passages, tapping on walls, whistling through cracks and slipping under doors.

'Stop them! Stop them!' shrieked old Ezekiel as he tried to wheel himself against the tide of leaves.

'What's happening?' Dr Bloor demanded, looking at his son.

'How should I know? We'd better stay where we are.' Manfred seized Ezekiel's wheelchair, pushed him into Dr Bloor's study and bolted the door. 'They can't get us now,' he said, rubbing his hands together until the sparks flew.

At the top of the Music Tower, Mr Pilgrim watched leaves dance like fireflies outside his window. Names stirred at the back of his mind. He struggled to remember them. He felt he was swimming up through deep, dark water. He saw a face. And then it was gone.

Outside the Pets' Café, parents and children had gathered in the open air to watch the fiery leaves stream through the sky.

Bartholomew Bloor was about to slip away with his family when Charlie caught him by the arm. 'Thank you, Mr Bloor,' he said. 'It was the spell in your diary that did it.'

'Did what, Charlie?' said the explorer. 'Better find out what's happened before you thank me.'

'OK. But goodnight anyway!'

This time Bartholomew smiled. 'Goodnight, Charlie.'

When he strode away, Naren skipped round and waved to Charlie. 'He's not so bad,' she called. 'See you, Charlie Bone!'

Other families were now hurrying away, the children still in very high spirits, their parents pleased, but eager for life to return to normal. A task had been completed, a wish fulfilled, but until Charlie Bone got home, no one would know the outcome.

Promising to call every one of his friends with good news or bad, Charlie and Uncle Paton set off for number nine.

As soon as they saw the candles lined up on the kitchen windowsill, they knew that a change had taken place. Grandma Bone would never have been so considerate. Charlie rushed up the steps, with his uncle striding behind.

They found Amy and Maisie having a nice cup of tea.

'Where have you been?' Charlie's mother hugged him tight. 'I was so worried.'

He didn't ask her where she had been. He knew she would never be able to tell him. 'Good to see you, Mum,' he murmured.

'I don't know what's happened to the weather,' said Maisie, 'but I feel awful queer. It's so hot in here.'

'It is NOT hot!' Grandma Bone shouted from the hall. 'It is ruddy well freezing. Someone tell that woman she's mad.'

'I wouldn't dream of it, Grizelda,' said Paton. 'I find it absolutely boiling.'

The kitchen erupted with joyful laughter, while

360

Grandma Bone stomped back to the sitting room and slammed the door.

Maisie had managed to make a large jam sponge – quite a feat for someone whose temperature an hour ago had been well below freezing.

The four of them sat down to an almost normal family tea, and then, when Paton judged the time was right, he took Amy's hand and said, very gently, 'Amy, we have found your husband.'

'Lyell?' Amy's hand flew to her heart. 'How?'

With Charlie's help, Paton told her everything that he thought she should know. How Lyell had been hypnotised by Manfred Bloor, at the height of his dreadful childish powers. And how Charlie had found his father with the help of the Mirror of Amoret. The enchanter was not mentioned by either Paton or Charlie and, for the time being, they thought it best not to speak of Maisie's deep-freezing.

'Will he wake up?' asked Amy. 'What shall we do?'

'I think he may be very close to waking,' Paton said solemnly. 'But something more might have to be done. After all, it's been ten years.'

Amy stood up. 'I must go to him, now.'

'No,' said Paton. 'Not yet. Lyell was hypnotised on the stroke of twelve. We must wait until it's close to midnight.

The cathedral clock will help to wake him. But there's something else.' He turned to Charlie and asked quietly, 'The king's tears?'

'I've got them,' said Charlie.

'And Amy,' Paton took her left hand. 'Could I ask you to put on your rings?'

Amy stared at her bare fingers. 'However did they come off?' She ran upstairs.

At ten minutes past eleven, Grandma Bone was snoozing in front of the television when a noise from the hall woke her up. She found Amy and Charlie putting on their boots and coats. It had started to snow again.

'Where are you two going at this hour?' Grandma Bone demanded.

Paton came out of the kitchen and said, 'We've found your son, Grizelda.'

Grandma Bone gave a stifled cry and stared at Paton in horror. Her mouth fell open and she clutched the doorframe.

Paton walked up to her. 'You hid him from us very well. What diabolical cunning it was, to keep him almost under our very noses. Well, we know where he is now, and Amy and Charlie are going to bring him home.'

Grandma Bone staggered back and dropped into a chair. 'I see,' she whispered.

Leopards!

The snow began to fall faster as Amy and Charlie walked towards Bloor's Academy.

'Real snow,' said Charlie, holding out his hand to catch the flakes. 'Not Tancred's magical stuff.'

Amy laughed. 'Come on, Charlie. We'd better run before we're buried.'

They had decided to knock until the Bloors let them in, but when they crossed the courtyard they saw that the tall doors were wide open. Leaves fluttered round the hall and snow lay on the flagstones. Light streamed into the courtyard through the stained glass windows of the chapel. Someone was playing the organ.

Taking his mother's hand, Charlie led her

round to the chapel entrance. Red and gold leaves drifted round the open doors; inside the chapel they floated in the air like brightly coloured butterflies. Lyell Bone was playing the organ at the far end.

Charlie's mother ran down the aisle, calling her husband's name. He looked up but gave no sign of recognition. Charlie followed his mother. They stood side by side while Lyell stared at them in bewilderment. 'Do I know you?' he asked.

The cathedral clock began to strike twelve. Charlie took out the small glass bottle. He uncorked the top and held it out to his father.

'For me?' Lyell frowned at the bottle. 'What should I do with it?'

Charlie wasn't sure. He was about to tell his father to pour the water into his palm, when a figure stepped out from behind the organ and, with a yell of triumph, knocked the bottle out of Charlie's hand.

'There!' Manfred kicked the broken bottle across the floor. 'That's put an end to your little game, Charlie Bone!'

The smile suddenly left Manfred's face and he stared in horror at the piles of drifting leaves. They had, somehow, become three huge cats. At first glance, their coats appeared to be dappled with the shadows of floating leaves,

but as they moved closer, it became clear that their spots were no mere shadows. The cats were leopards. The three bright creatures ran down the aisle, with their golden eyes fixed on Manfred.

Whimpering in terror, Manfred tore round the pews, pursued by the leopards. With thunderous roars they chased him out of the chapel and then, above the midnight chimes, there came a single, dreadful scream – followed by silence.

Lyell Bone stood up and shook his head, as though he couldn't quite understand what he had seen.

'Lyell!' Amy said in a desolate voice. 'Oh, Lyell, will you never wake up?'

Charlie looked at the empty broken bottle. The king's tears had gone.

Lyell gave a faint smile. His eye had been caught by the glint of wet glass. He bent down to pick up the broken bottle, but cut his finger on the jagged edge.

'Ouch!' Lyell sat down and put his bleeding finger into his mouth. He tasted something utterly strange; it was warm and infinitely comforting. He looked at the two people standing before him. One of them he knew, so very well. The other must be . . .

'Charlie?' he said. 'And Amy.'

Charlie watched his parents fall into each other's arms. He felt that he could stand there forever, just watching. But then his father beckoned to him.